MOBILE SUIT GUNDAM 0079

BY KAZUHISA KONDO

Based on the anime TV series MOBILE SUIT GUNDAM created by Hajime YATATE and Yoshiyuki TOMINO

Cover Illustration/Kazuhisa Kondo
Layout & Design/Sean Lee
Translation/William Flanagan
Script Consultant/Mark Simmons
Touch-Up Art & Lettering/Bill Schuch
Contributing Editor/Mark Simmons
Editor/Ian Robertson

Managing Editor/Annette Roman
V.P. of Sales & Marketing/Rick Bauer
V.P. of Editorial/Hyoe Narita
Publisher/Seiji Horibuchi

© SOTSU AGENCY/SUNRISE
© KAZUHISA KONDO 2001
First published in 2001 by Media Works Inc., Tokyo, Japan.
English translation rights arranged with Media Works, Inc.

Printed in Canada

Published by Viz Communications, Inc.
P.O. Box 77010 • San Francisco, CA 94107
www.viz.com • www.j-pop.com

Go to store.viz.com for your free
Viz Shop-By-Mail catalog.

10 9 8 7 6 5 4 3 2 1
First printing, December 2002

**MOBILE SUIT GUNDAM 0079
GRAPHIC NOVELS TO DATE:**

VIZ GRAPHIC NOVEL

MOBILE SUIT
GUNDAM
0079

VOL. 8

VIZ GRAPHIC NOVEL

MOBILE SUIT GUNDAM 0079

VOL. 8

By KAZUHISA KONDO

MOBILE SUIT
GUNDAM 0079

The official adaptation of the anime series Mobile Suit Gundam

A 43-episode animated series that began airing in Japan in 1979, **Mobile Suit Gundam** was unusual for a Japanese "giant robot" show in its grim war story and its then-revolutionary concept of using the robots (or "mobile suits," in this case) as mass-produced war machines, like tanks or planes, rather than more colorful, superhero-like, transforming robots. Edited together into three two-hour movies (**Gundam I, II** and **III**), the **Gundam** saga was released in theaters in 1981 and 1982 to enthusiastic crowds. The resulting boom in toy model kits from the series elevated **Gundam** to legendary status, and animated sequels, comics, and merchandise have been continuously produced for over 20 years to this day.

In condensing the series into six hours, the movie editions removed many of the nuances of the TV series version, as well as several of the more colorful machines. **Gundam 0079**, by using the TV series continuity for much of its story, gives readers who may have only seen the movie editions a look at the whole story with which Japanese viewers are familar. The **Mobile Suit Gundam** TV series is still often rerun on Japanese TV.

STORY

In the not-so-far-off future, Earth's increasing population forces mankind to emigrate into space. Gigantic, orbiting space colonies are built around the Earth to house humanity's billions, and within half a century, entire nations of human beings call these space colonies their homeland.

In the calendar year of the Universal Century 0079, the furthest group of colonies from Earth, Side 3, under the name "Principality of Zeon," began a war of independence against the Earth Federation government. In slightly over a month of battle, both the Principality of Zeon and the Federation saw half their populations die. The Zeon forces' use of a new weapon, a humanoid-shaped fighting unit called a "mobile suit," gave it the advantage in battle. A temporary truce was called, a treaty was signed to prevent the use of nuclear weapons and poison gas, and the war came to a stalemate for a little more than eight months.

A Zeon attack on the space colony of Side 7 forced many of the colonists to seek refuge on the Federation mobile suit carrier *White Base*. Some of those civilians are called upon to help the Earth Federation defend itself against the Zeon enemy. Piloting a mobile suit salvaged from the Side 7 colony, the Earth Federation's new "Gundam," 15-year-old Amuro Ray finds himself on the front line of battle.

Now the *White Base* heads toward Earth, hoping to bring its precious cargo of mobile suits across enemy lines to the Federation high command on the planet's surface. But safety is yet a long way off....

CHARACTERS

AMURO RAY

A 15-year-old civilian from the Side 7 space colony. The son of the Federation engineer who designed the Gundam, Amuro has demonstrated a knack for piloting this prototype mobile suit.

BRIGHT NOAH

One of the few surviving crew members of the Federation mobile suit carrier *White Base*, this former cadet has become the ship's acting captain.

SAYLA MASS

A mysterious refugee from Side 7, who now serves as the *White Base*'s communications officer. She appears to have some connection to enemy ace Char Aznable.

MIRAI YASHIMA

A member of the influential Yashima family, and part of the Federation's social elite. After the escape from Side 7, Mirai becomes the *White Base*'s pilot.

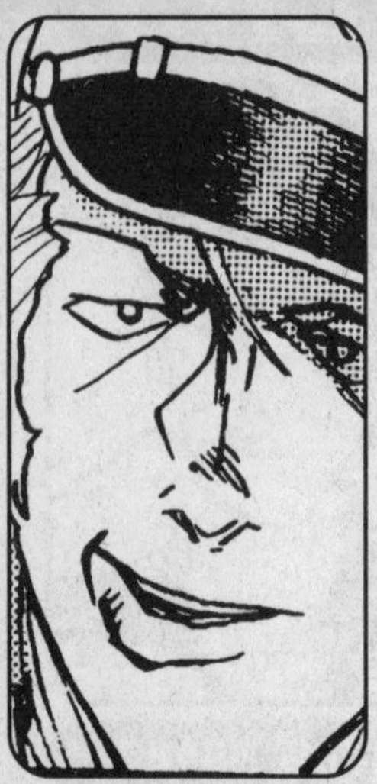

SLEGGAR LAW

A happy-go-lucky guy who has come to the *White Base* to replace Ryu Jose, who` was killed in battle.

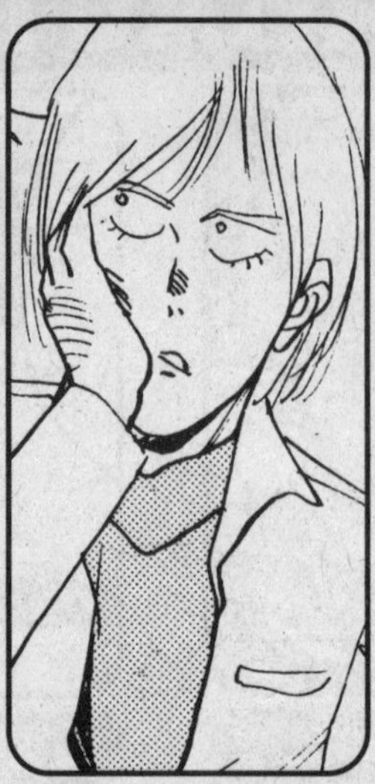

KAI SHIDEN

A cynical civilian from Side 7, and the pilot of the mobile suit Guncannon.

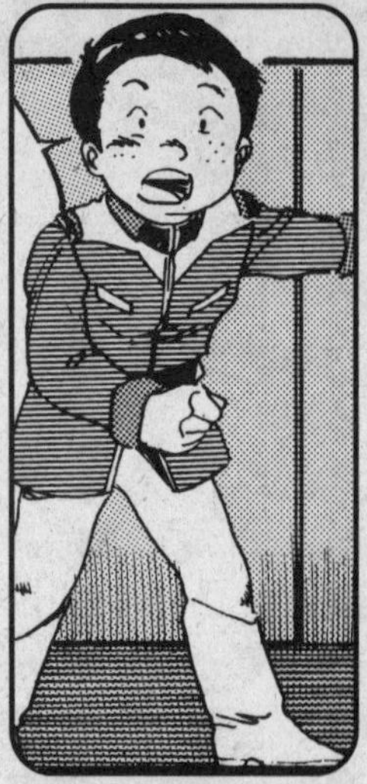

HAYATO KOBAYASHI

Amuro's hot-tempered Side 7 neighbor, who teams up with Ryu to operate the mobile suit Guntank.

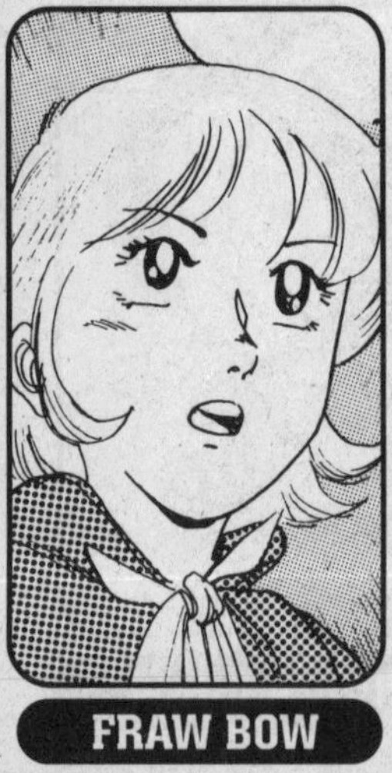

FRAW BOW

Amuro's would-be girlfriend helps out by serving food and riding herd on the younger refugees.

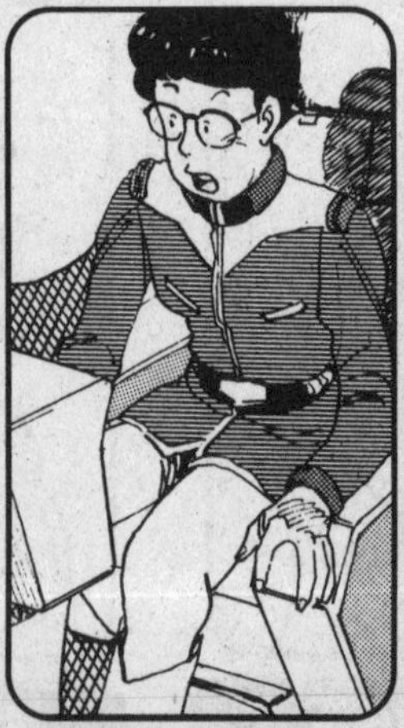

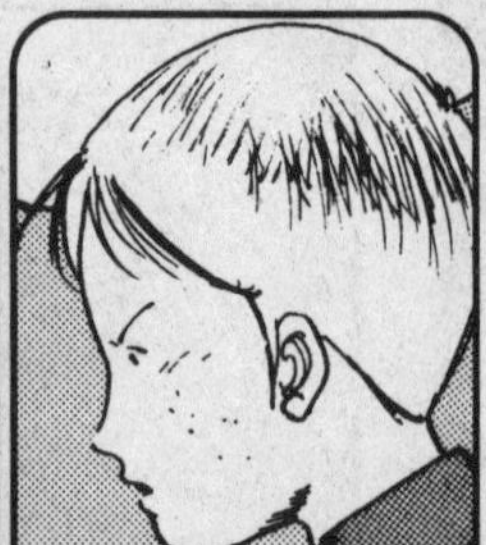

MARKER CLAN AND OSCAR DUBLIN

The *White Base*'s ever-reliable bridge operators.

CHAR AZNABLE

Zeon's famous "Red Comet" is a legendary ace mobile suit pilot, with a sinister secret agenda of his own. Char's dismissal from the Space Attack Force, for his failure to protect Garma Zabi, complicates both his career and his private schemes.

KYCILIA ZABI

The eldest daughter of Zeon's ruling Zabi family. Kycilia commands the Mobile Assault Force from her headquarters on the moon.

LALAH

Like Amuro, she is a "Newtype", one of the new breed of humans with superhuman mental powers. Char is planning to use her in the war against the Federation Forces.

DOZLE ZABI

Commander of Zeon's Space Attack Force and younger son of Soverign Degwin Sodo Zabi.

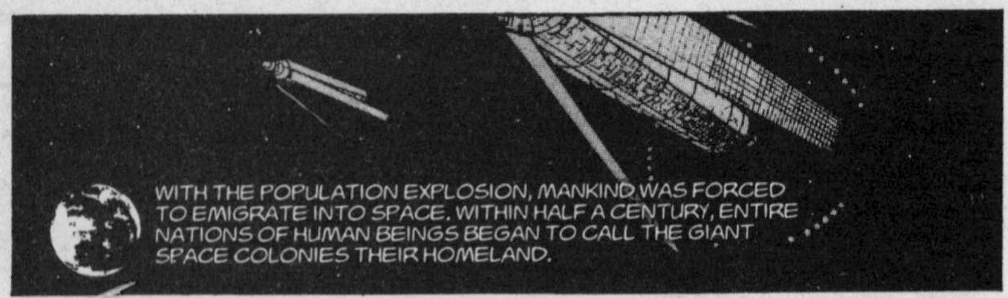
WITH THE POPULATION EXPLOSION, MANKIND WAS FORCED TO EMIGRATE INTO SPACE. WITHIN HALF A CENTURY, ENTIRE NATIONS OF HUMAN BEINGS BEGAN TO CALL THE GIANT SPACE COLONIES THEIR HOMELAND.

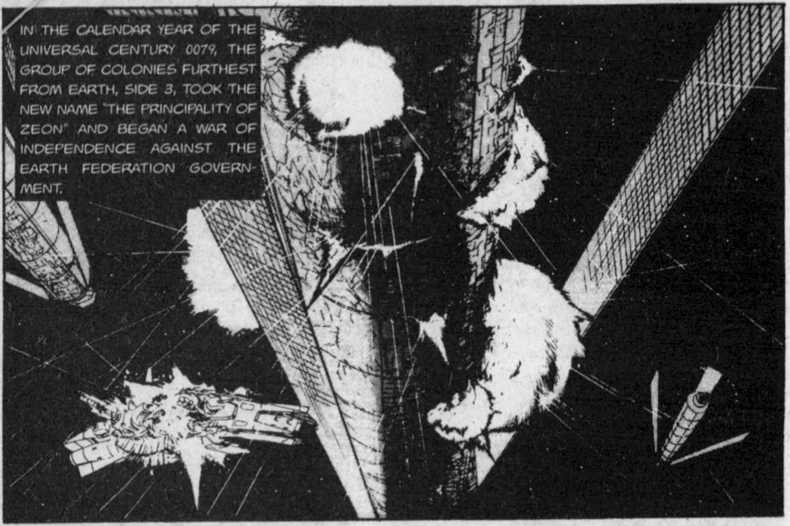
IN THE CALENDAR YEAR OF THE UNIVERSAL CENTURY 0079, THE GROUP OF COLONIES FURTHEST FROM EARTH, SIDE 3, TOOK THE NEW NAME "THE PRINCIPALITY OF ZEON" AND BEGAN A WAR OF INDEPENDENCE AGAINST THE EARTH FEDERATION GOVERNMENT.

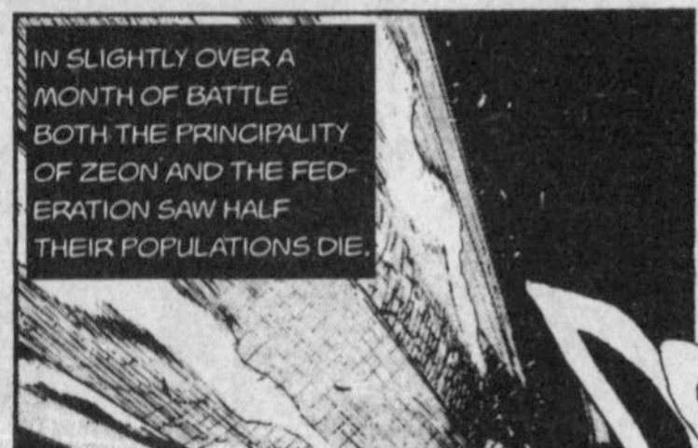
IN SLIGHTLY OVER A MONTH OF BATTLE BOTH THE PRINCIPALITY OF ZEON AND THE FEDERATION SAW HALF THEIR POPULATIONS DIE.

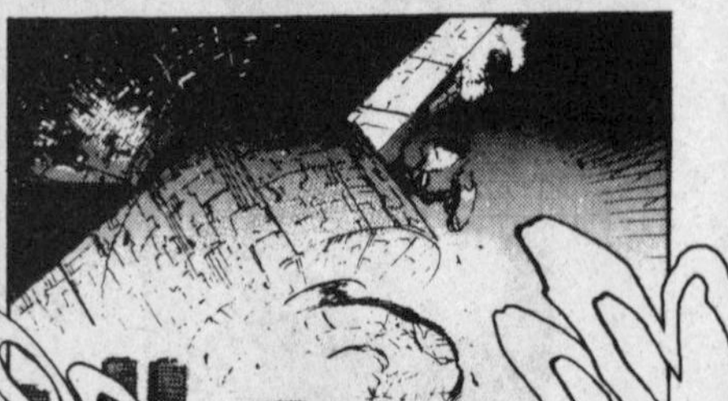
MANKIND WAS HORRIFIED AT ITS OWN ATROCITIES, AND THE WAR CAME TO A STALEMATE FOR A LITTLE MORE THAN EIGHT MONTHS.

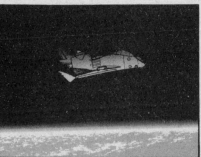

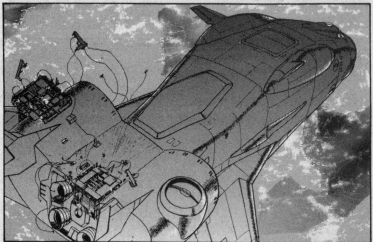

CAPTAIN CHAR?

!

WE'VE ALMOST FINISHED REPAIRS ON THE SHIP.

WE CAN GET UNDER-WAY SOON.

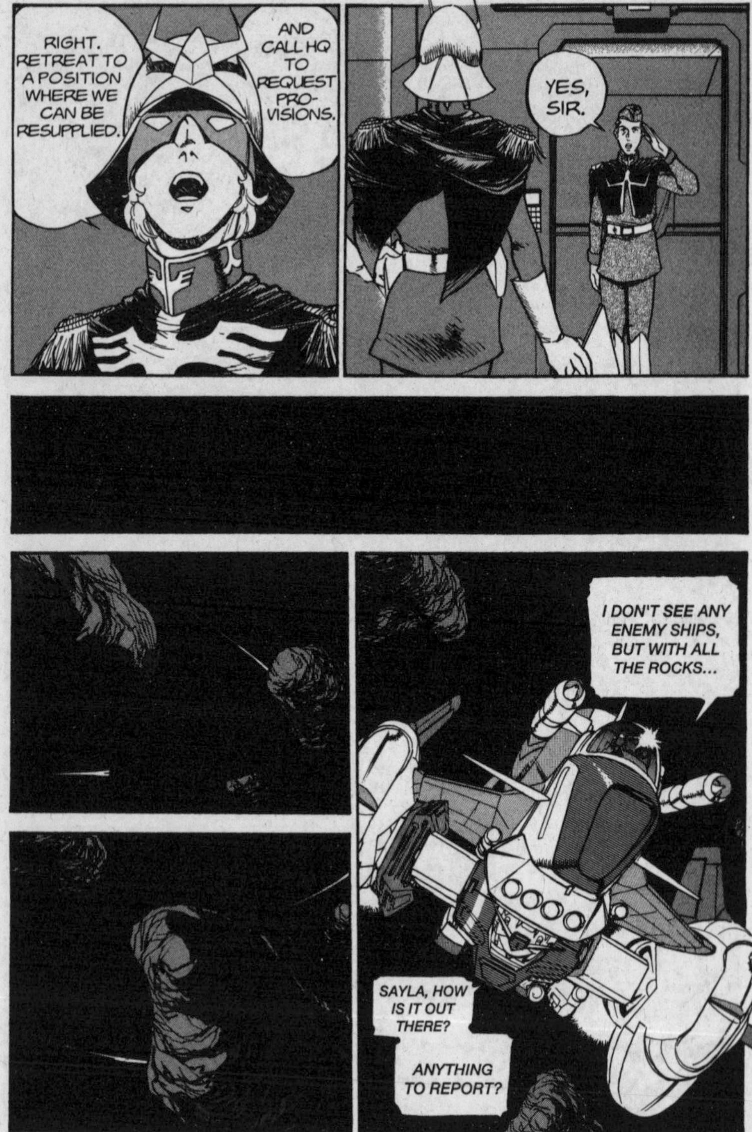
RIGHT. RETREAT TO A POSITION WHERE WE CAN BE RESUPPLIED.
AND CALL HQ TO REQUEST PRO-VISIONS.
YES, SIR.
I DON'T SEE ANY ENEMY SHIPS, BUT WITH ALL THE ROCKS...
SAYLA, HOW IS IT OUT THERE?
ANYTHING TO REPORT?

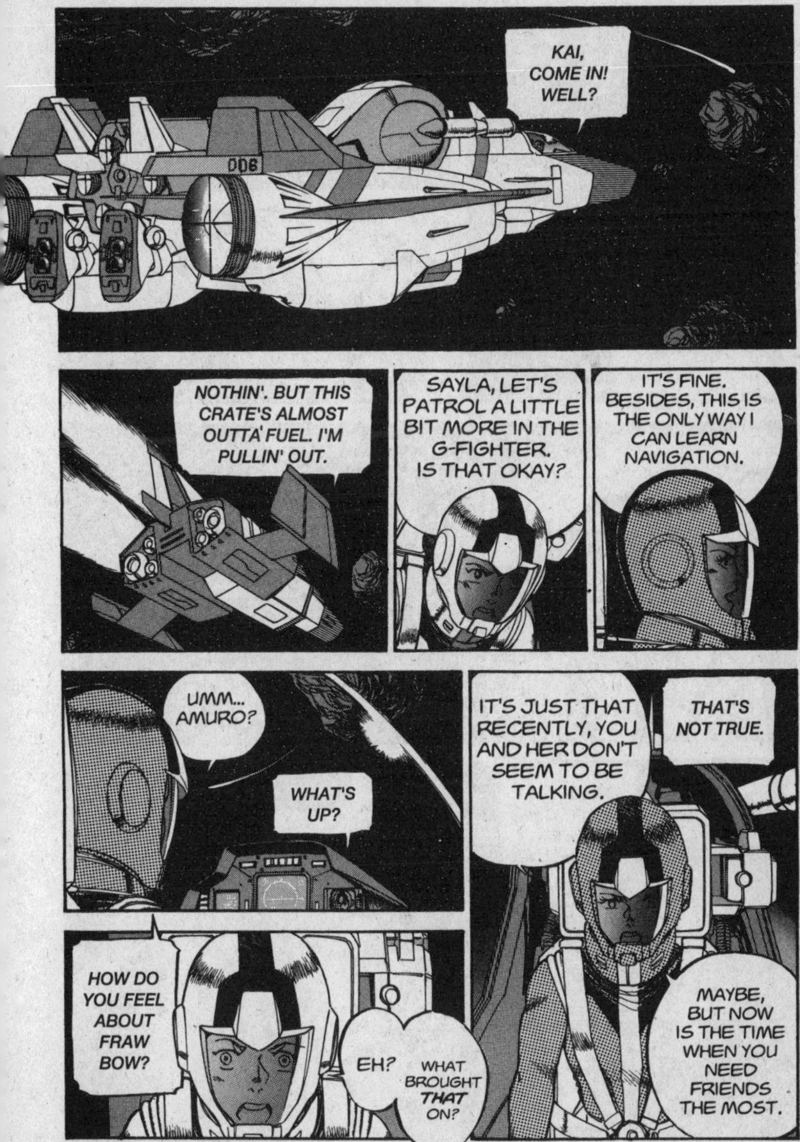
KAI, COME IN! WELL?
NOTHIN'. BUT THIS CRATE'S ALMOST OUTTA' FUEL. I'M PULLIN' OUT.
SAYLA, LET'S PATROL A LITTLE BIT MORE IN THE G-FIGHTER. IS THAT OKAY?
IT'S FINE. BESIDES, THIS IS THE ONLY WAY I CAN LEARN NAVIGATION.
UMM... AMURO?
WHAT'S UP?
HOW DO YOU FEEL ABOUT FRAW BOW?
EH?
WHAT BROUGHT THAT ON?
IT'S JUST THAT RECENTLY, YOU AND HER DON'T SEEM TO BE TALKING.
THAT'S NOT TRUE.
MAYBE, BUT NOW IS THE TIME WHEN YOU NEED FRIENDS THE MOST.

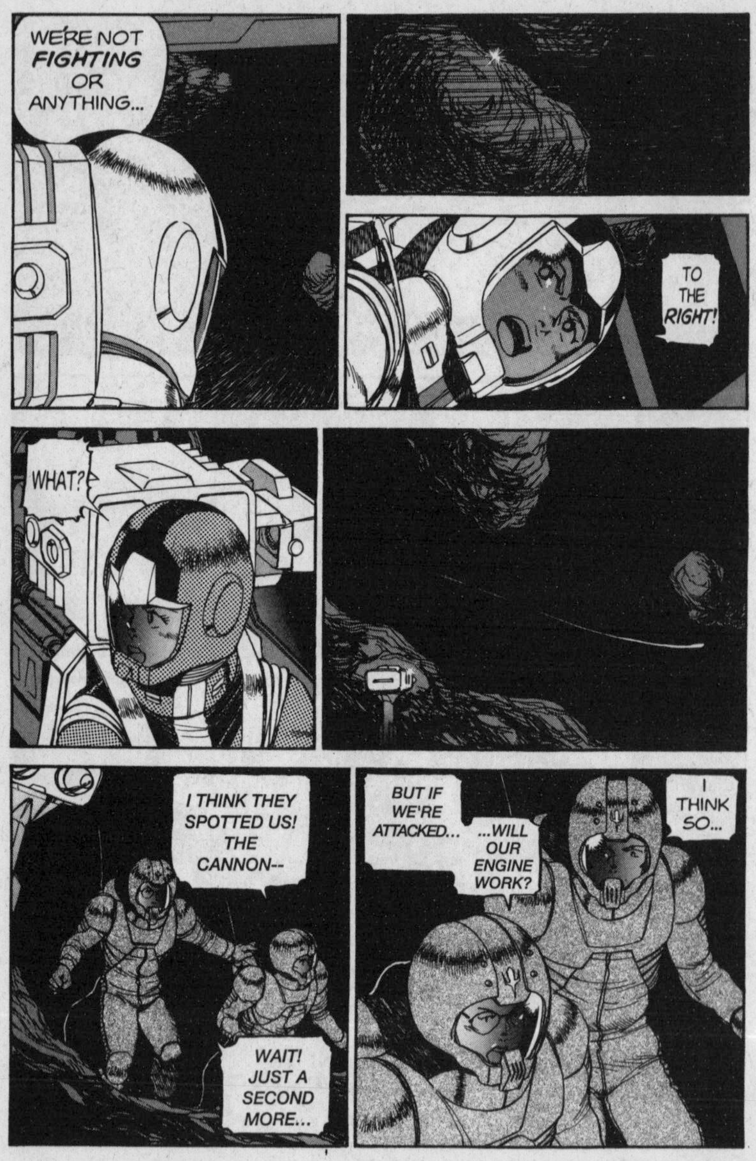
WE'RE NOT FIGHTING OR ANYTHING...
TO THE RIGHT!
WHAT?
I THINK THEY SPOTTED US! THE CANNON--
WAIT! JUST A SECOND MORE...
BUT IF WE'RE ATTACKED...
...WILL OUR ENGINE WORK?
I THINK SO...

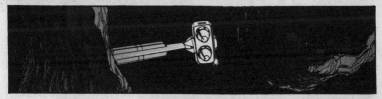

OH, *NO!*
SAYLA,
PULL US
BACK!

WHA~?

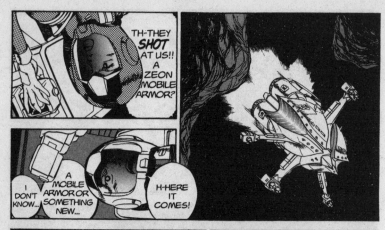

TH-THEY *SHOT* AT US!! A ZEON MOBILE ARMOR?

I DON'T KNOW...

A MOBILE ARMOR OR SOMETHING NEW...

H-HERE IT COMES!

YOU *IDIOT!!* WHY'D YOU SHOOT?

TH-THEY WERE ATTACKING, SO...

NO, THEY *WEREN'T!*

WAKE UP!

14

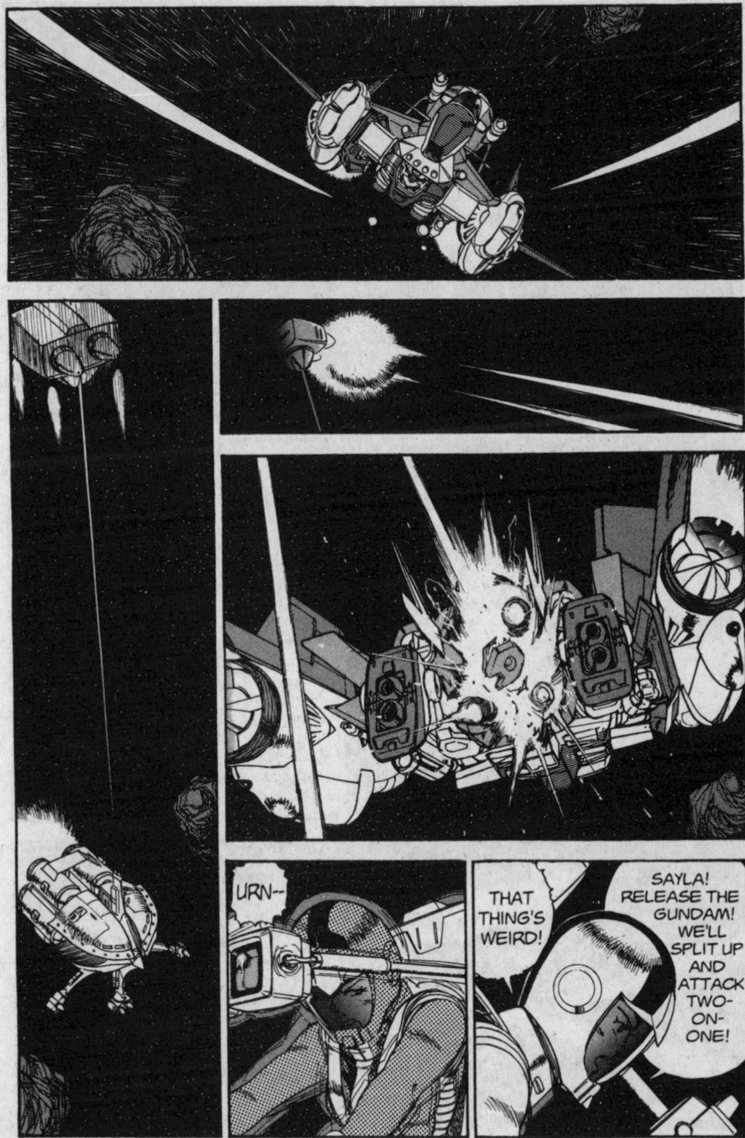
URN--
THAT THING'S WEIRD!
SAYLA! RELEASE THE GUNDAM! WE'LL SPLIT UP AND ATTACK TWO-ON-ONE!

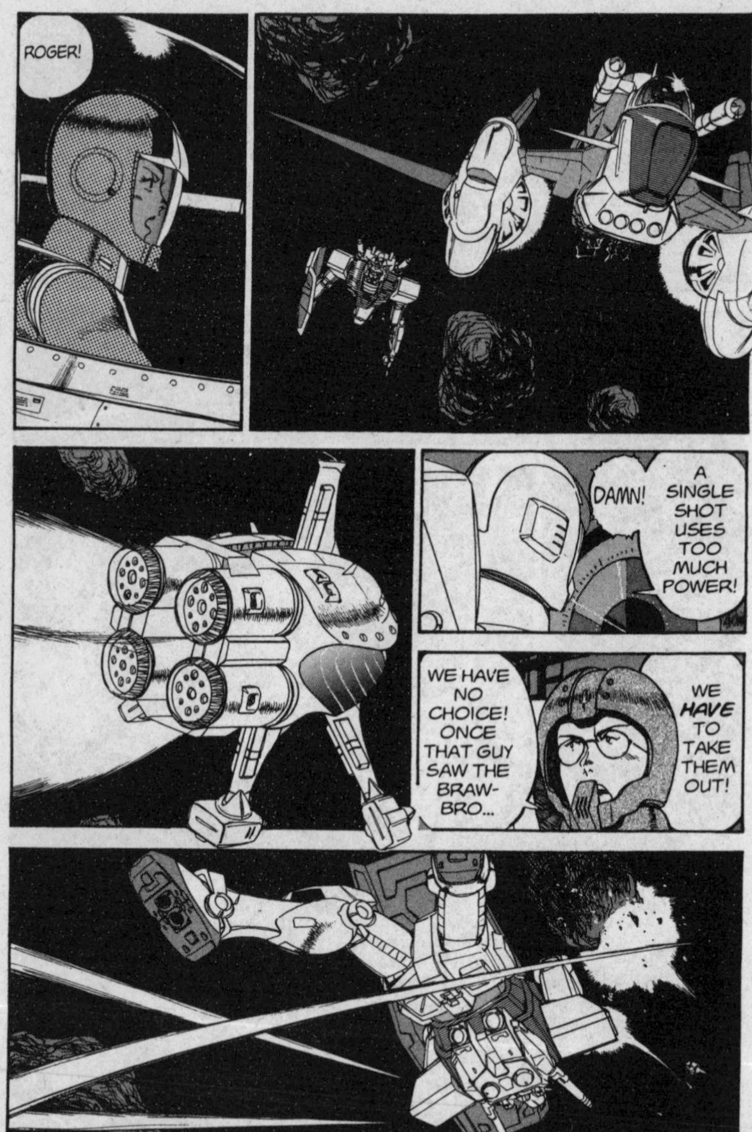
ROGER!
DAMN!
A SINGLE SHOT USES TOO MUCH POWER!
WE HAVE NO CHOICE! ONCE THAT GUY SAW THE BRAW-BRO...
WE *HAVE* TO TAKE THEM OUT!

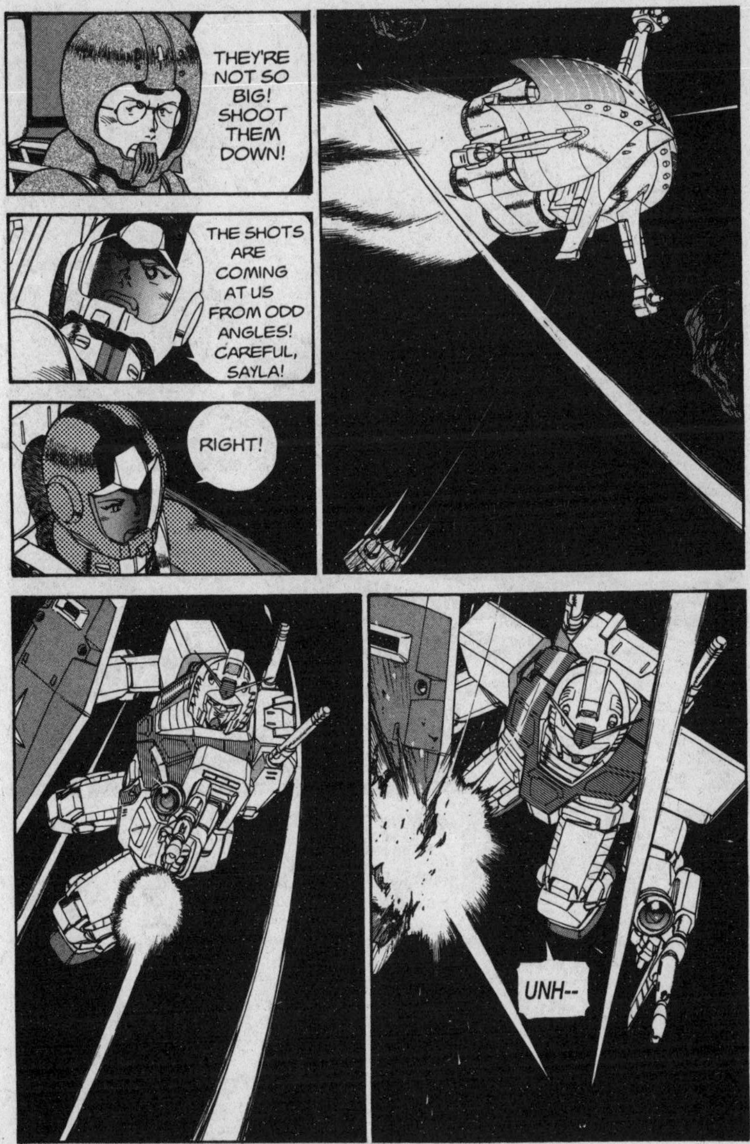
THEY'RE NOT SO BIG! SHOOT THEM DOWN!
THE SHOTS ARE COMING AT US FROM ODD ANGLES! CAREFUL, SAYLA!
RIGHT!
UNH--

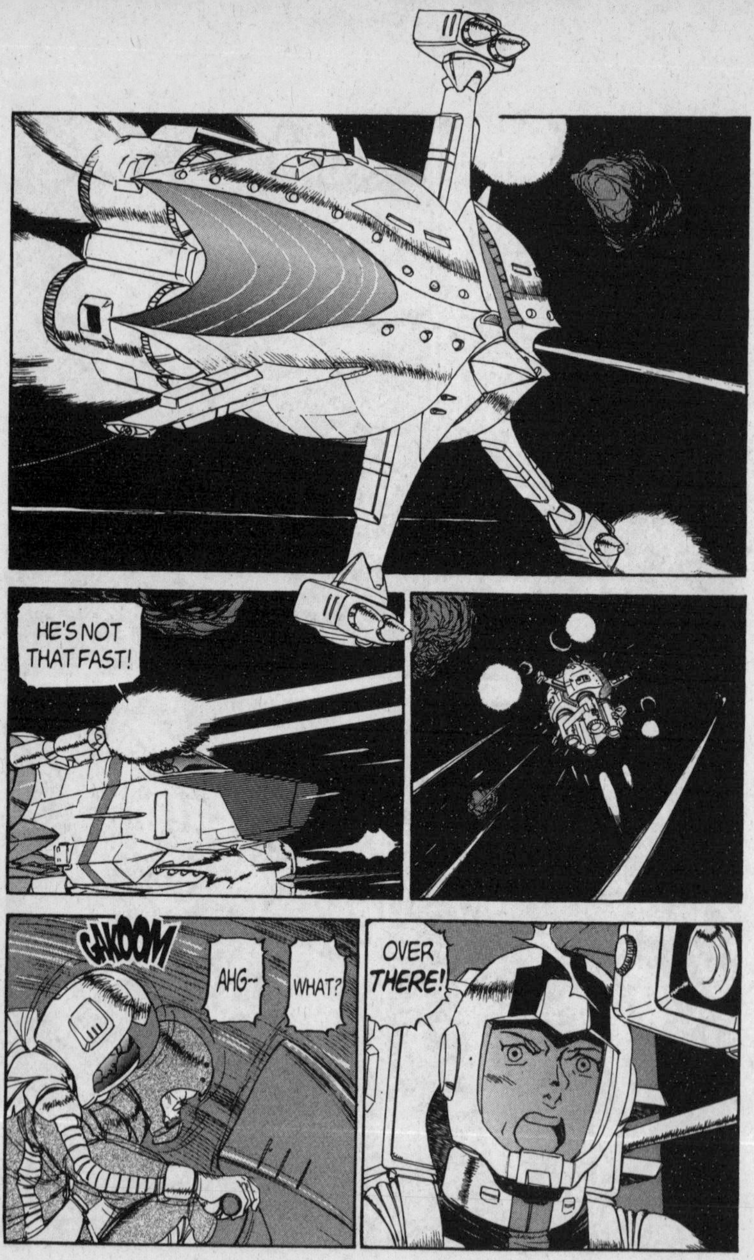
HE'S NOT THAT FAST!
GAKOOM
AHG--
WHAT?
OVER THERE!

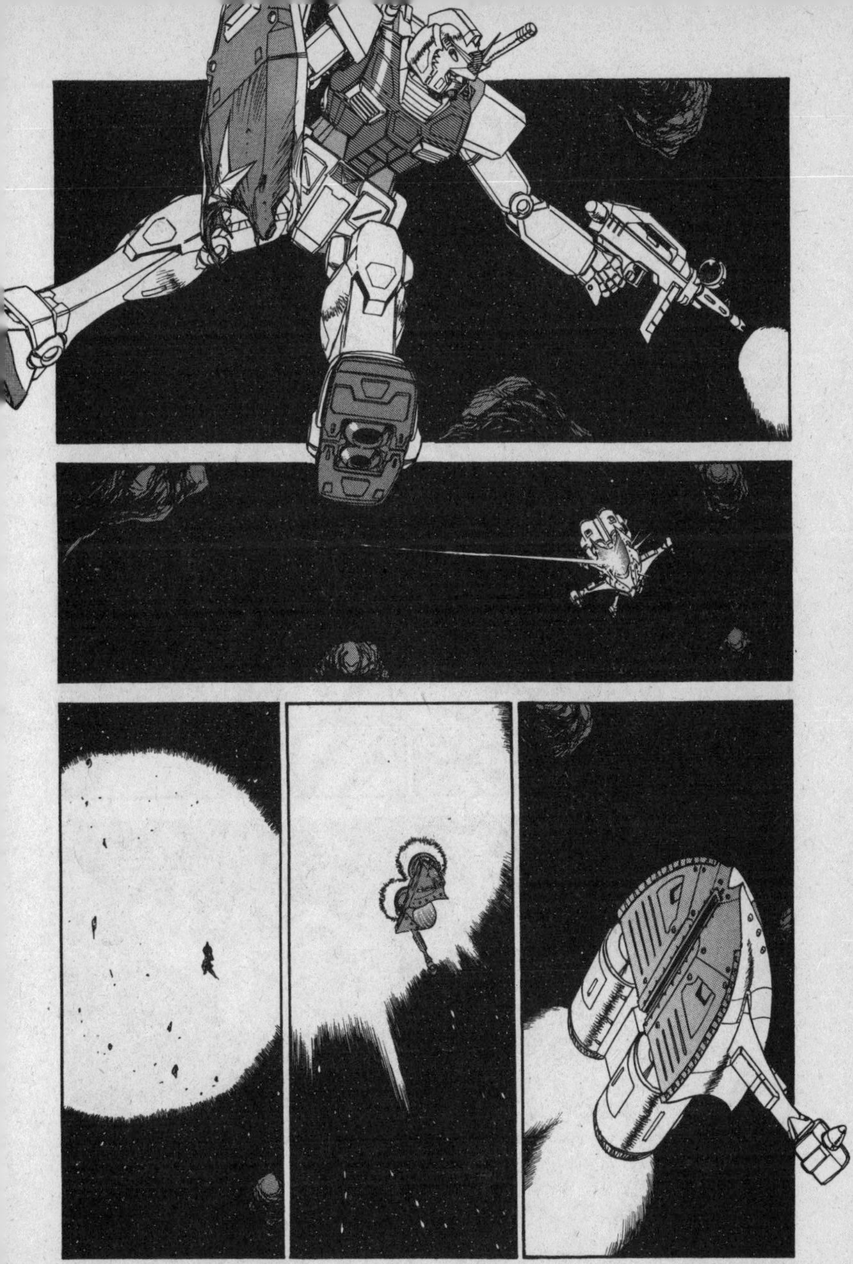

FINALLY, THEY GAVE US A TEST SHIP WE CAN WORK WITH!

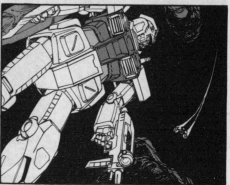

AMURO, WE'RE OUT OF TIME! WE HAVE TO DOCK WITH THE WHITE BASE...

...BEFORE IT ENTERS SIDE 6 AIR SPACE.

ROGER

I'M SET, SAYLA.

D06

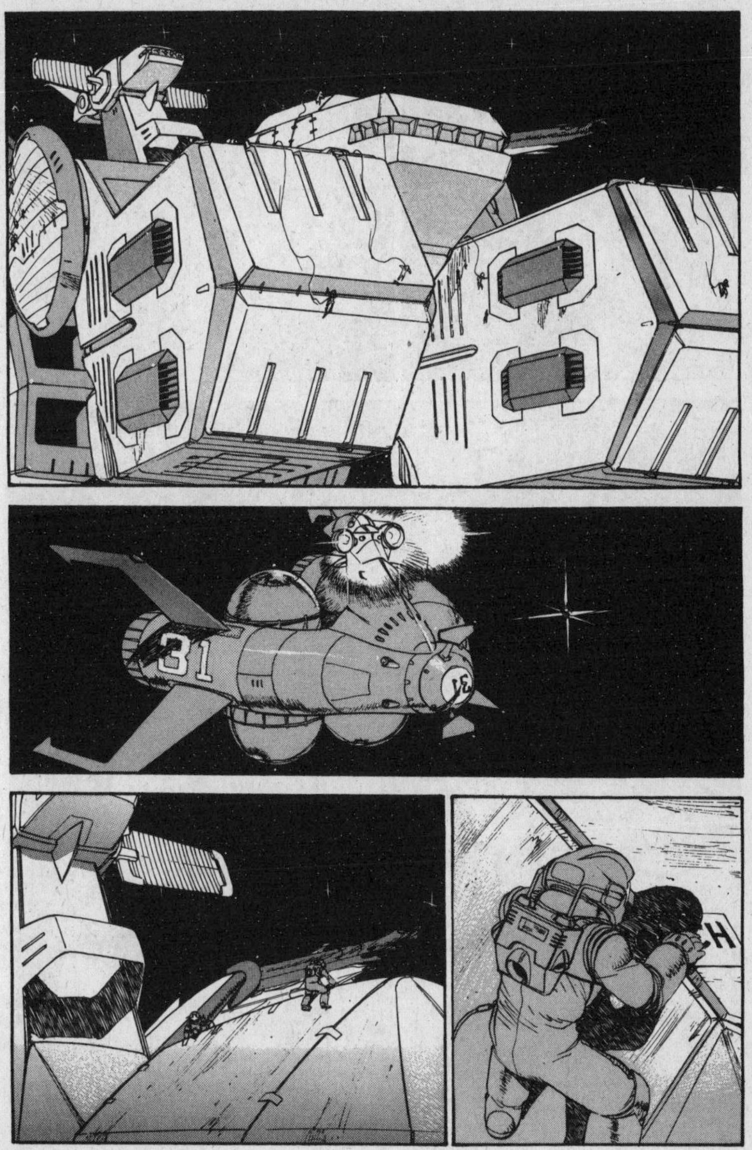
31

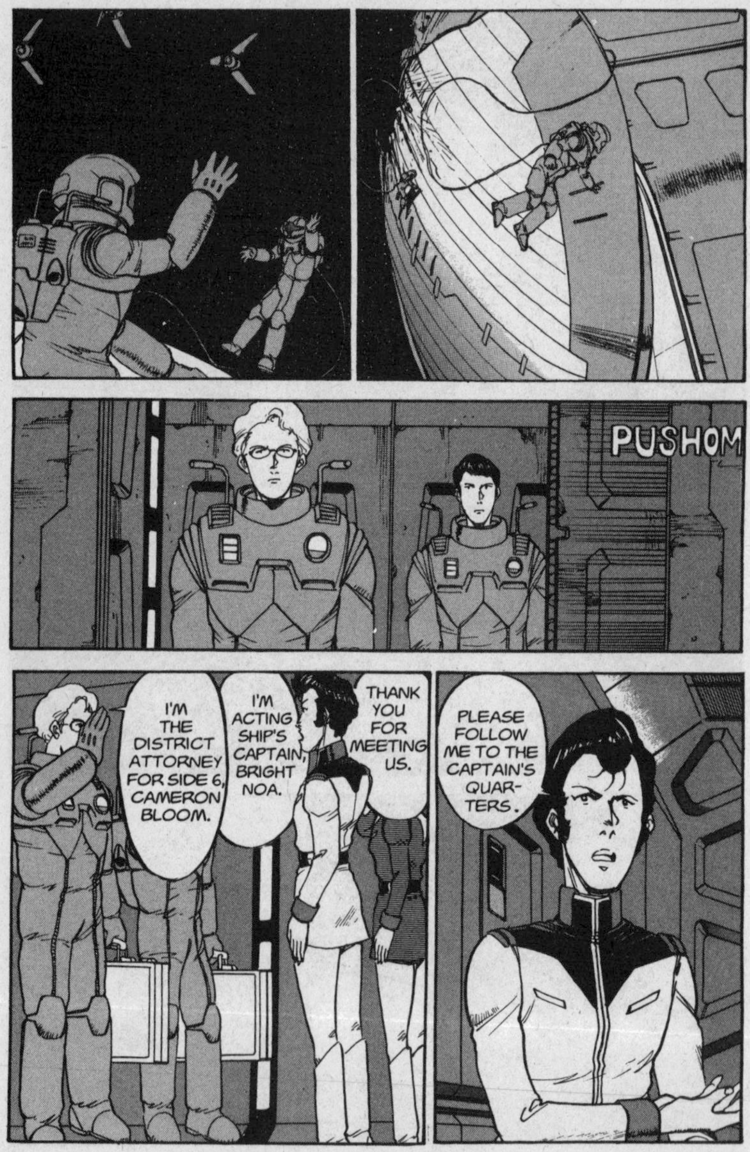
PUSHOM
I'M THE DISTRICT ATTORNEY FOR SIDE 6, CAMERON BLOOM.
I'M ACTING SHIP'S CAPTAIN, BRIGHT NOA.
THANK YOU FOR MEETING US.
PLEASE FOLLOW ME TO THE CAPTAIN'S QUARTERS.

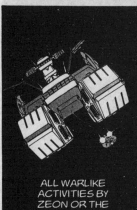

ALL WARLIKE
ACTIVITIES BY
ZEON OR THE
FEDERATION
ARE STRICTLY
FORBIDDEN IN
SIDE 6
CONTROLLED
AIRSPACE.

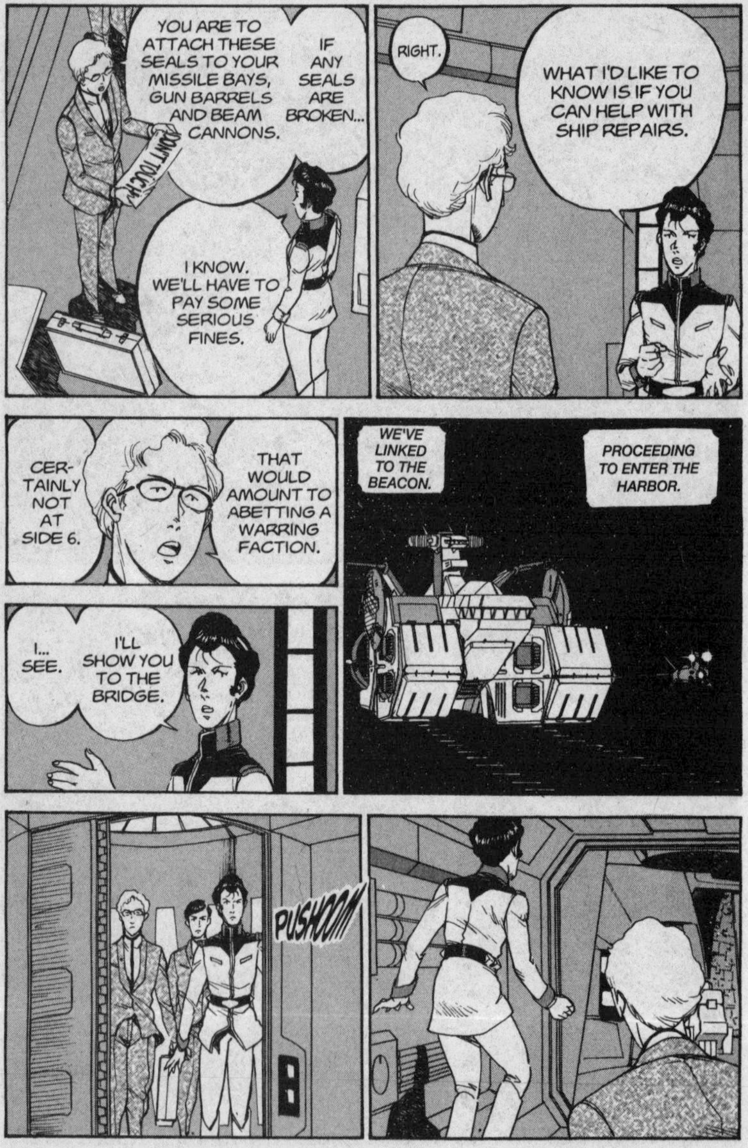
YOU ARE TO ATTACH THESE SEALS TO YOUR MISSILE BAYS, GUN BARRELS AND BEAM CANNONS.
DON'T TOUCH
IF ANY SEALS ARE BROKEN...
I KNOW. WE'LL HAVE TO PAY SOME SERIOUS FINES.
RIGHT.
WHAT I'D LIKE TO KNOW IS IF YOU CAN HELP WITH SHIP REPAIRS.
CER-TAINLY NOT AT SIDE 6.
THAT WOULD AMOUNT TO ABETTING A WARRING FACTION.
I... SEE.
I'LL SHOW YOU TO THE BRIDGE.
WE'VE LINKED TO THE BEACON.
PROCEEDING TO ENTER THE HARBOR.
PUSHOOM

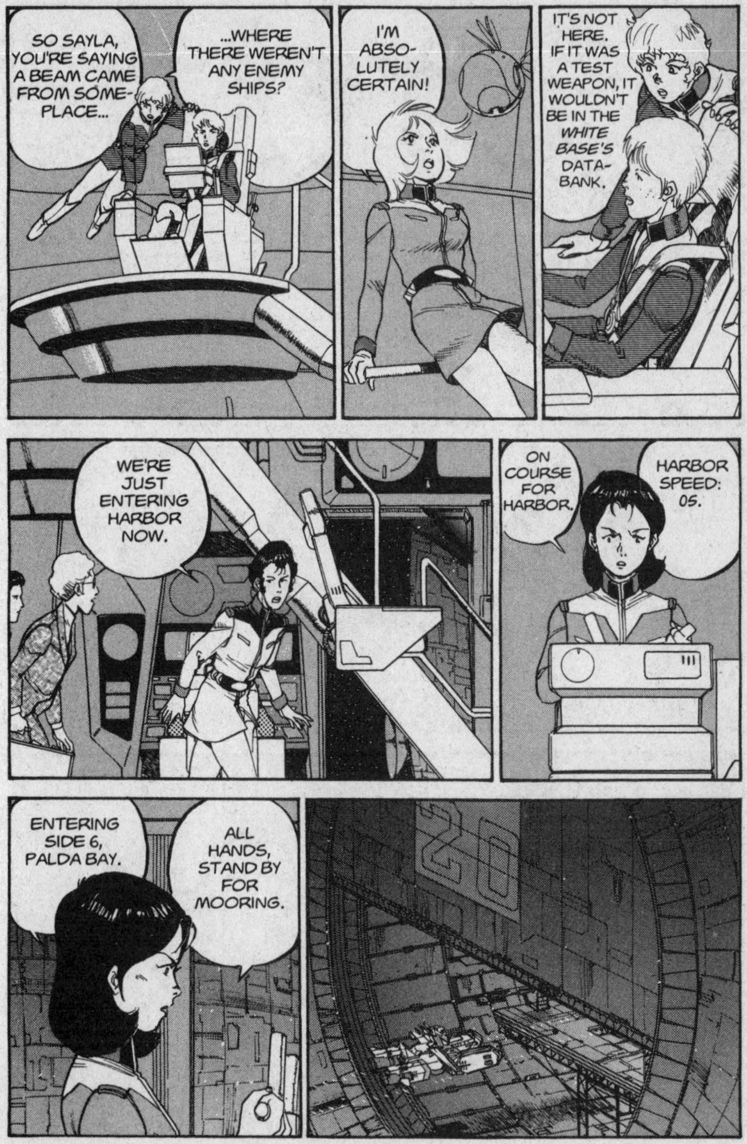
SO SAYLA, YOU'RE SAYING A BEAM CAME FROM SOME-PLACE...
...WHERE THERE WEREN'T ANY ENEMY SHIPS?
I'M ABSO-LUTELY CERTAIN!
IT'S NOT HERE. IF IT WAS A TEST WEAPON, IT WOULDN'T BE IN THE *WHITE BASE'S* DATA-BANK.
WE'RE JUST ENTERING HARBOR NOW.
ON COURSE FOR HARBOR.
HARBOR SPEED: 05.
ENTERING SIDE 6, PALDA BAY.
ALL HANDS, STAND BY FOR MOORING.

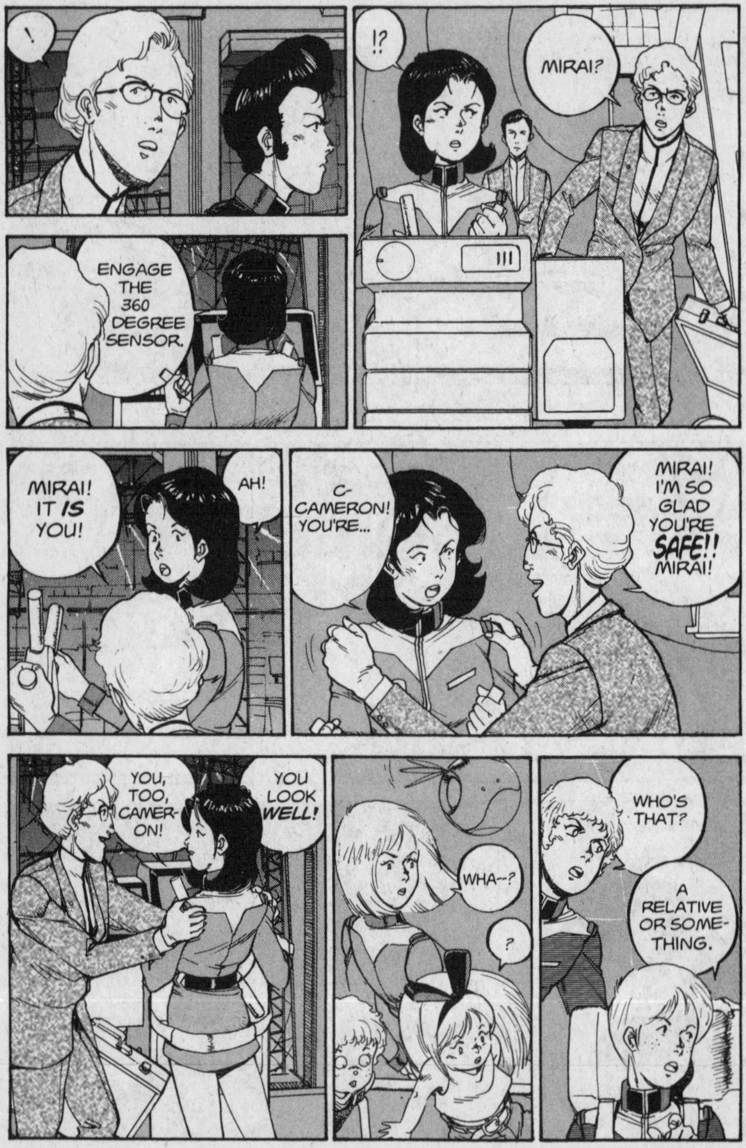
!
!?
MIRAI?
ENGAGE THE 360 DEGREE SENSOR.
MIRAI! IT *IS* YOU!
AH!
C-CAMERON! YOU'RE...
MIRAI! I'M SO GLAD YOU'RE **SAFE!!** MIRAI!
YOU, TOO, CAMER-ON!
YOU LOOK **WELL!**
WHA--?
?
WHO'S THAT?
A RELATIVE OR SOME-THING.

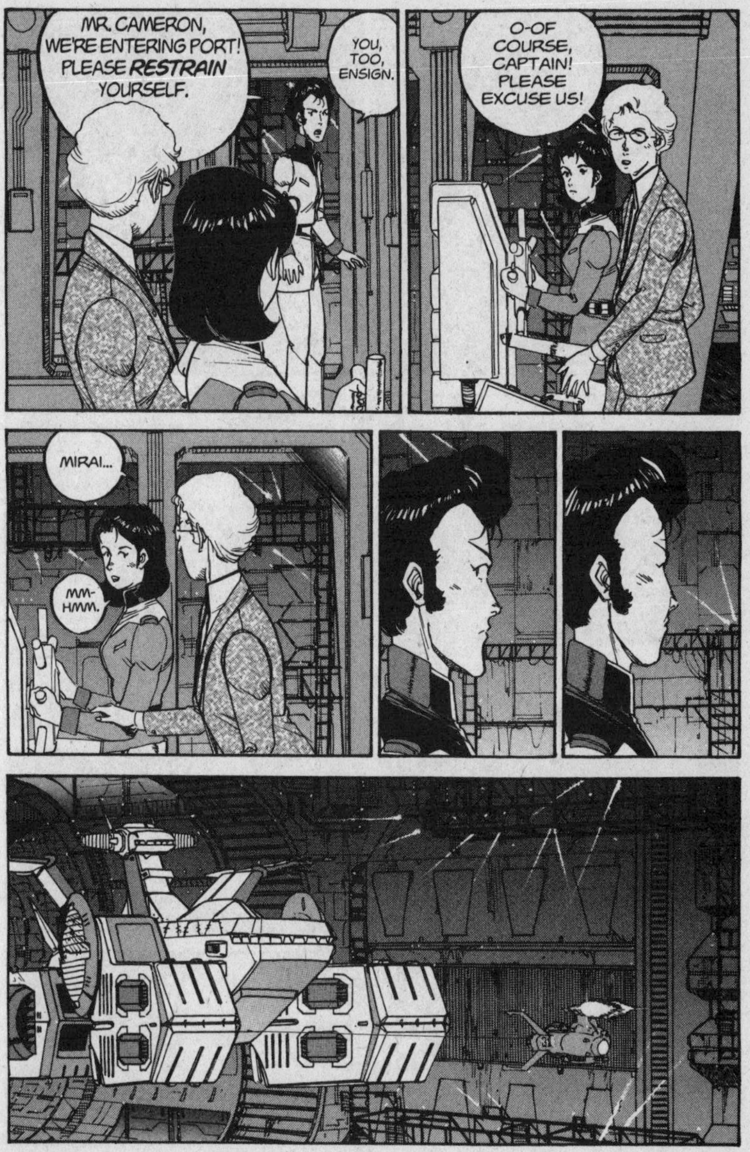
MR. CAMERON, WE'RE ENTERING PORT! PLEASE **RESTRAIN** YOURSELF.
YOU, TOO, ENSIGN.
O-OF COURSE, CAPTAIN! PLEASE EXCUSE US!
MIRAI...
MM-HMM.

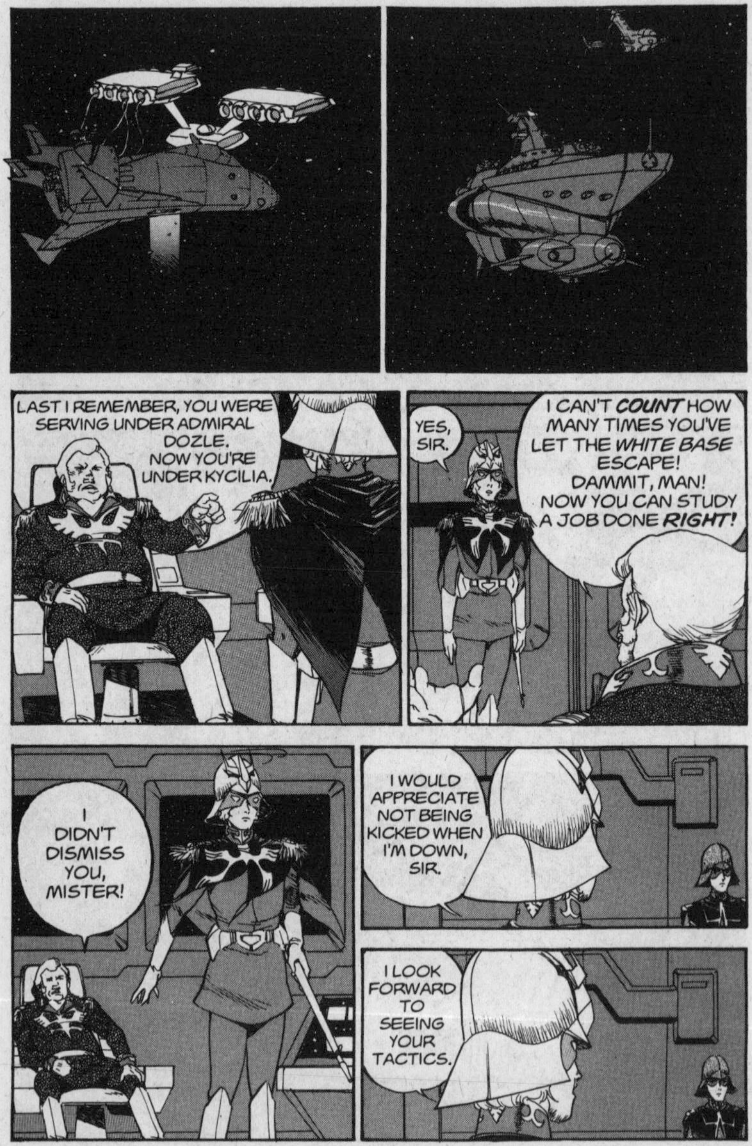
LAST I REMEMBER, YOU WERE SERVING UNDER ADMIRAL DOZLE. NOW YOU'RE UNDER KYCILIA.
YES, SIR.
I CAN'T **COUNT** HOW MANY TIMES YOU'VE LET THE *WHITE BASE* ESCAPE! DAMMIT, MAN! NOW YOU CAN STUDY A JOB DONE ***RIGHT!***
I DIDN'T DISMISS YOU, MISTER!
I WOULD APPRECIATE NOT BEING KICKED WHEN I'M DOWN, SIR.
I LOOK FORWARD TO SEEING YOUR TACTICS.

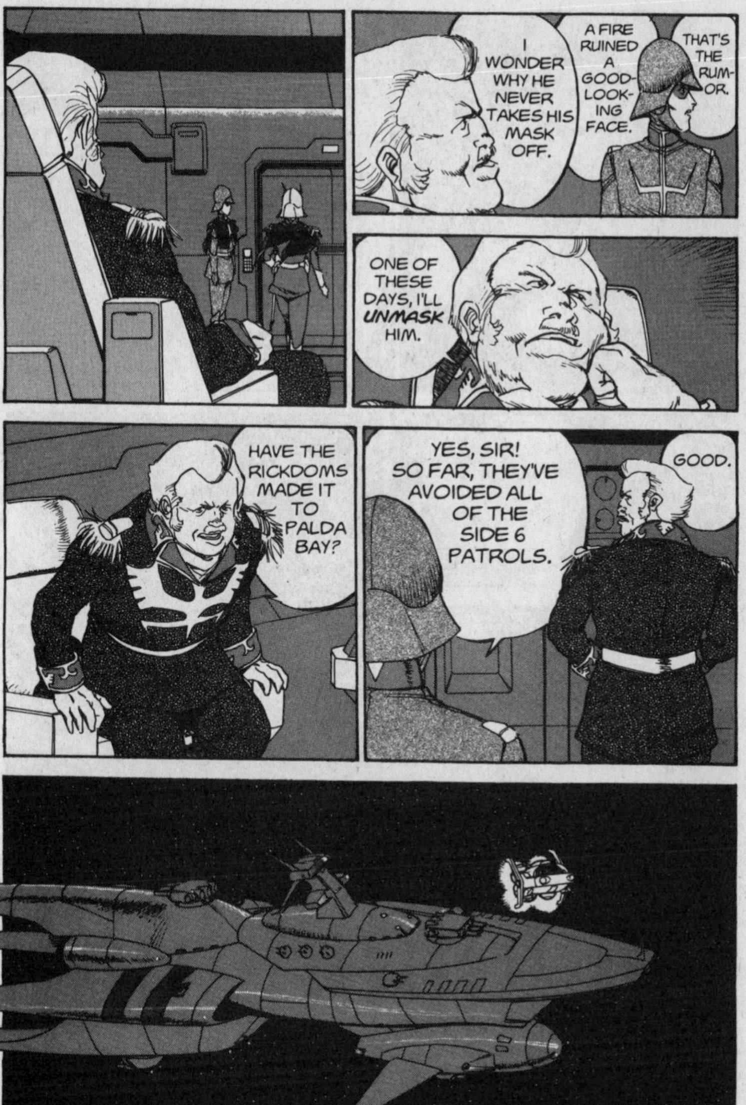
I WONDER WHY HE NEVER TAKES HIS MASK OFF.
A FIRE RUINED A GOOD-LOOKING FACE.
THAT'S THE RUMOR.
ONE OF THESE DAYS, I'LL *UNMASK* HIM.
HAVE THE RICKDOMS MADE IT TO PALDA BAY?
YES, SIR! SO FAR, THEY'VE AVOIDED ALL OF THE SIDE 6 PATROLS.
GOOD.

MULLIGAN, WHEN WE RETURN TO THE ZANZIBAR, SEND A CODED MESSAGE TO ADMIRAL KYCILIA.

YES, SIR.

"PARAROM ZU, CHAR."

GOT IT?

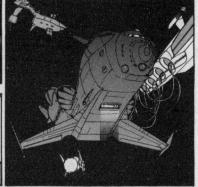

IS THAT ALL?

DON'T ASK QUESTIONS. IT'S A MILITARY SECRET.

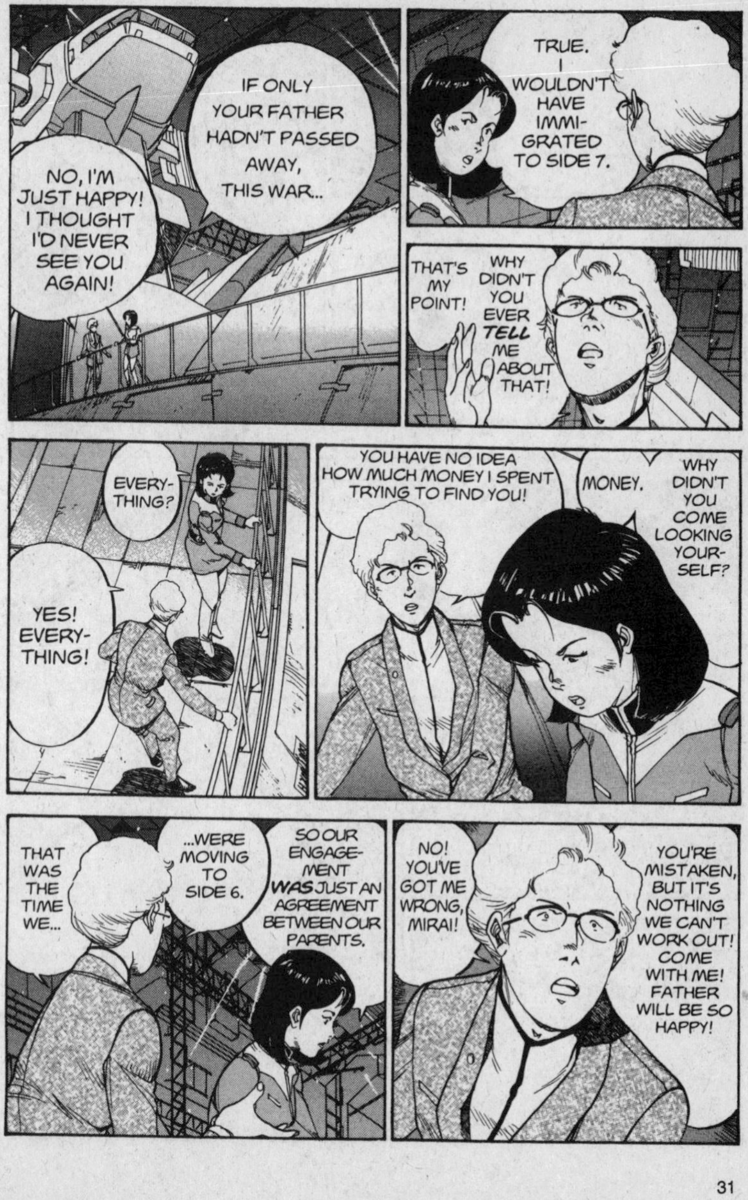
IF ONLY YOUR FATHER HADN'T PASSED AWAY, THIS WAR...
NO, I'M JUST HAPPY! I THOUGHT I'D NEVER SEE YOU AGAIN!
TRUE. I WOULDN'T HAVE IMMI-GRATED TO SIDE 7.
THAT'S MY POINT!
WHY DIDN'T YOU EVER **TELL** ME ABOUT THAT!
EVERY-THING?
YES! EVERY-THING!
YOU HAVE NO IDEA HOW MUCH MONEY I SPENT TRYING TO FIND YOU!
MONEY.
WHY DIDN'T YOU COME LOOKING YOUR-SELF?
THAT WAS THE TIME WE...
...WERE MOVING TO SIDE 6.
SO OUR ENGAGE-MENT **WAS** JUST AN AGREEMENT BETWEEN OUR PARENTS.
NO! YOU'VE GOT ME WRONG, MIRAI!
YOU'RE MISTAKEN, BUT IT'S NOTHING WE CAN'T WORK OUT! COME WITH ME! FATHER WILL BE SO HAPPY!

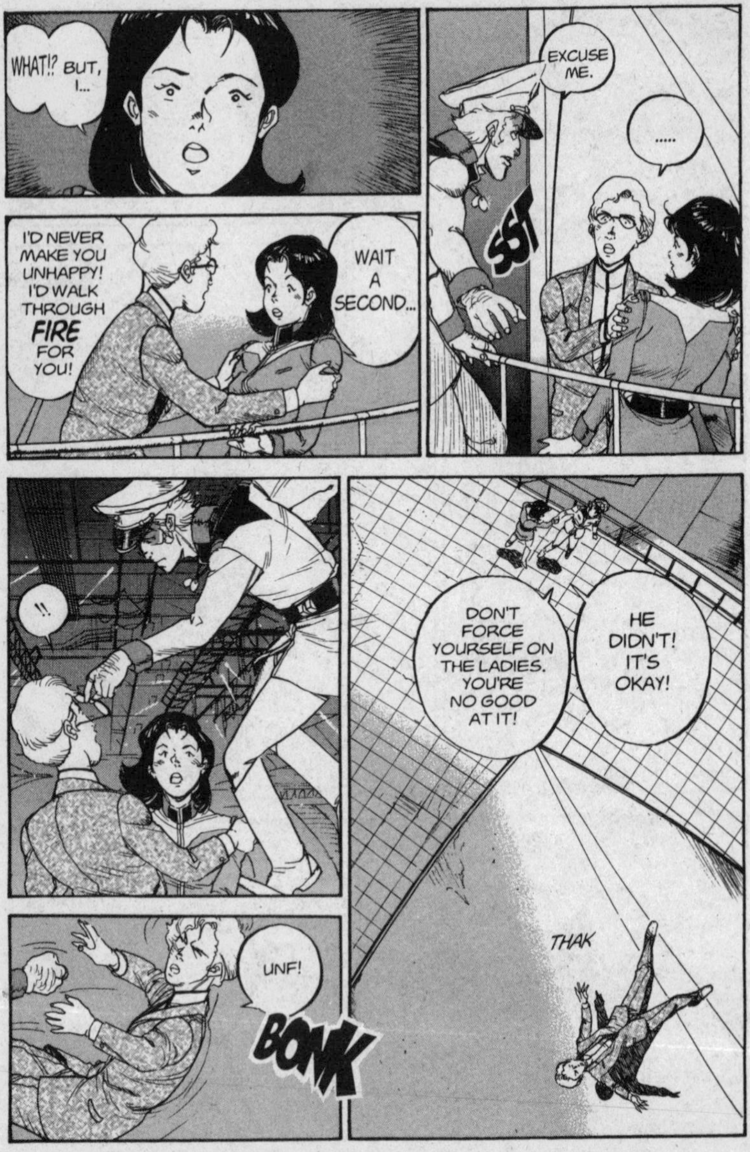
WHAT!? BUT, I...
EXCUSE ME.
.....
I'D NEVER MAKE YOU UNHAPPY! I'D WALK THROUGH FIRE FOR YOU!
WAIT A SECOND...
SST
!!
DON'T FORCE YOURSELF ON THE LADIES. YOU'RE NO GOOD AT IT!
HE DIDN'T! IT'S OKAY!
UNF!
BONK
THAK

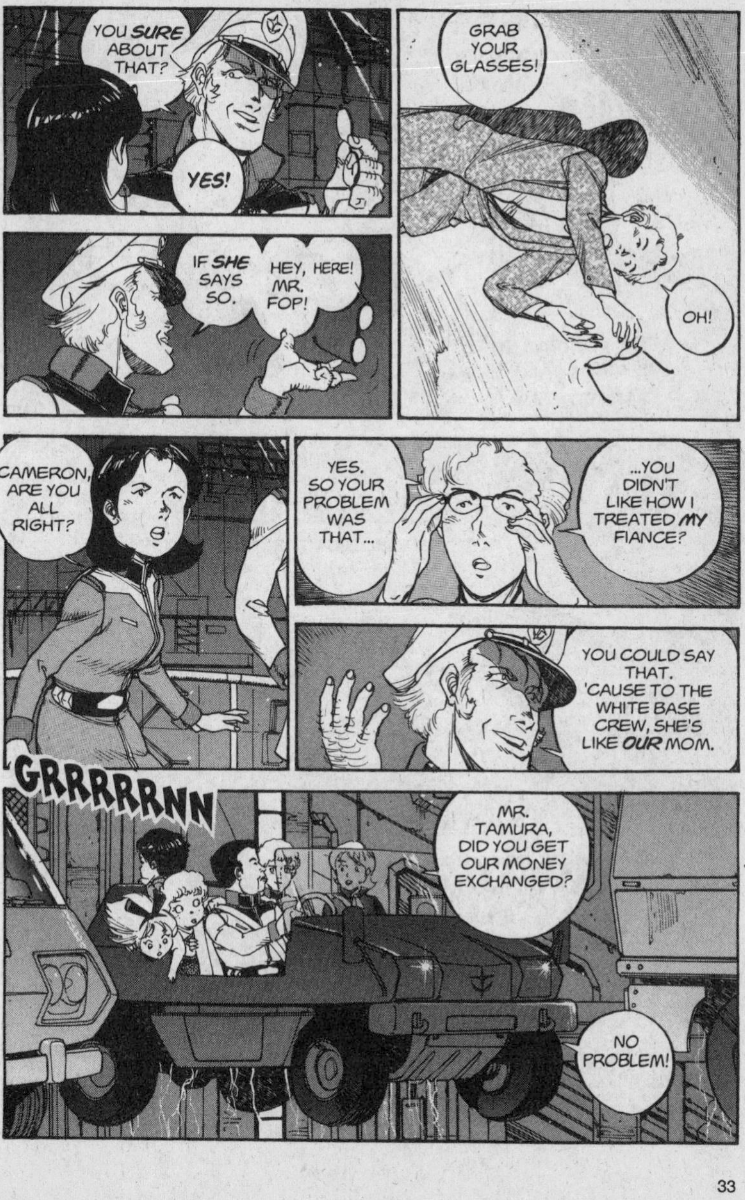
YOU **SURE** ABOUT THAT?
YES!
GRAB YOUR GLASSES!
IF **SHE** SAYS SO.
HEY, HERE! MR. FOP!
OH!
CAMERON, ARE YOU ALL RIGHT?
YES. SO YOUR PROBLEM WAS THAT...
...YOU DIDN'T LIKE HOW I TREATED **MY** FIANCE?
YOU COULD SAY THAT. 'CAUSE TO THE WHITE BASE CREW, SHE'S LIKE **OUR** MOM.
GRRRRRNN
MR. TAMURA, DID YOU GET OUR MONEY EXCHANGED?
NO PROBLEM!

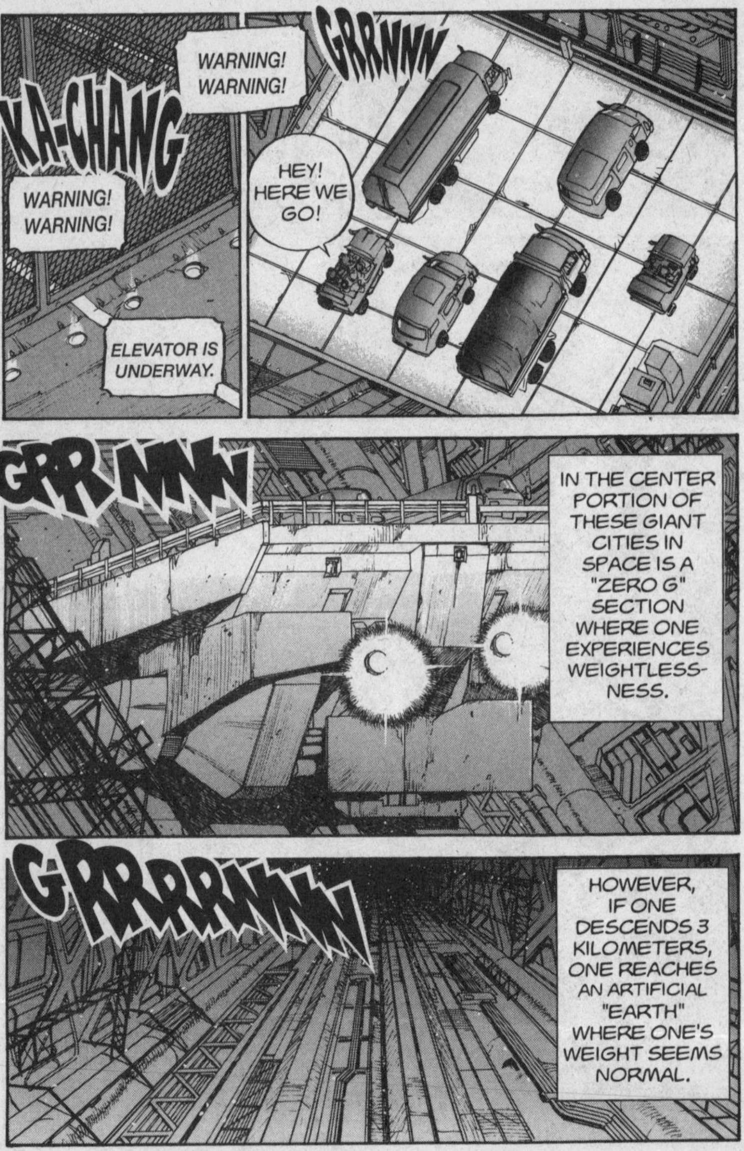
KA-CHANG
WARNING! WARNING!
WARNING! WARNING!
ELEVATOR IS UNDERWAY.
GRRNNN
HEY! HERE WE GO!
GRR NNN
IN THE CENTER PORTION OF THESE GIANT CITIES IN SPACE IS A "ZERO G" SECTION WHERE ONE EXPERIENCES WEIGHTLESS-NESS.
GRRRRNNN
HOWEVER, IF ONE DESCENDS 3 KILOMETERS, ONE REACHES AN ARTIFICIAL "EARTH" WHERE ONE'S WEIGHT SEEMS NORMAL.

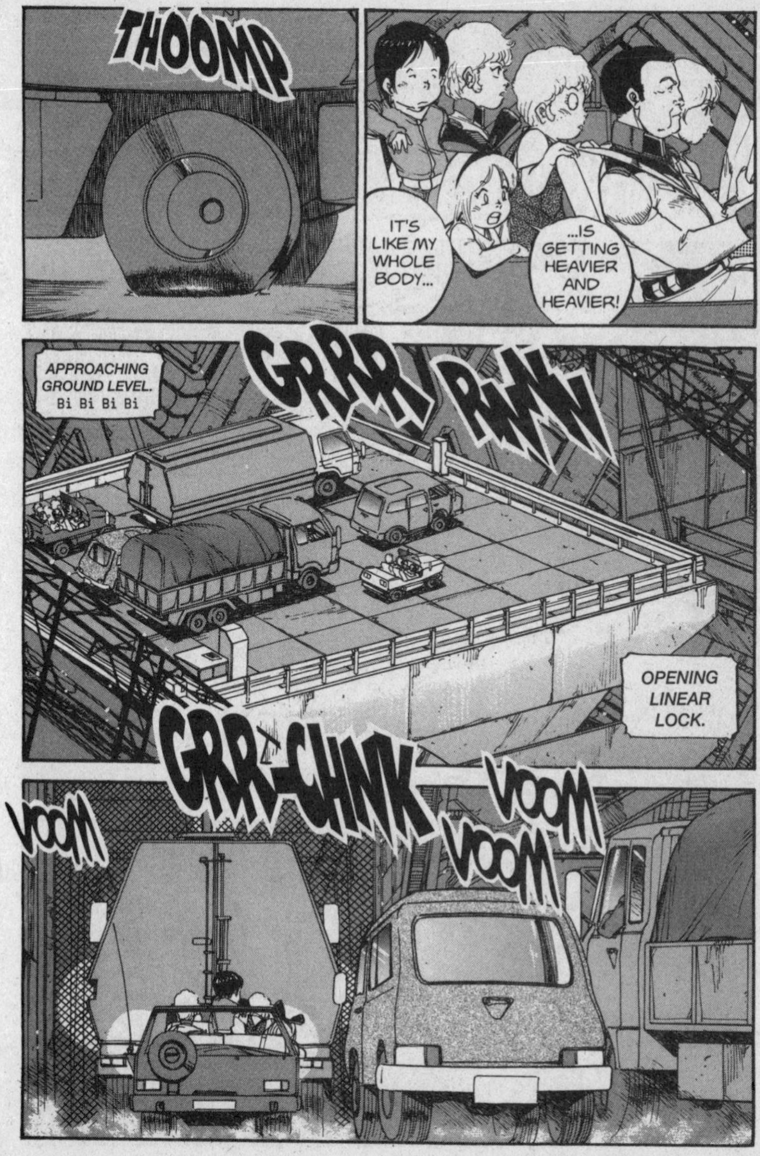
THOOMP
IT'S LIKE MY WHOLE BODY...
...IS GETTING HEAVIER AND HEAVIER!
APPROACHING GROUND LEVEL. Bi Bi Bi Bi
GRRR
OPENING LINEAR LOCK.
GRR-CHNK
VOOM
VOOM
VOOM

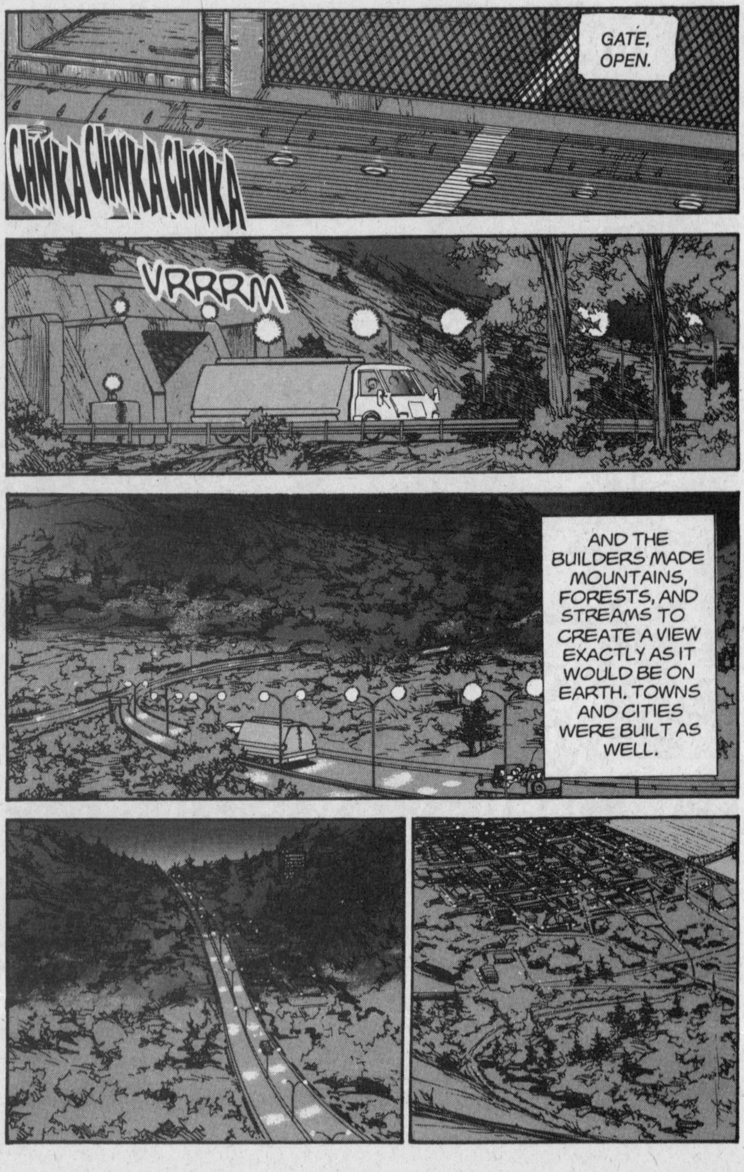
GATE, OPEN.
CHNKA CHNKA CHNKA
VRRRM
AND THE BUILDERS MADE MOUNTAINS, FORESTS, AND STREAMS TO CREATE A VIEW EXACTLY AS IT WOULD BE ON EARTH. TOWNS AND CITIES WERE BUILT AS WELL.

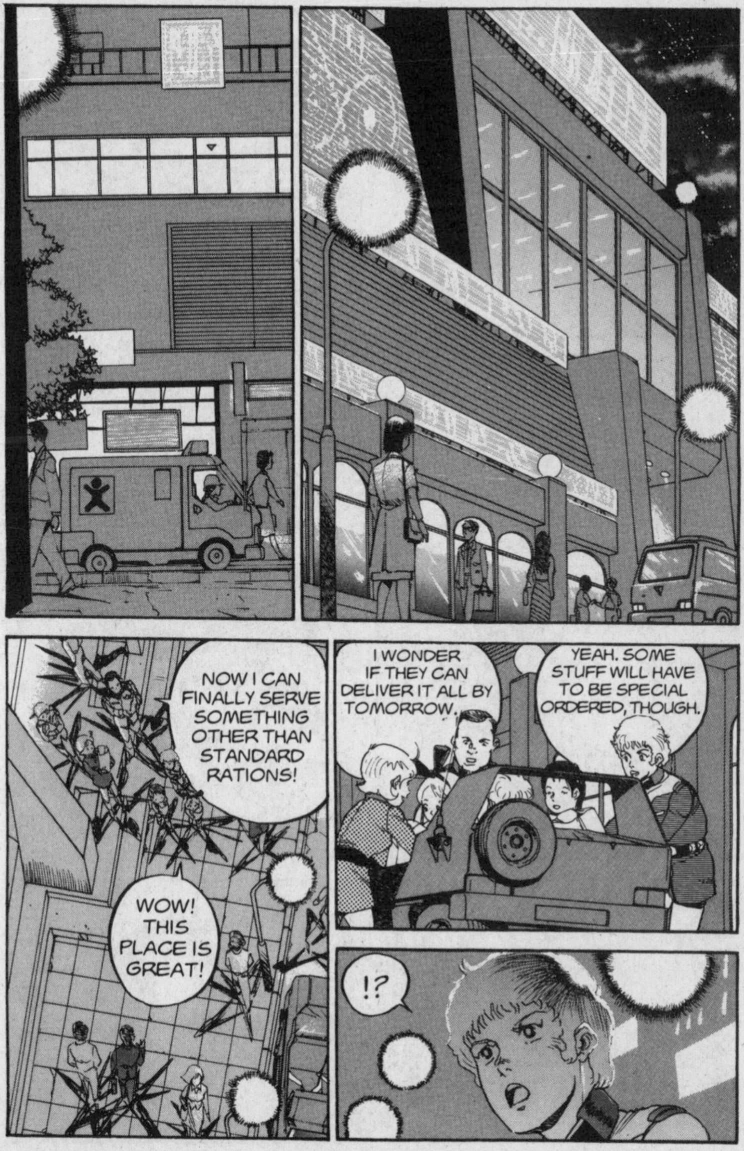
NOW I CAN FINALLY SERVE SOMETHING OTHER THAN STANDARD RATIONS!
WOW! THIS PLACE IS GREAT!
I WONDER IF THEY CAN DELIVER IT ALL BY TOMORROW.
YEAH. SOME STUFF WILL HAVE TO BE SPECIAL ORDERED, THOUGH.
!?

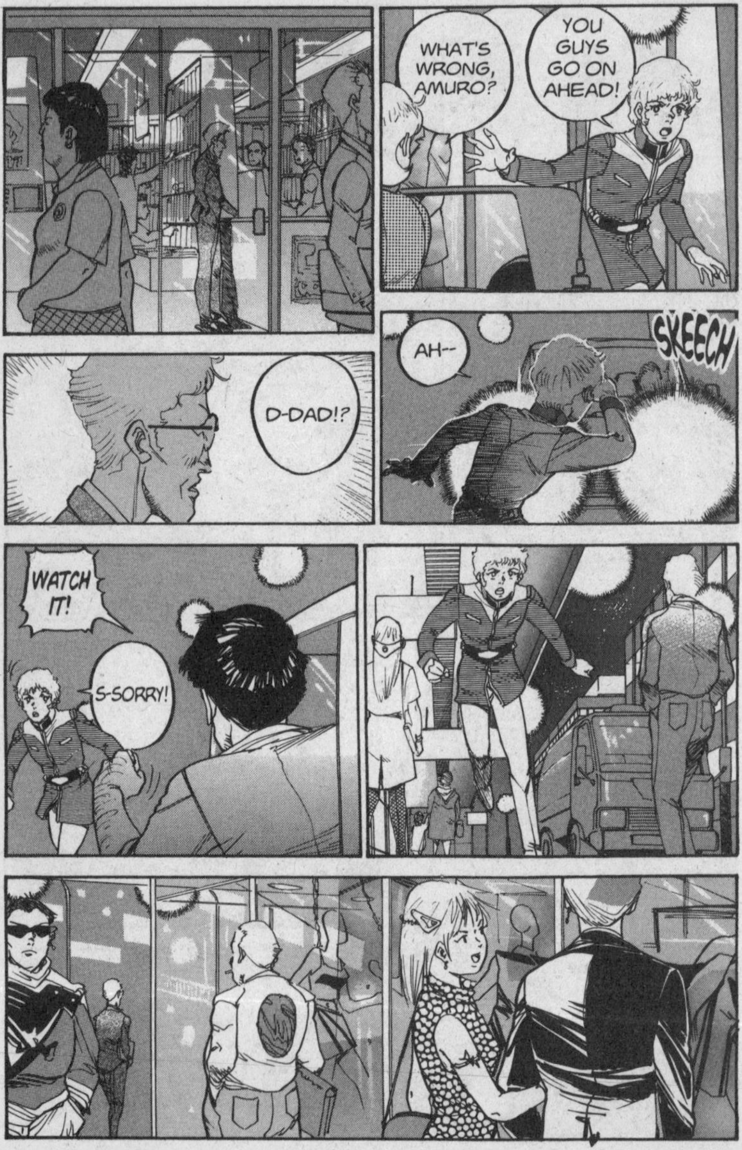
WHAT'S WRONG, AMURO?
YOU GUYS GO ON AHEAD!
D-DAD!?
AH--
SKEECH
WATCH IT!
S-SORRY!

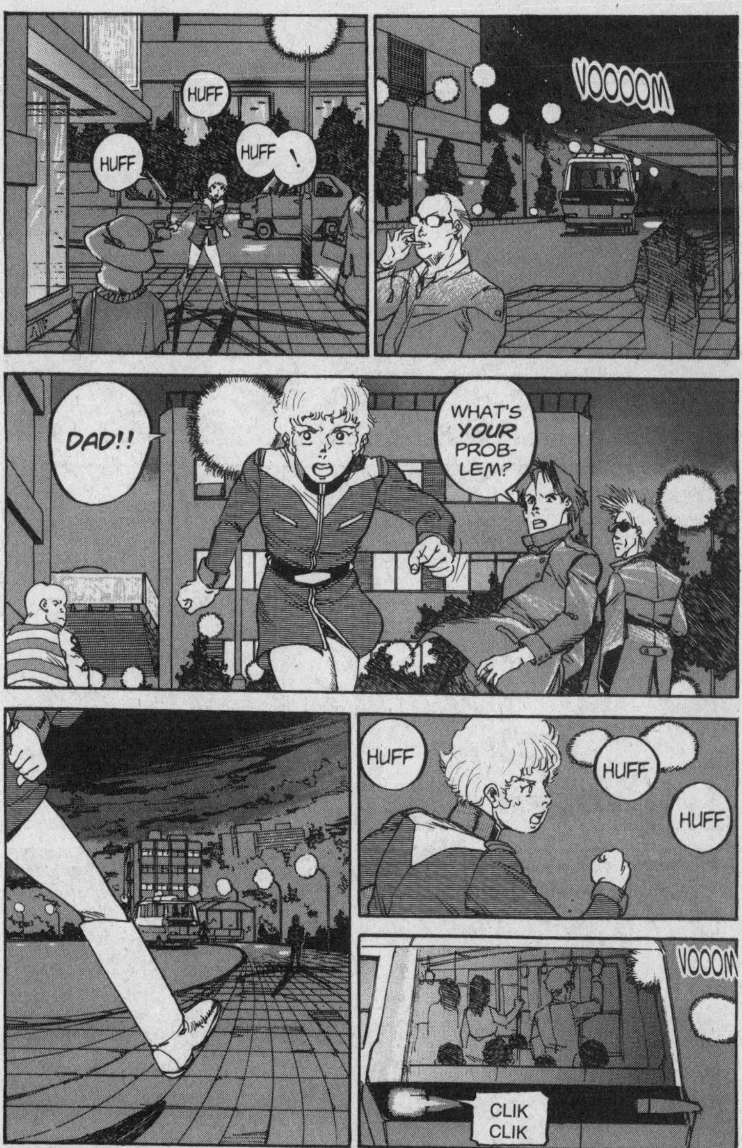
HUFF
HUFF
HUFF
!
VOOOOM
DAD!!
WHAT'S YOUR PROB-LEM?
HUFF
HUFF
HUFF
VOOOM
CLIK
CLIK

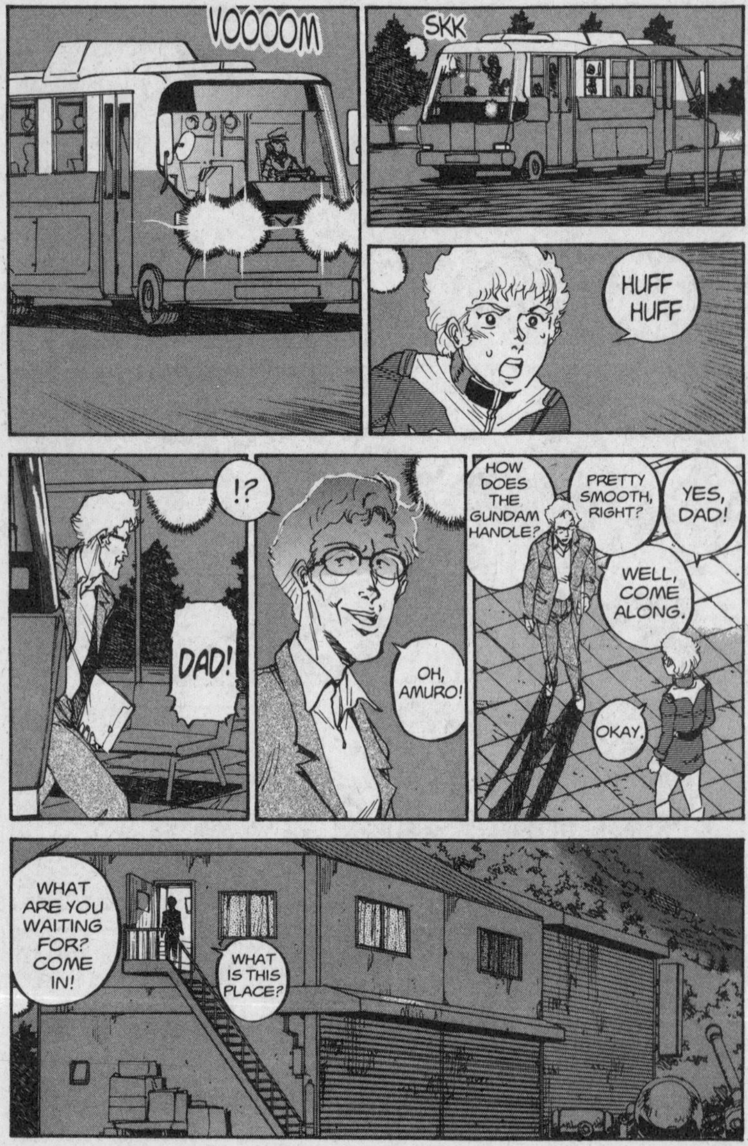
VOOOOM
SKK
HUFF HUFF
!?
DAD!
OH, AMURO!
HOW DOES THE GUNDAM HANDLE?
PRETTY SMOOTH, RIGHT?
YES, DAD!
WELL, COME ALONG.
OKAY.
WHAT ARE YOU WAITING FOR? COME IN!
WHAT IS THIS PLACE?

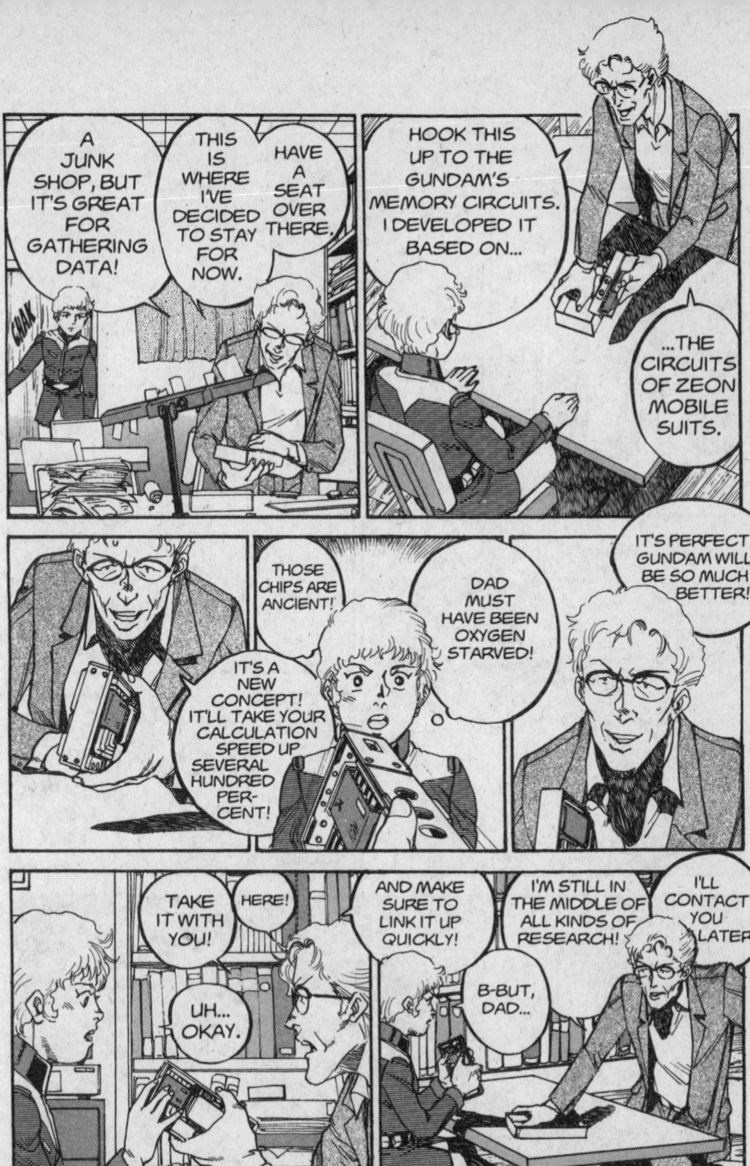
CHAK
A JUNK SHOP, BUT IT'S GREAT FOR GATHERING DATA!
THIS IS WHERE I'VE DECIDED TO STAY FOR NOW.
HAVE A SEAT OVER THERE.
HOOK THIS UP TO THE GUNDAM'S MEMORY CIRCUITS. I DEVELOPED IT BASED ON...
...THE CIRCUITS OF ZEON MOBILE SUITS.
IT'S A NEW CONCEPT! IT'LL TAKE YOUR CALCULATION SPEED UP SEVERAL HUNDRED PER-CENT!
THOSE CHIPS ARE ANCIENT!
DAD MUST HAVE BEEN OXYGEN STARVED!
IT'S PERFECT! GUNDAM WILL BE SO MUCH BETTER!
TAKE IT WITH YOU!
HERE!
UH... OKAY.
AND MAKE SURE TO LINK IT UP QUICKLY!
I'M STILL IN THE MIDDLE OF ALL KINDS OF RESEARCH!
I'LL CONTACT YOU LATER.
B-BUT, DAD...

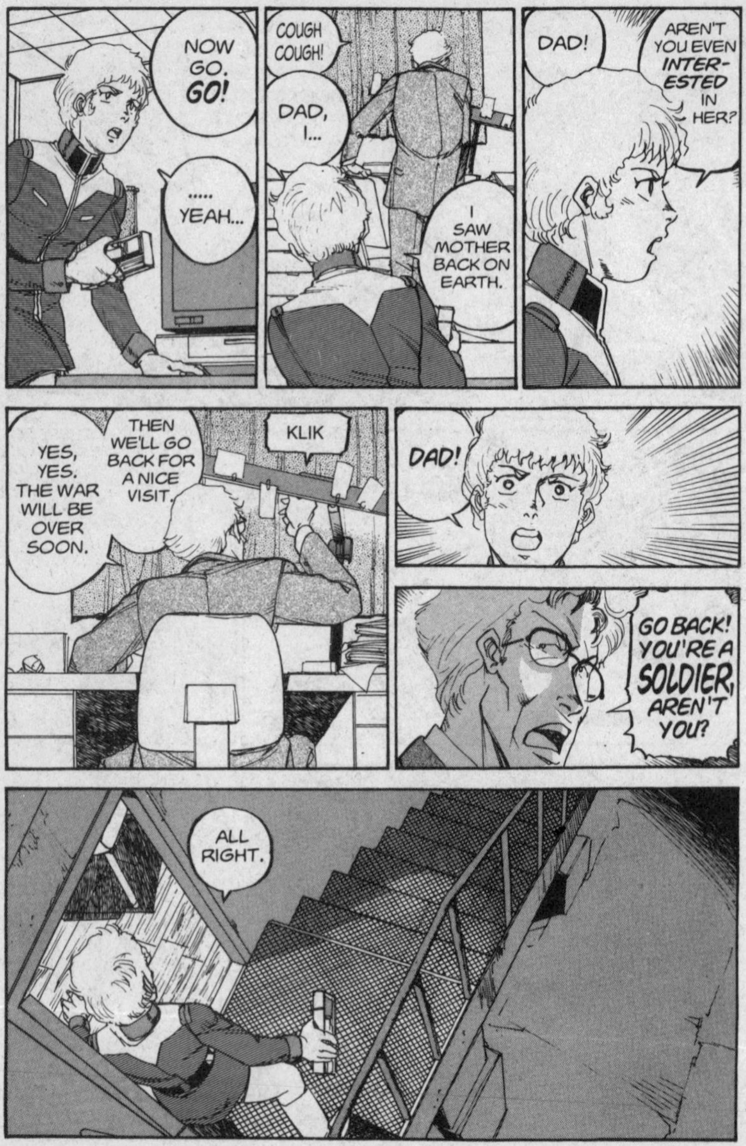
NOW GO. GO!
..... YEAH...
COUGH COUGH!
DAD, I...
I SAW MOTHER BACK ON EARTH.
DAD!
AREN'T YOU EVEN INTER-ESTED IN HER?
YES, YES. THE WAR WILL BE OVER SOON.
THEN WE'LL GO BACK FOR A NICE VISIT.
KLIK
DAD!
GO BACK! YOU'RE A SOLDIER, AREN'T YOU?
ALL RIGHT.

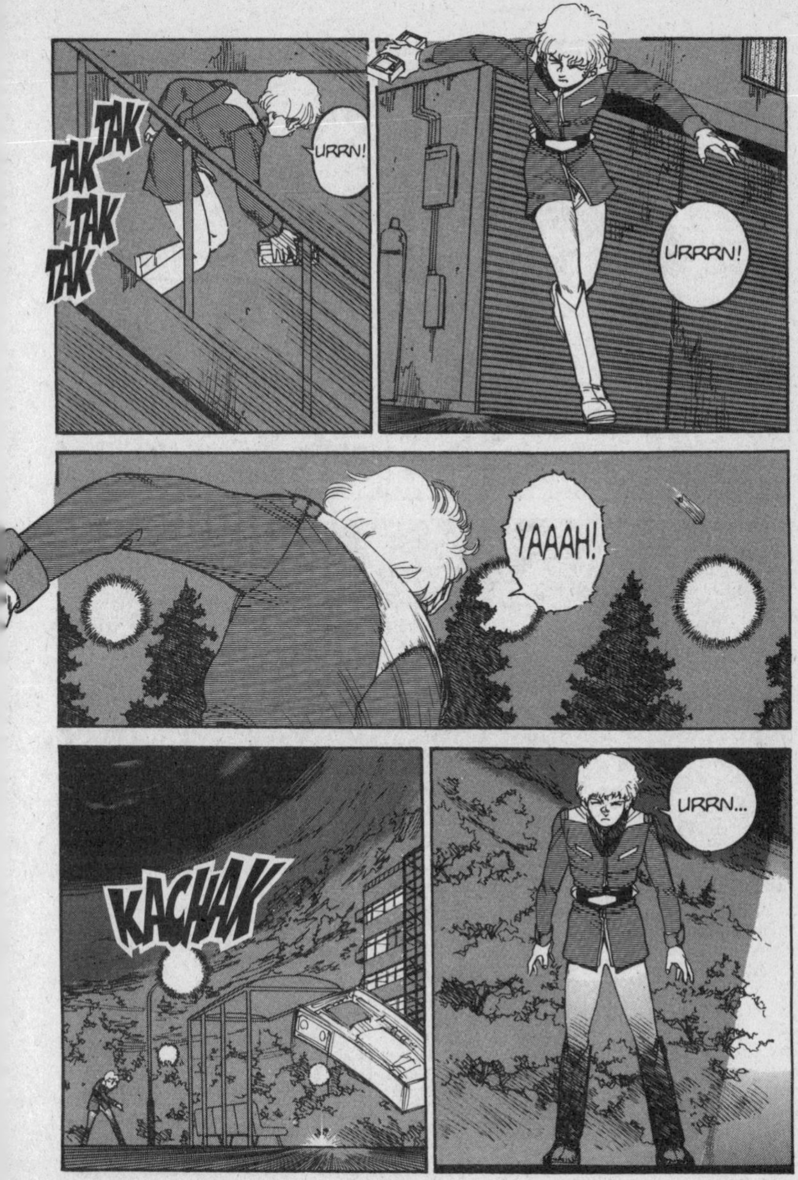
TAK TAK TAK TAK TAK
URRN!
URRRN!
YAAAH!
KACHAK
URRN...

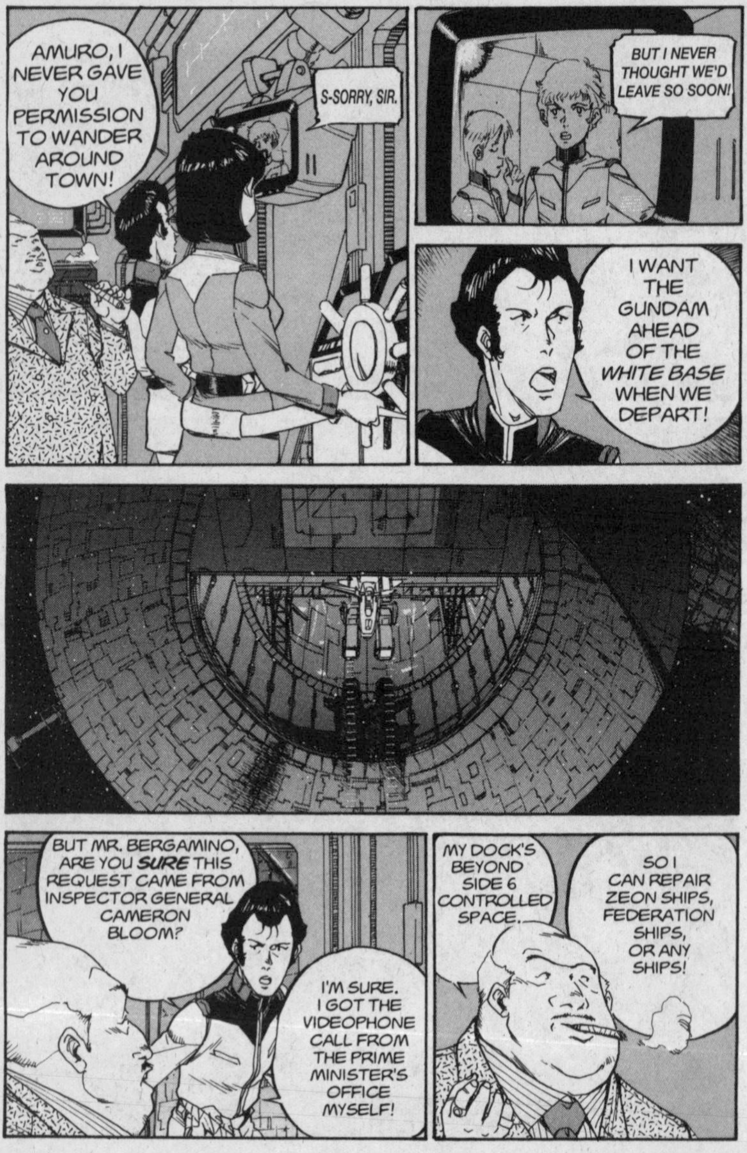
AMURO, I NEVER GAVE YOU PERMISSION TO WANDER AROUND TOWN!
S-SORRY, SIR.
BUT I NEVER THOUGHT WE'D LEAVE SO SOON!
I WANT THE GUNDAM AHEAD OF THE WHITE BASE WHEN WE DEPART!
BUT MR. BERGAMINO, ARE YOU SURE THIS REQUEST CAME FROM INSPECTOR GENERAL CAMERON BLOOM?
I'M SURE. I GOT THE VIDEOPHONE CALL FROM THE PRIME MINISTER'S OFFICE MYSELF!
MY DOCK'S BEYOND SIDE 6 CONTROLLED SPACE.
SO I CAN REPAIR ZEON SHIPS, FEDERATION SHIPS, OR ANY SHIPS!

WE'RE BEING FOLLOWED BY THE ZEONS.

IS THAT A PROBLEM?

FOR ME? I GOT FRIENDS IN HIGH PLACES...

...ON BOTH SIDES OF THE CONFLICT.

SO *THIS* YOUNG LADY CAN FEEL AT EASE.

THANK YOU, MR. BERGAMINO.

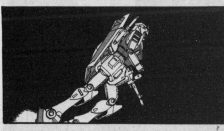

YO, AMURO. YOU'RE LOOKIN' A LITTLE DOWN.

ME? NO, I'M FINE.

THAT'S THE RIGHT ATTITUDE. GOOD BOY!

LT. SLEGGAR, COULD YOU STOP CALLING ME A BOY?

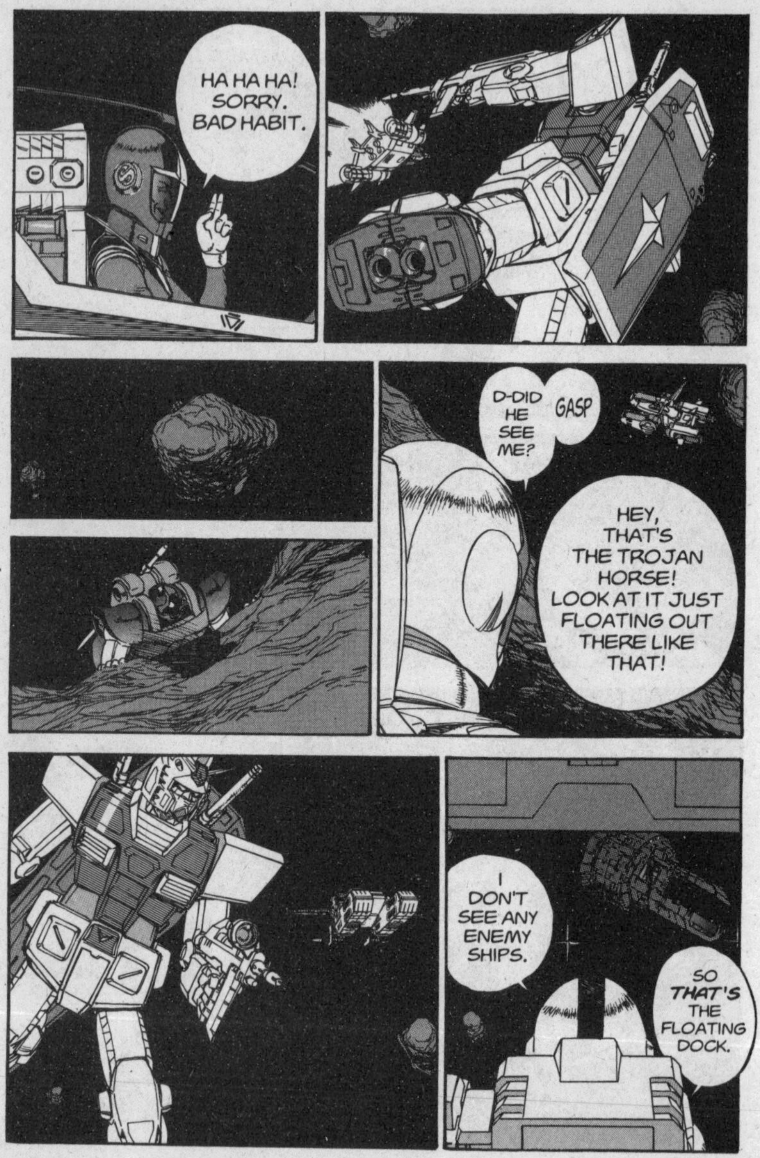
HA HA HA! SORRY. BAD HABIT.
D-DID HE SEE ME?
GASP
HEY, THAT'S THE TROJAN HORSE! LOOK AT IT JUST FLOATING OUT THERE LIKE THAT!
I DON'T SEE ANY ENEMY SHIPS.
SO *THAT'S* THE FLOATING DOCK.

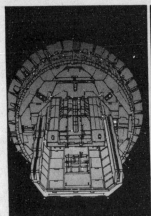

HM? WHAT'S THAT?

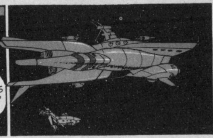

WE GOT A SIGNAL FROM KAYAHAWA?

SHHT

THE SIGNAL SAYS THAT THE TROJAN HORSE *LEFT* SIDE 6 AIRSPACE!

CONFIRM ITS POSITION! START THE EN-GINES!

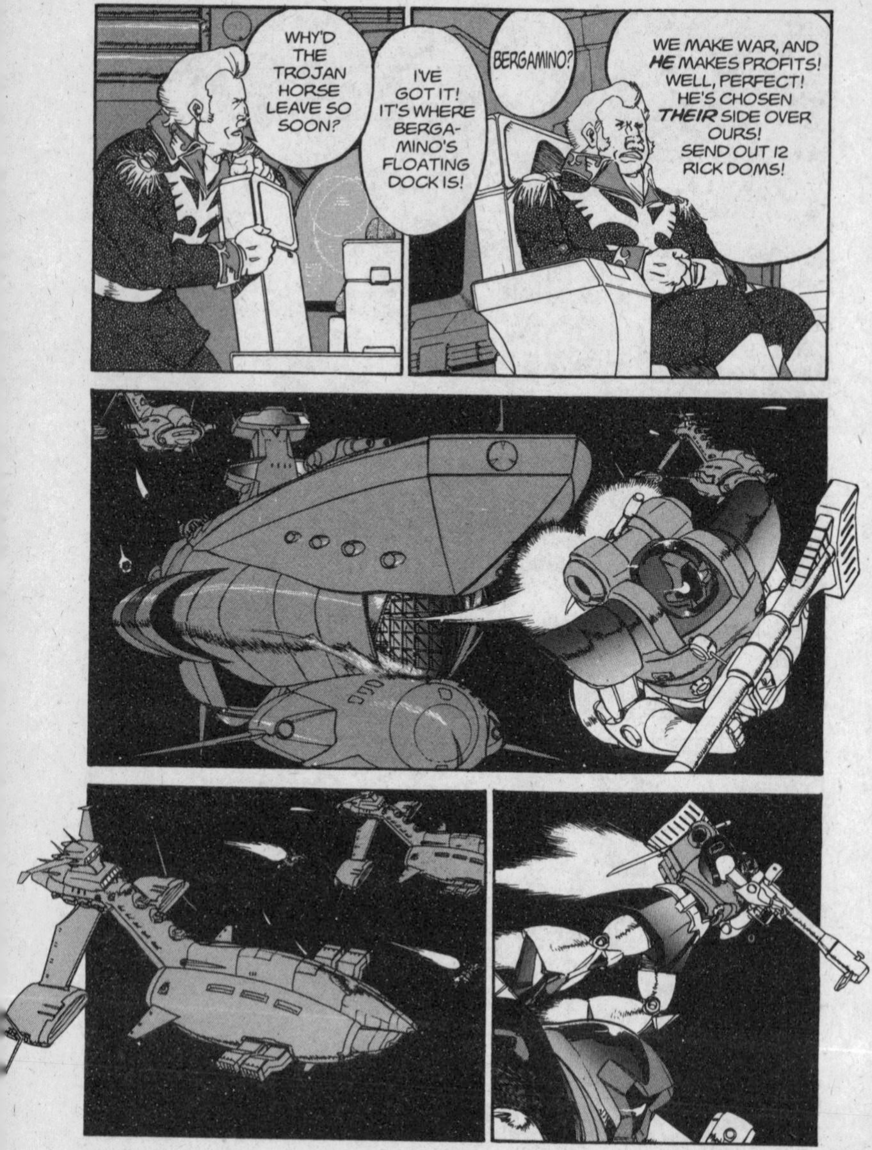
WHY'D THE TROJAN HORSE LEAVE SO SOON?
I'VE GOT IT! IT'S WHERE BERGA-MINO'S FLOATING DOCK IS!
BERGAMINO?
WE MAKE WAR, AND **HE** MAKES PROFITS! WELL, PERFECT! HE'S CHOSEN **THEIR** SIDE OVER OURS! SEND OUT 12 RICK DOMS!

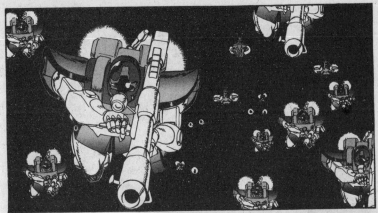

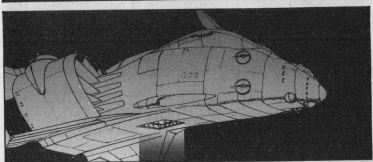

CONSCON FOUND THE TROJAN HORSE'S POSITION?

SIR.

I THINK SO, SIR. AND HE'S SENT OUT RICK DOMS TO ATTACK THEM.

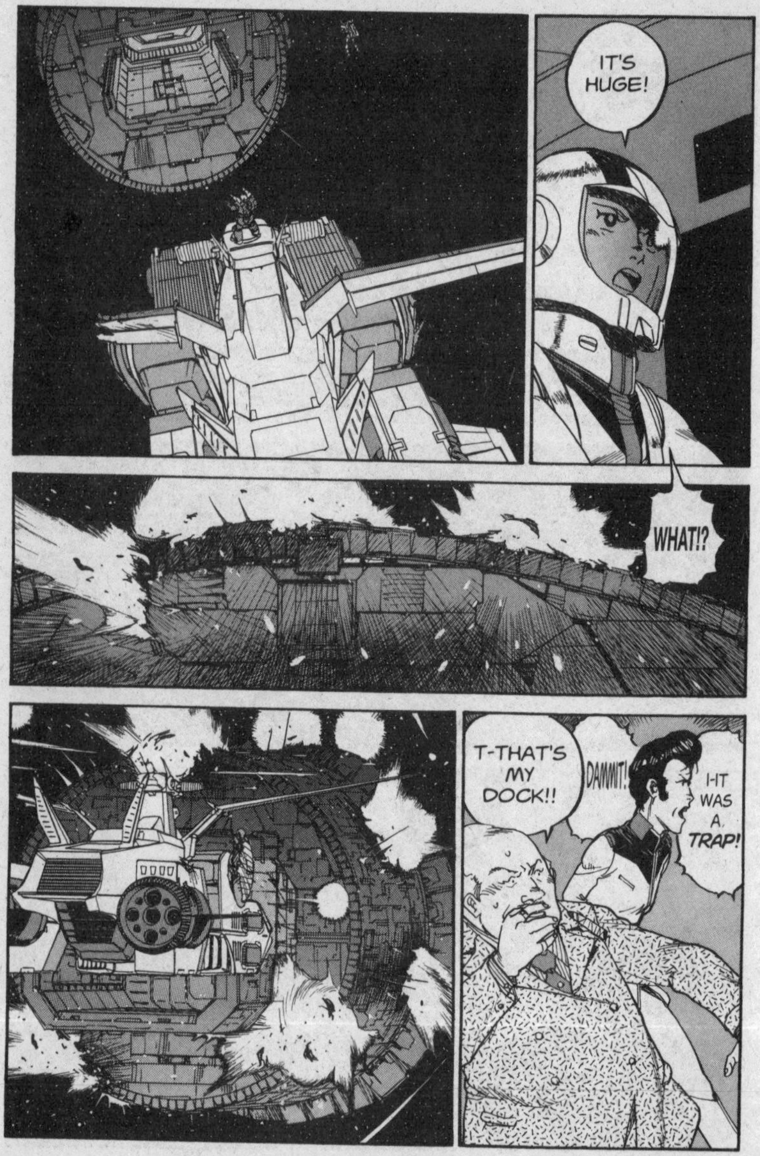
IT'S HUGE!
WHAT!?
T-THAT'S MY DOCK!!
DAMMIT!
I-IT WAS A TRAP!

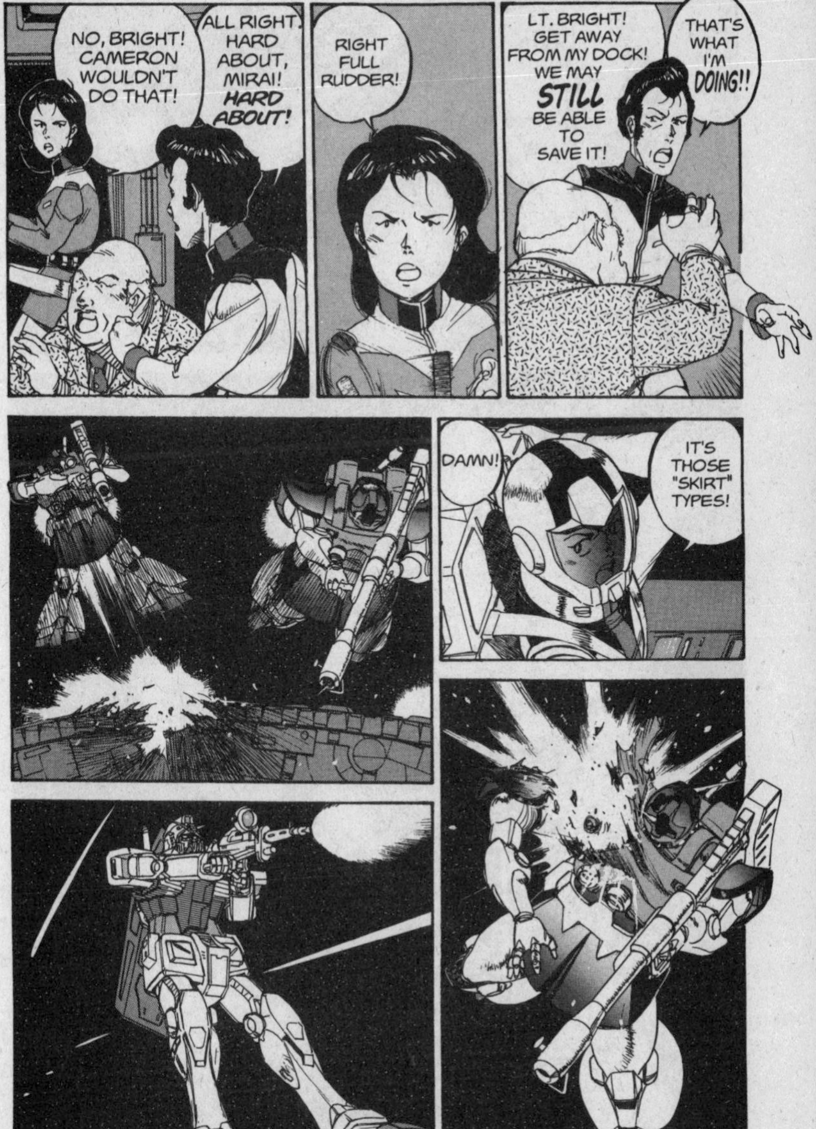
NO, BRIGHT! CAMERON WOULDN'T DO THAT!
ALL RIGHT. HARD ABOUT, MIRAI! HARD ABOUT!
RIGHT FULL RUDDER!
LT. BRIGHT! GET AWAY FROM MY DOCK! WE MAY STILL BE ABLE TO SAVE IT!
THAT'S WHAT I'M DOING!!
DAMN!
IT'S THOSE "SKIRT" TYPES!

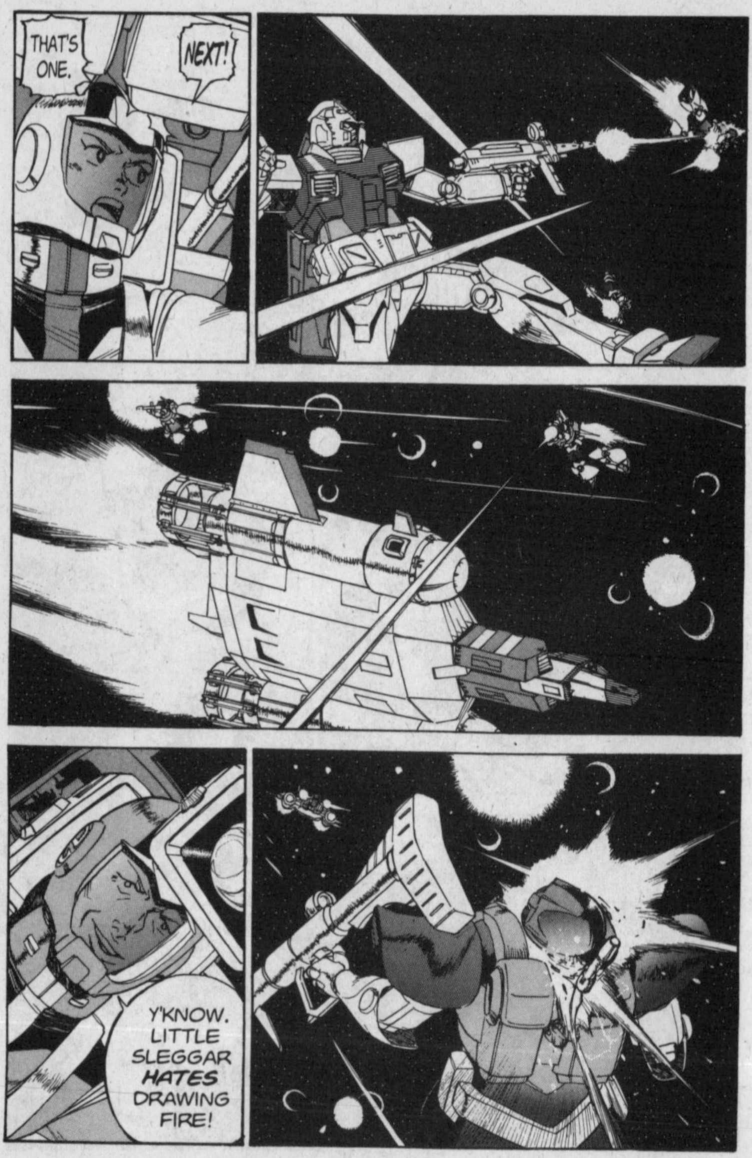
THAT'S ONE.
NEXT!
Y'KNOW. LITTLE SLEGGAR HATES DRAWING FIRE!

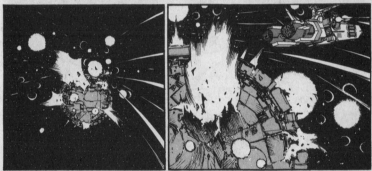

CONCEN-
TRATE ALL
FIRE ON THE
CENTER
SHIP!

WHERE
ARE OUR
MOBILE
SUITS?

THE GUNDAM AND THE CORE BOOSTER HAS THEM IN A DOGFIGHT!

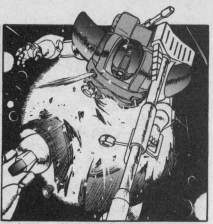

THAT'S *THREE!*

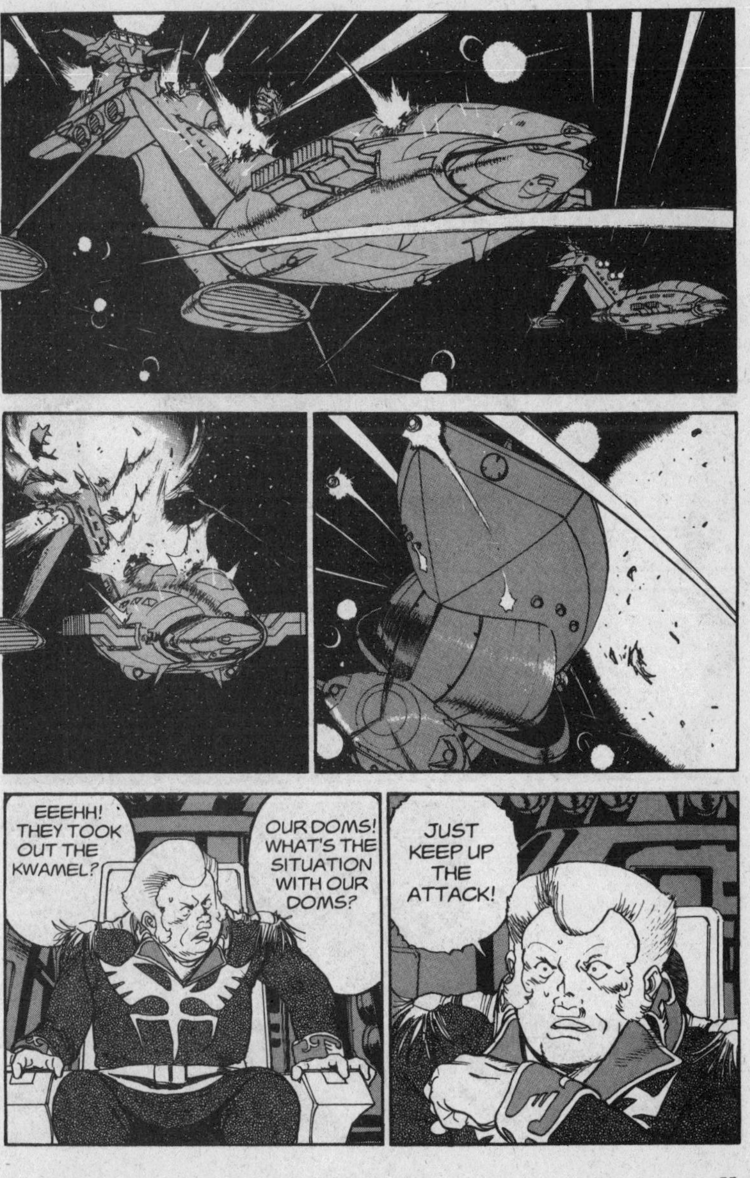
EEEHH! THEY TOOK OUT THE KWAMEL?
OUR DOMS! WHAT'S THE SITUATION WITH OUR DOMS?
JUST KEEP UP THE ATTACK!

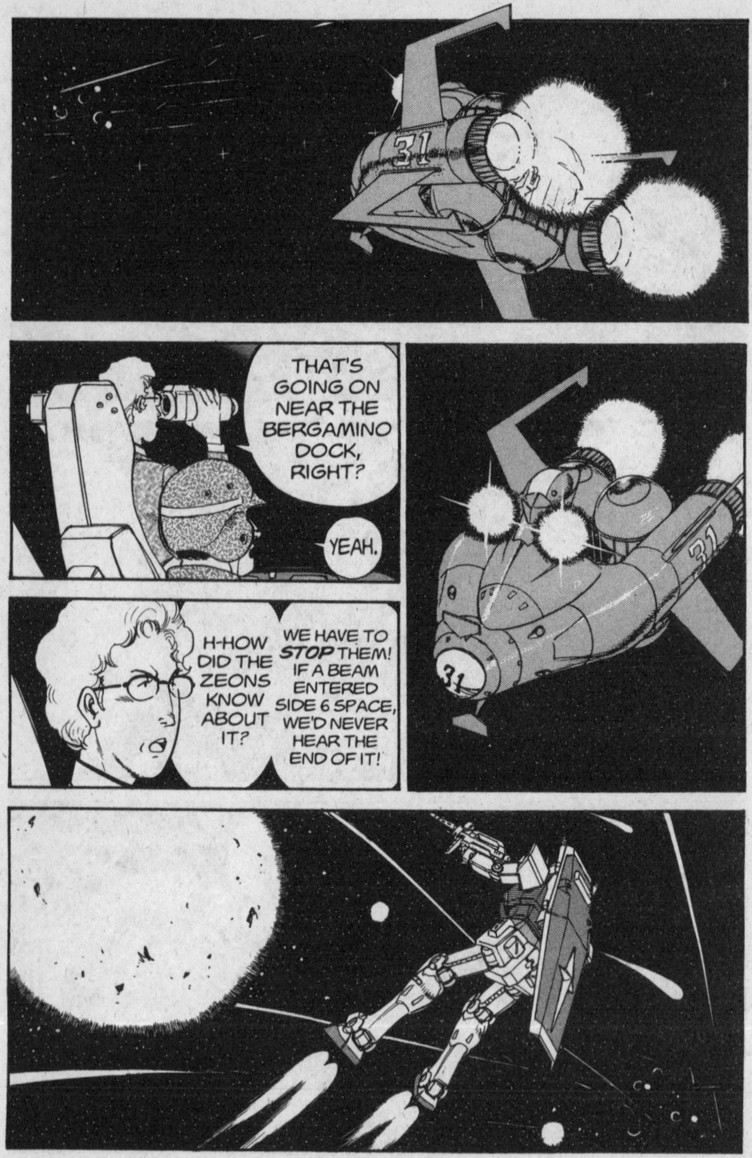
THAT'S GOING ON NEAR THE BERGAMINO DOCK, RIGHT?
YEAH.
H-HOW DID THE ZEONS KNOW ABOUT IT?
WE HAVE TO **STOP** THEM! IF A BEAM ENTERED SIDE 6 SPACE, WE'D NEVER HEAR THE END OF IT!

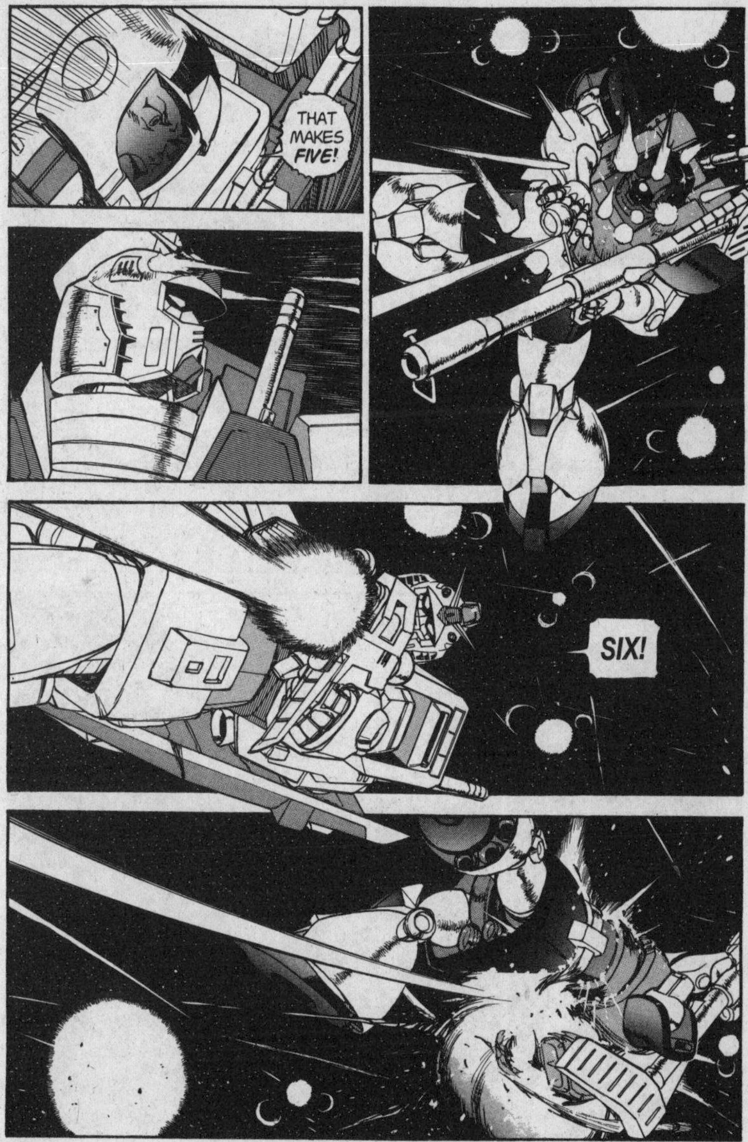
THAT MAKES FIVE!
SIX!

YOU LITTLE...

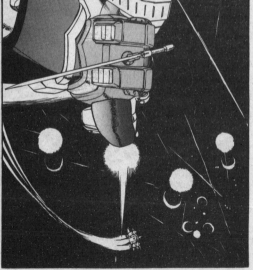

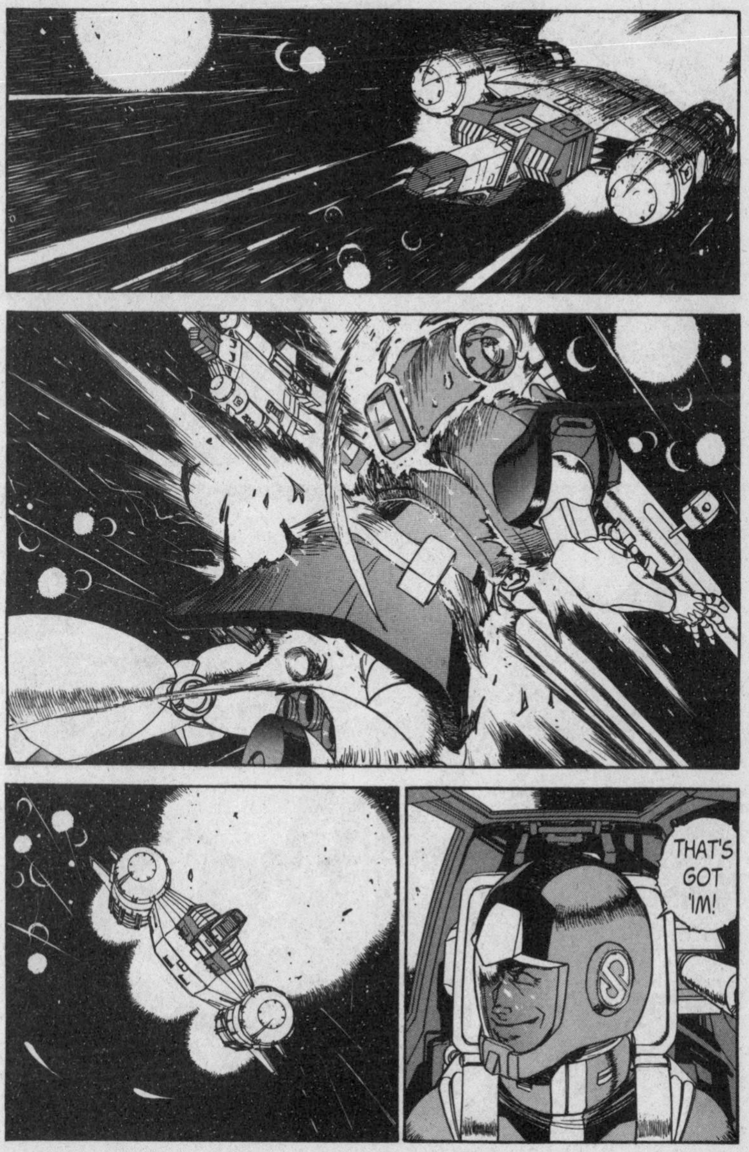
THAT'S GOT 'IM!

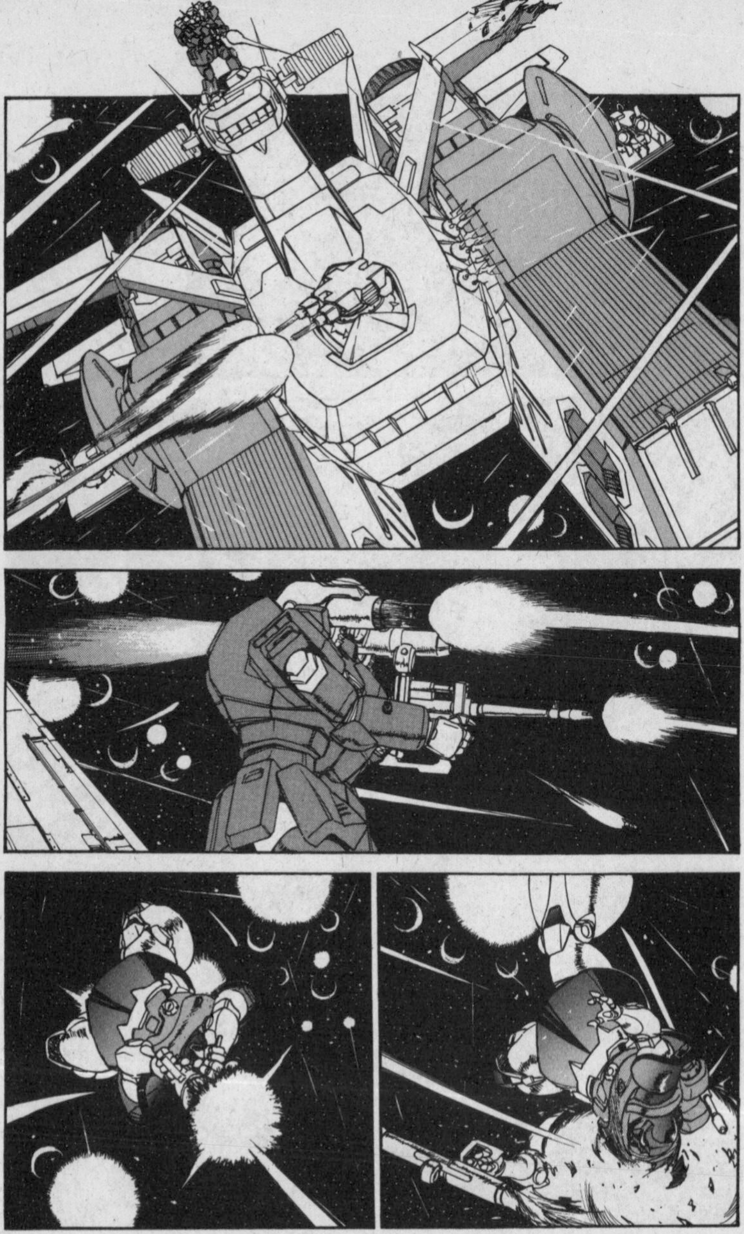

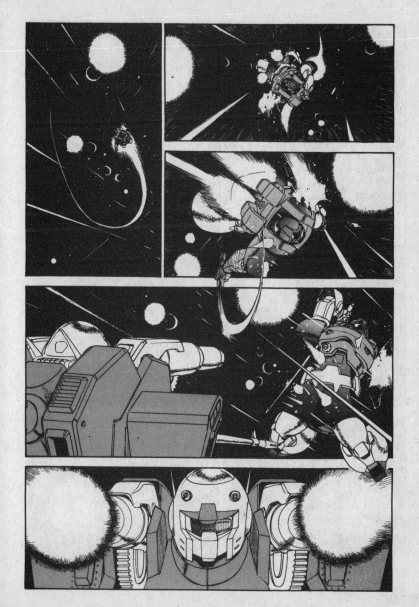

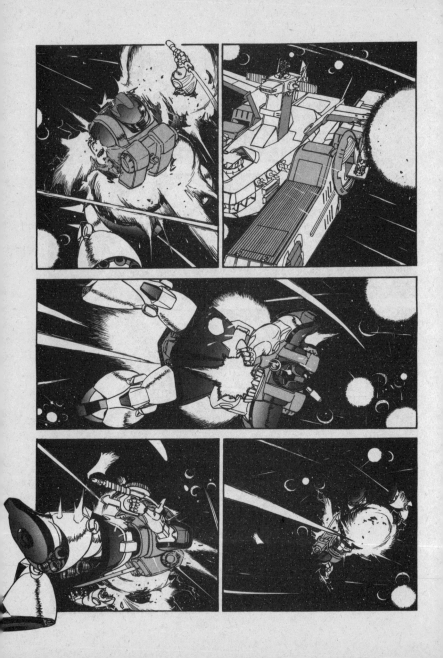

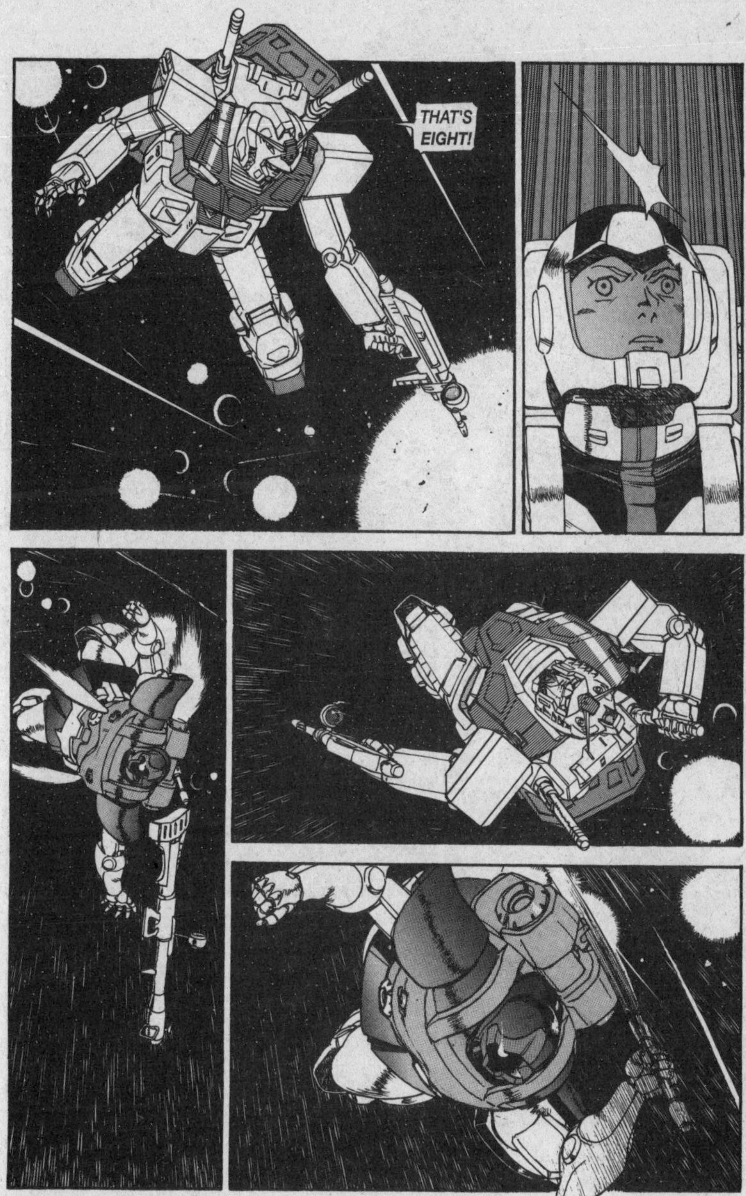
THAT'S EIGHT!

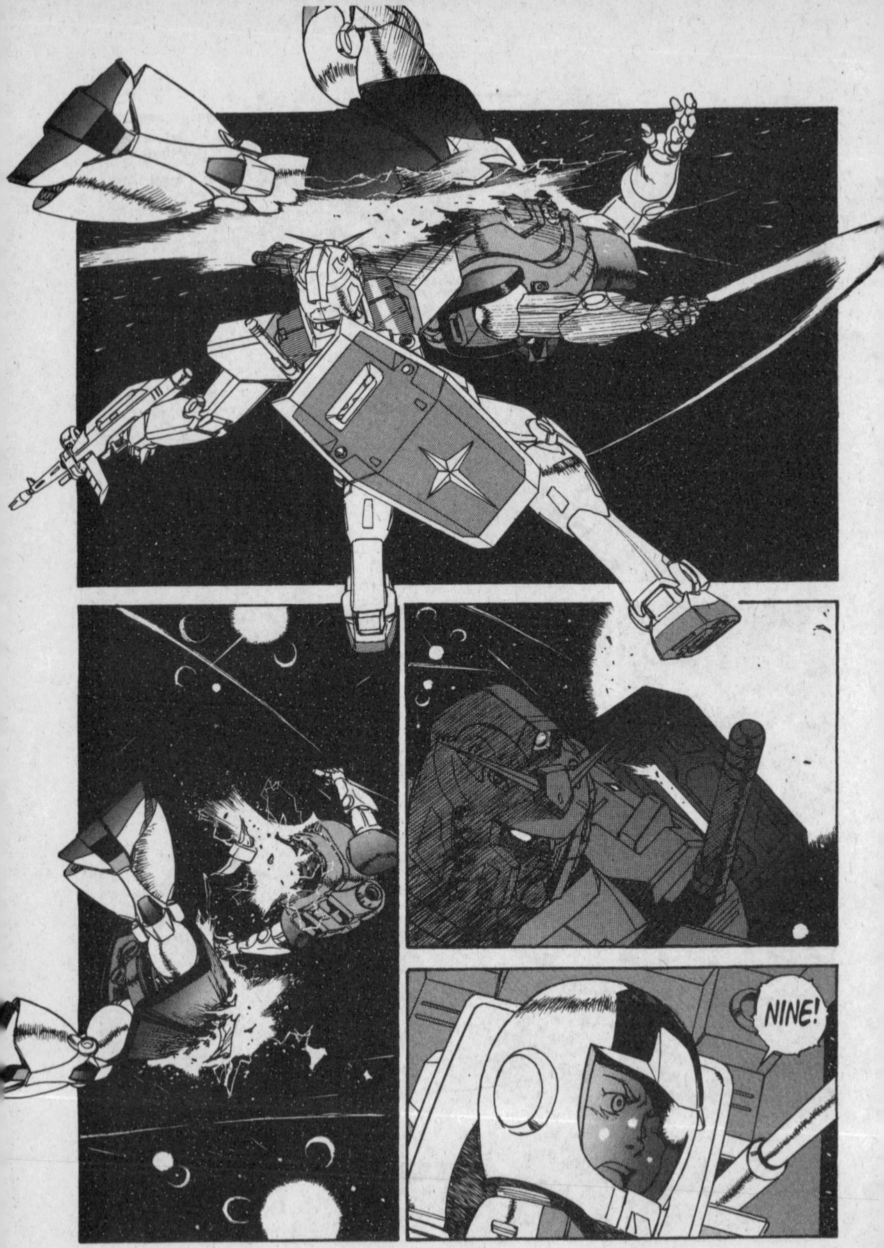
NINE!

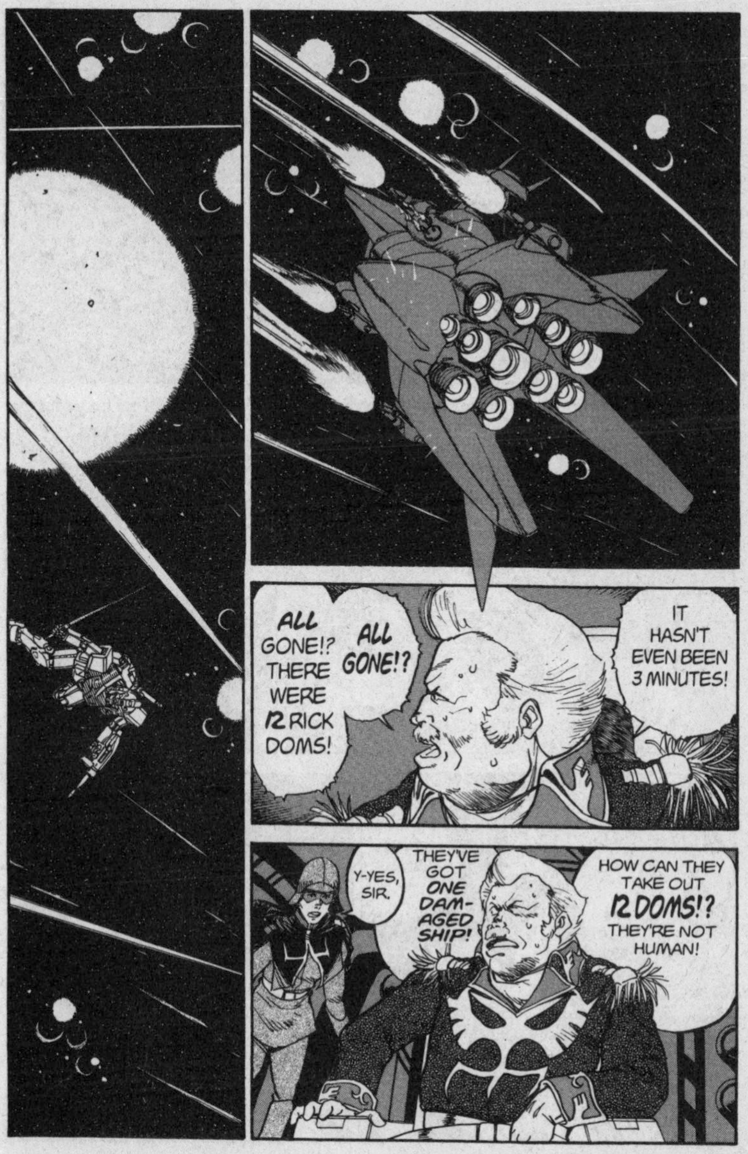
ALL GONE!? THERE WERE 12 RICK DOMS!
ALL GONE!?
IT HASN'T EVEN BEEN 3 MINUTES!
Y-YES, SIR.
THEY'VE GOT ONE DAMAGED SHIP!
HOW CAN THEY TAKE OUT 12 DOMS!? THEY'RE NOT HUMAN!

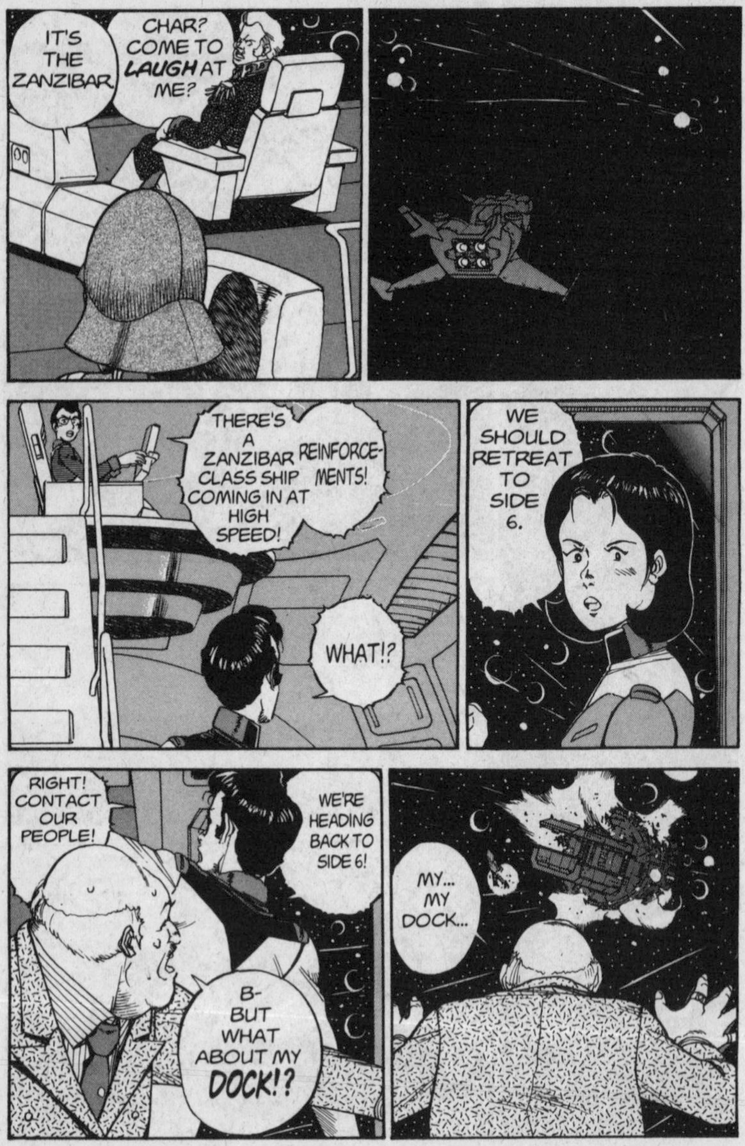

IT'S THE ZANZIBAR.
CHAR? COME TO **LAUGH** AT ME?
THERE'S A ZANZIBAR CLASS SHIP COMING IN AT HIGH SPEED!
REINFORCE-MENTS!
WHAT!?
WE SHOULD RETREAT TO SIDE 6.
RIGHT! CONTACT OUR PEOPLE!
WE'RE HEADING BACK TO SIDE 6!
B- BUT WHAT ABOUT MY **DOCK!?**
MY... MY DOCK...

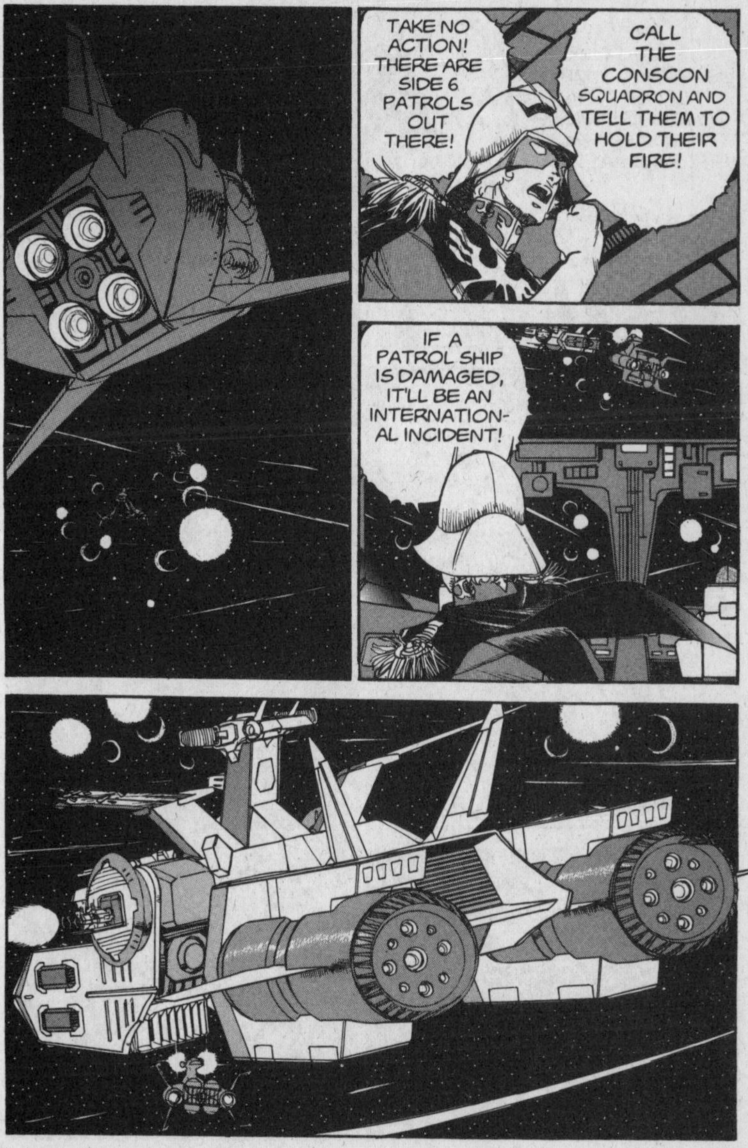
TAKE NO ACTION! THERE ARE SIDE 6 PATROLS OUT THERE!
CALL THE CONSCON SQUADRON AND TELL THEM TO HOLD THEIR FIRE!
IF A PATROL SHIP IS DAMAGED, IT'LL BE AN INTERNATION-AL INCIDENT!

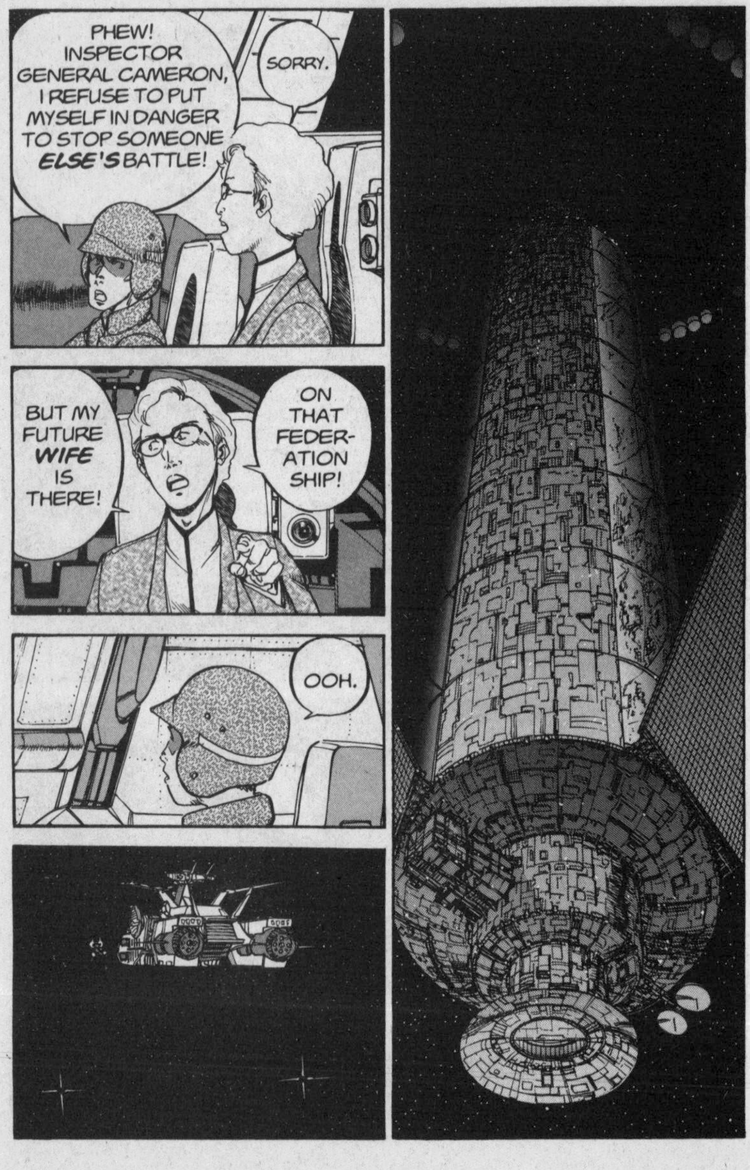
PHEW! INSPECTOR GENERAL CAMERON, I REFUSE TO PUT MYSELF IN DANGER TO STOP SOMEONE ELSE'S BATTLE!
SORRY.
BUT MY FUTURE WIFE IS THERE!
ON THAT FEDER-ATION SHIP!
OOH.

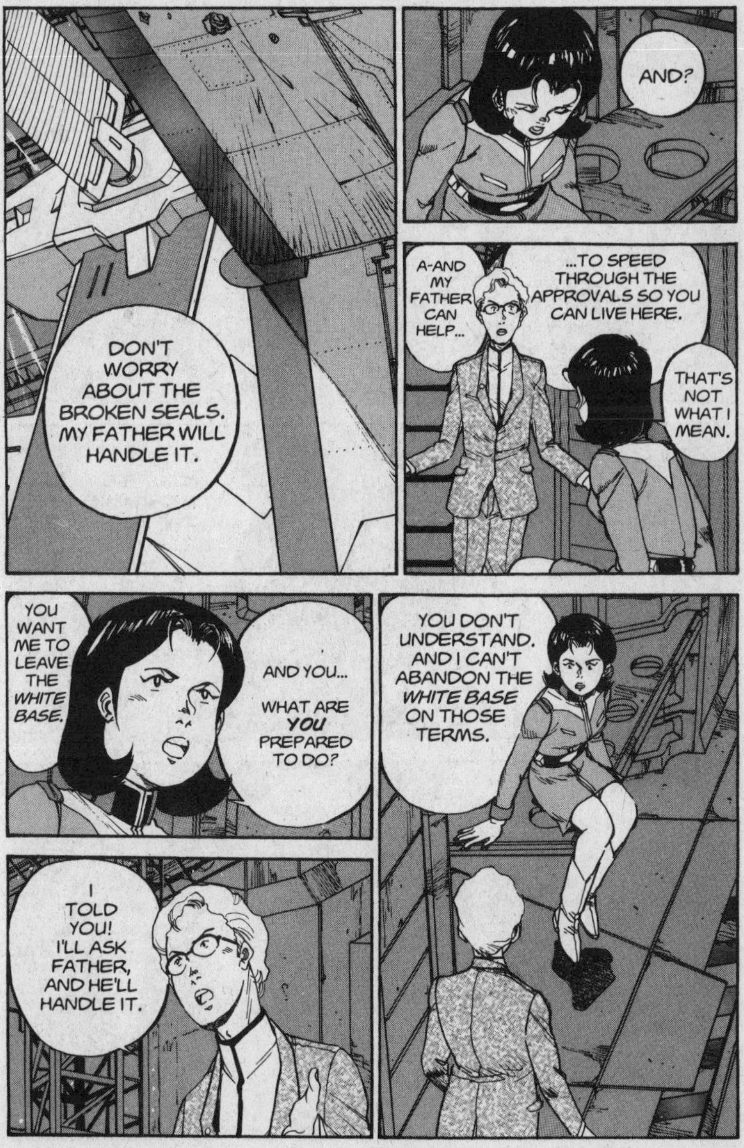
DON'T WORRY ABOUT THE BROKEN SEALS. MY FATHER WILL HANDLE IT.
AND?
A-AND MY FATHER CAN HELP...
...TO SPEED THROUGH THE APPROVALS SO YOU CAN LIVE HERE.
THAT'S NOT WHAT I MEAN.
YOU WANT ME TO LEAVE THE *WHITE BASE.*
AND YOU...
WHAT ARE ***YOU*** PREPARED TO DO?
YOU DON'T UNDERSTAND. AND I CAN'T ABANDON THE *WHITE BASE* ON THOSE TERMS.
I TOLD YOU! I'LL ASK FATHER, AND HE'LL HANDLE IT.

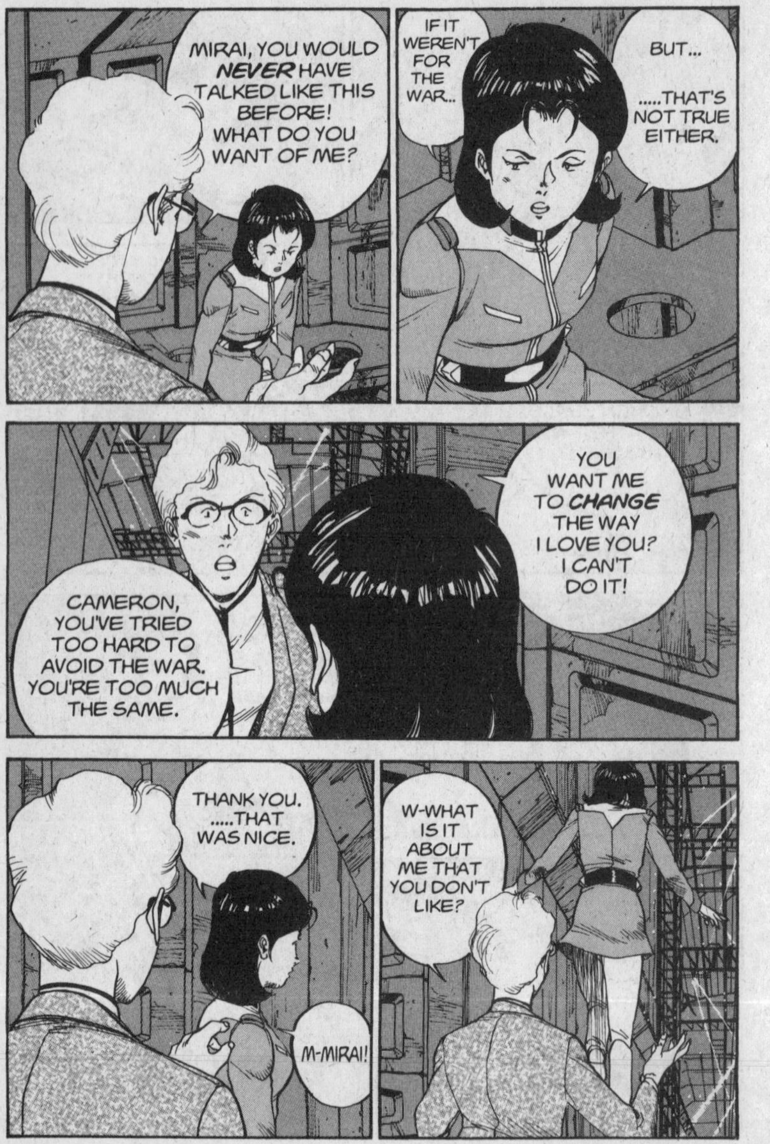
MIRAI, YOU WOULD **NEVER** HAVE TALKED LIKE THIS BEFORE! WHAT DO YOU WANT OF ME?
IF IT WEREN'T FOR THE WAR...
BUT...
.....THAT'S NOT TRUE EITHER.
CAMERON, YOU'VE TRIED TOO HARD TO AVOID THE WAR. YOU'RE TOO MUCH THE SAME.
YOU WANT ME TO **CHANGE** THE WAY I LOVE YOU? I CAN'T DO IT!
THANK YOU. .....THAT WAS NICE.
M-MIRAI!
W-WHAT IS IT ABOUT ME THAT YOU DON'T LIKE?

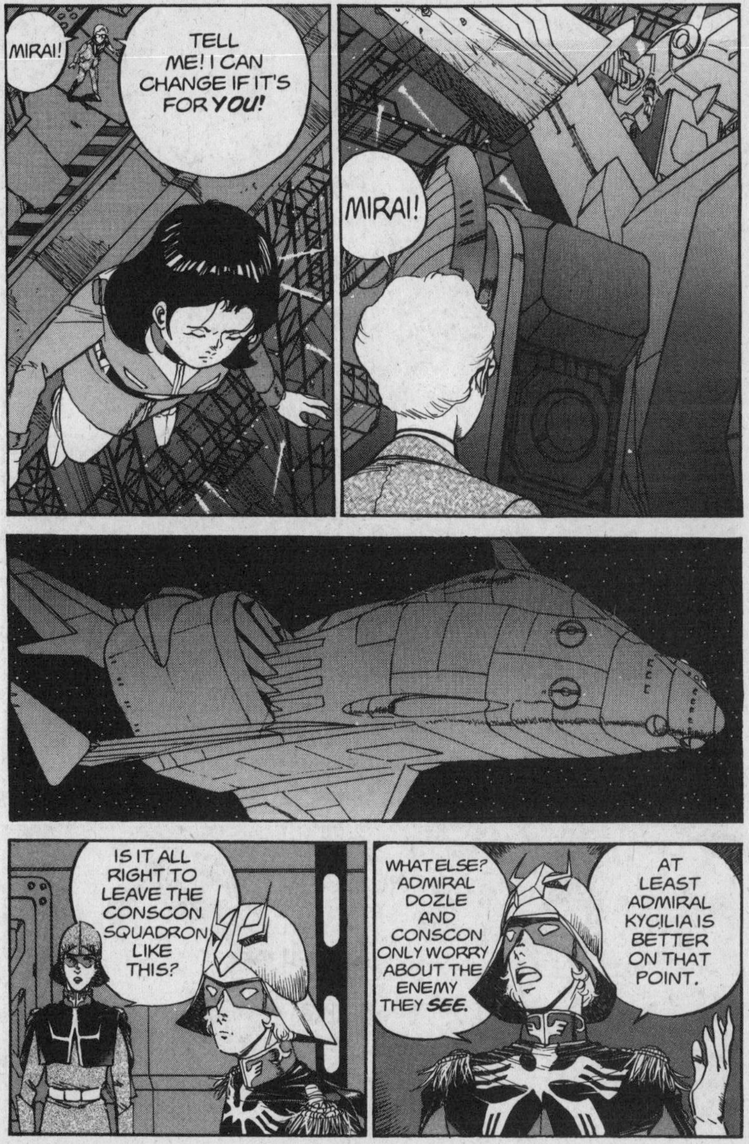
MIRAI!
TELL ME! I CAN CHANGE IF IT'S FOR YOU!
MIRAI!
IS IT ALL RIGHT TO LEAVE THE CONSCON SQUADRON LIKE THIS?
WHAT ELSE? ADMIRAL DOZLE AND CONSCON ONLY WORRY ABOUT THE ENEMY THEY SEE.
AT LEAST ADMIRAL KYCILIA IS BETTER ON THAT POINT.

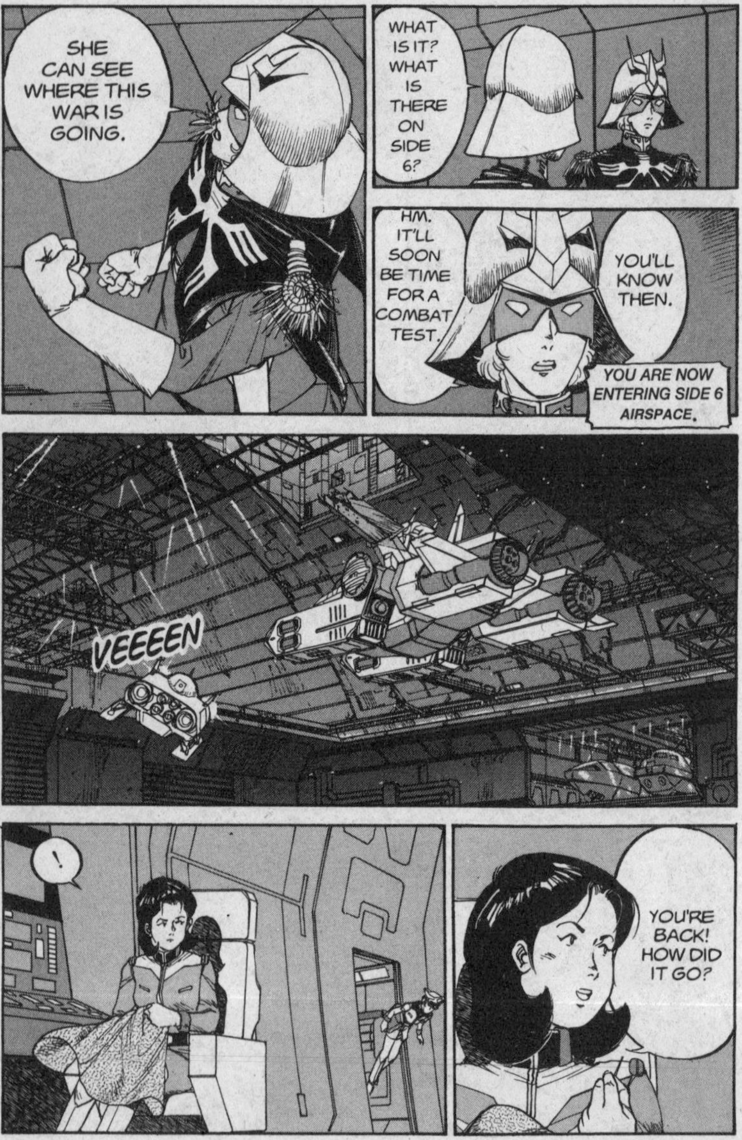
SHE CAN SEE WHERE THIS WAR IS GOING.
WHAT IS IT? WHAT IS THERE ON SIDE 6?
HM. IT'LL SOON BE TIME FOR A COMBAT TEST.
YOU'LL KNOW THEN.
YOU ARE NOW ENTERING SIDE 6 AIRSPACE.
VEEEEN
!
YOU'RE BACK! HOW DID IT GO?

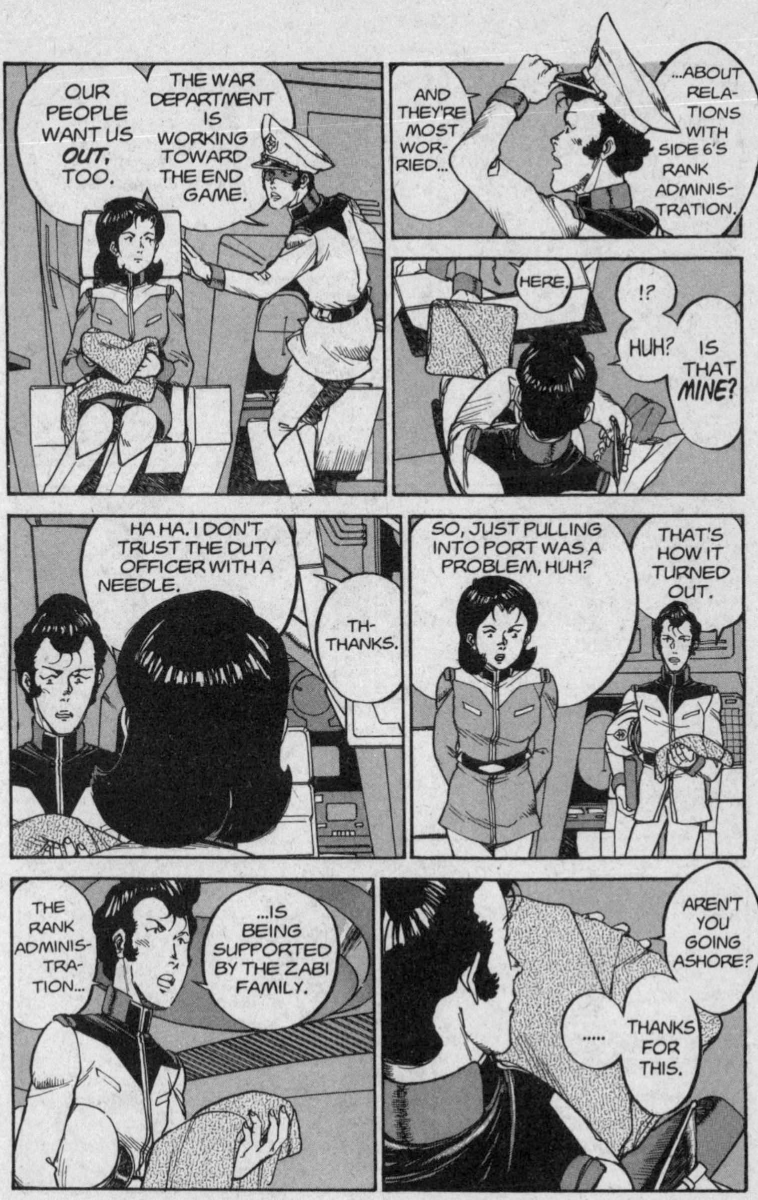
OUR PEOPLE WANT US *OUT,* TOO.
THE WAR DEPARTMENT IS WORKING TOWARD THE END GAME.
AND THEY'RE MOST WORRIED...
...ABOUT RELATIONS WITH SIDE 6'S RANK ADMINISTRATION.
HERE.
!?
HUH?
IS THAT *MINE?*
HA HA. I DON'T TRUST THE DUTY OFFICER WITH A NEEDLE.
TH-THANKS.
SO, JUST PULLING INTO PORT WAS A PROBLEM, HUH?
THAT'S HOW IT TURNED OUT.
THE RANK ADMINISTRATION...
...IS BEING SUPPORTED BY THE ZABI FAMILY.
AREN'T YOU GOING ASHORE?
.....
THANKS FOR THIS.

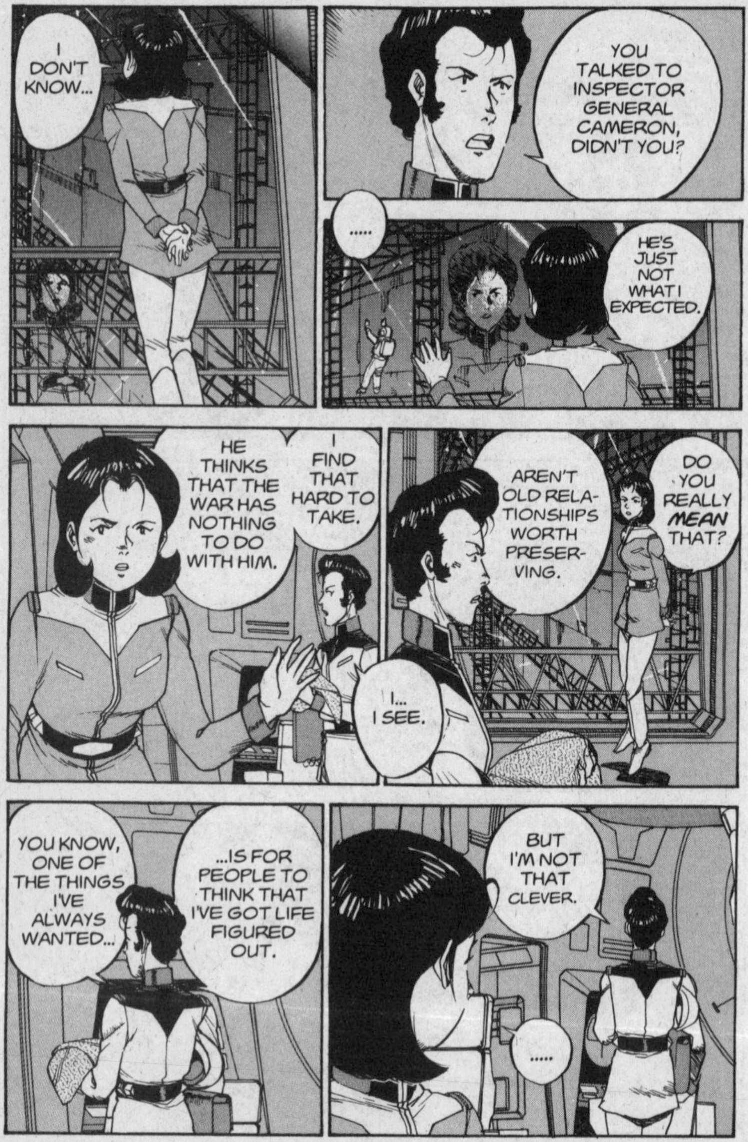
I DON'T KNOW...
YOU TALKED TO INSPECTOR GENERAL CAMERON, DIDN'T YOU?
.....
HE'S JUST NOT WHAT I EXPECTED.
HE THINKS THAT THE WAR HAS NOTHING TO DO WITH HIM.
I FIND THAT HARD TO TAKE.
I... I SEE.
AREN'T OLD RELA-TIONSHIPS WORTH PRESER-VING.
DO YOU REALLY *MEAN* THAT?
YOU KNOW, ONE OF THE THINGS I'VE ALWAYS WANTED...
...IS FOR PEOPLE TO THINK THAT I'VE GOT LIFE FIGURED OUT.
BUT I'M NOT THAT CLEVER.
.....

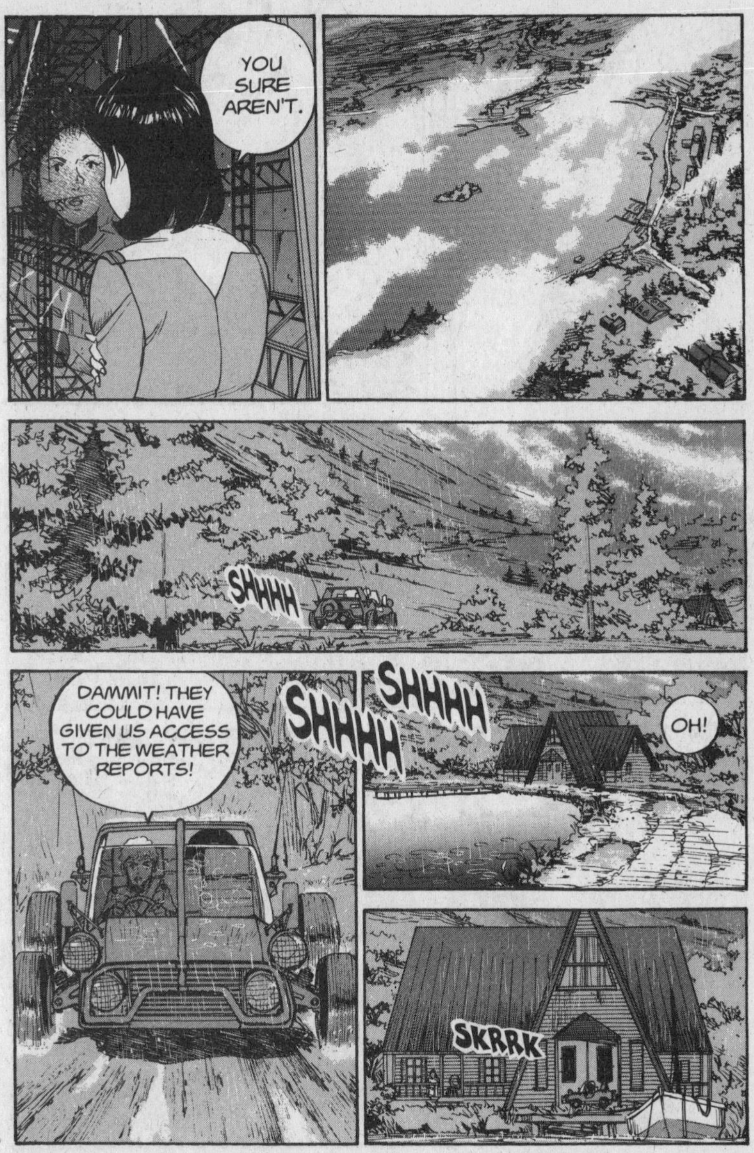
YOU SURE AREN'T.
SHHHH
DAMMIT! THEY COULD HAVE GIVEN US ACCESS TO THE WEATHER REPORTS!
SHHHH
SHHHH
OH!
SKRRK

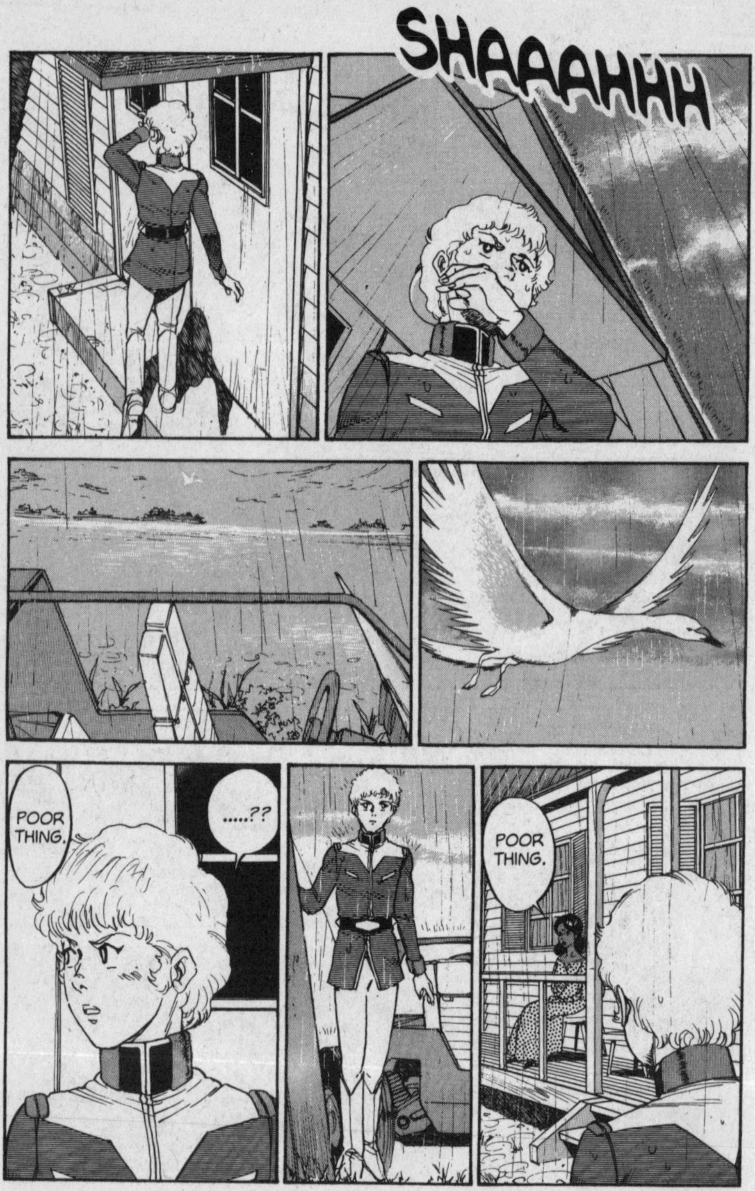

SHAAAAHHH
POOR THING.
.....??
POOR THING.

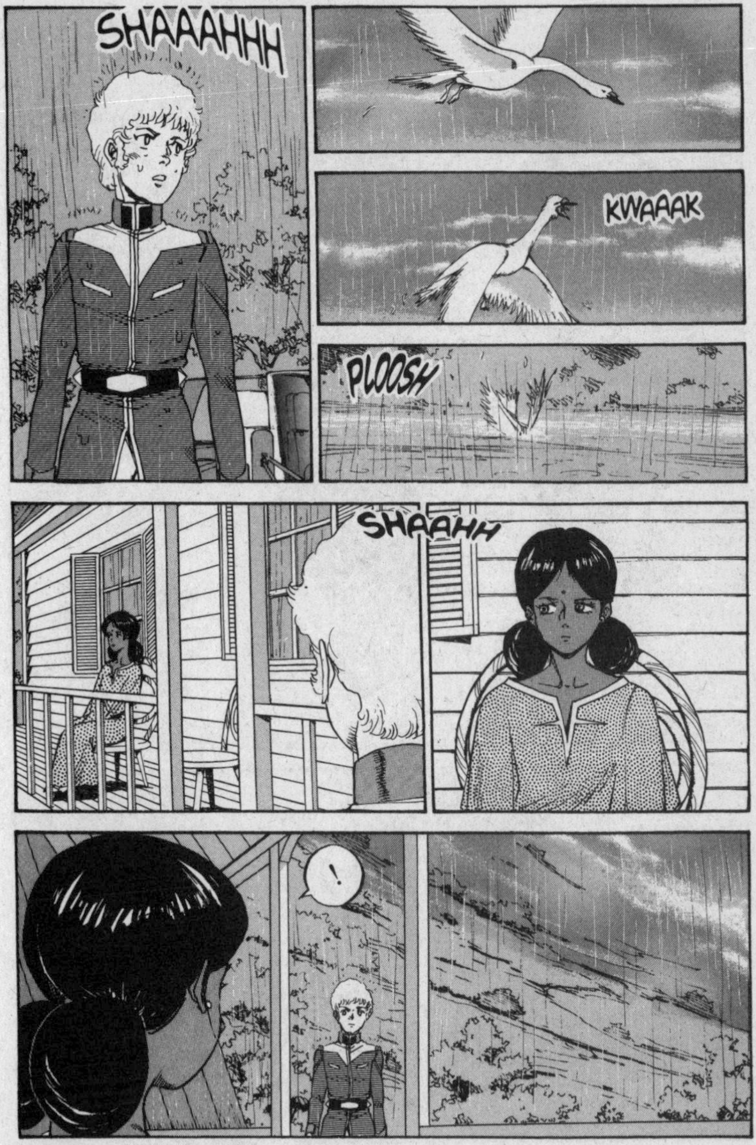
SHAAAHHH
KWAAAK
PLOOSH
SHAAHH
!

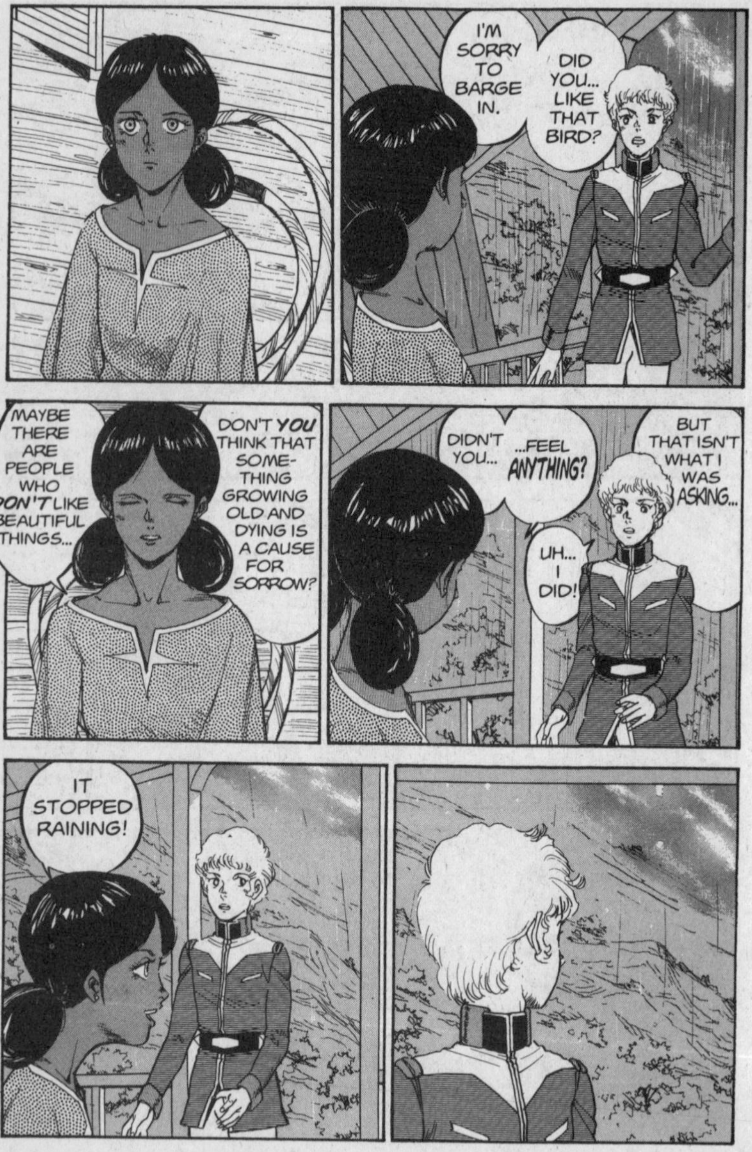
I'M SORRY TO BARGE IN.
DID YOU... LIKE THAT BIRD?
MAYBE THERE ARE PEOPLE WHO DON'T LIKE BEAUTIFUL THINGS...
DON'T YOU THINK THAT SOME-THING GROWING OLD AND DYING IS A CAUSE FOR SORROW?
DIDN'T YOU...
...FEEL ANYTHING?
UH... I DID!
BUT THAT ISN'T WHAT I WAS ASKING...
IT STOPPED RAINING!

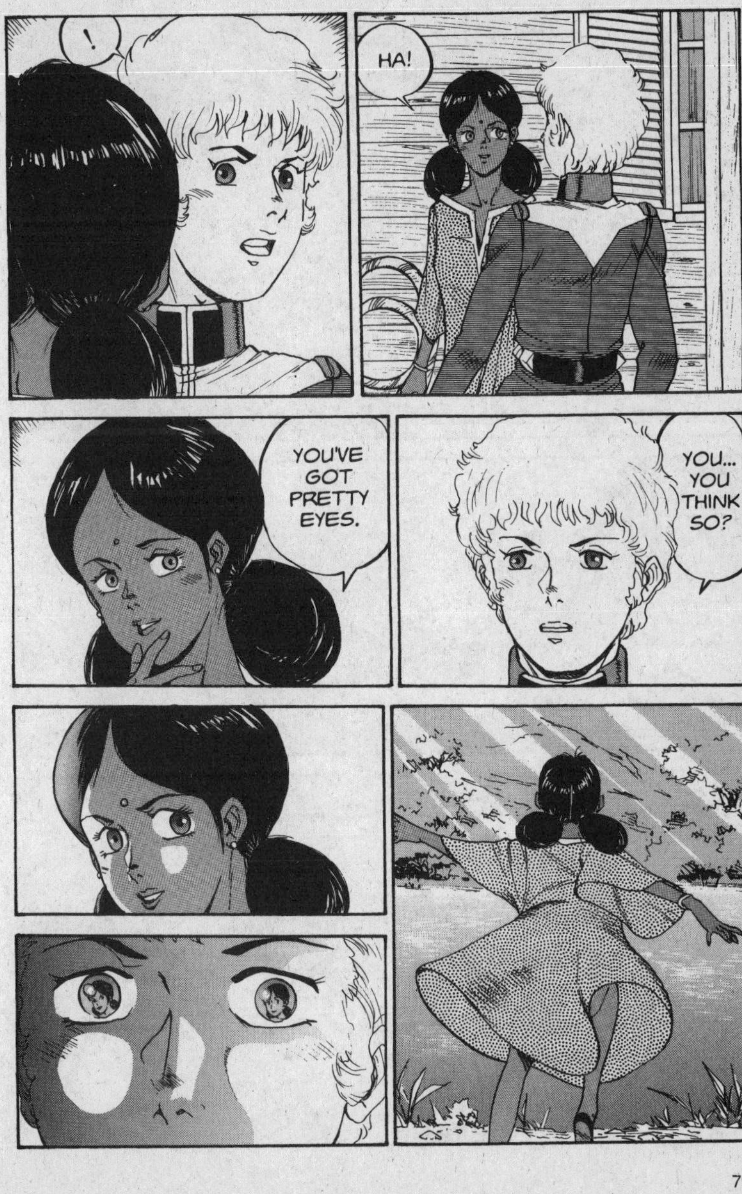
!
HA!
YOU'VE GOT PRETTY EYES.
YOU... YOU THINK SO?

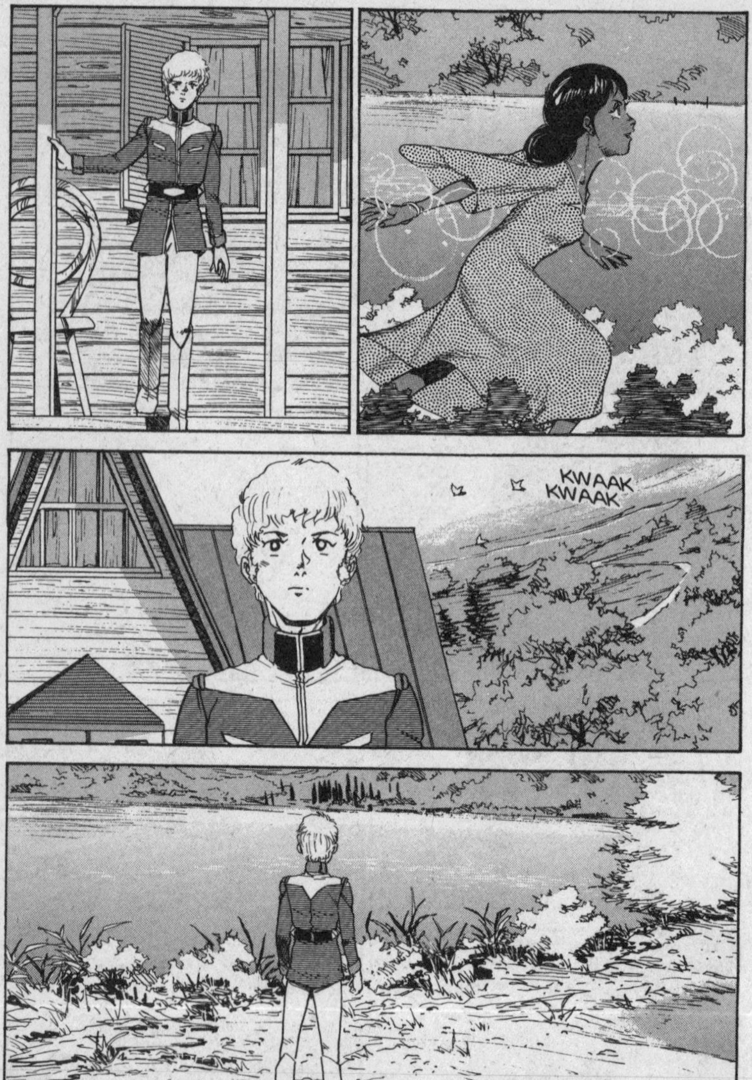
KWAAK
KWAAK

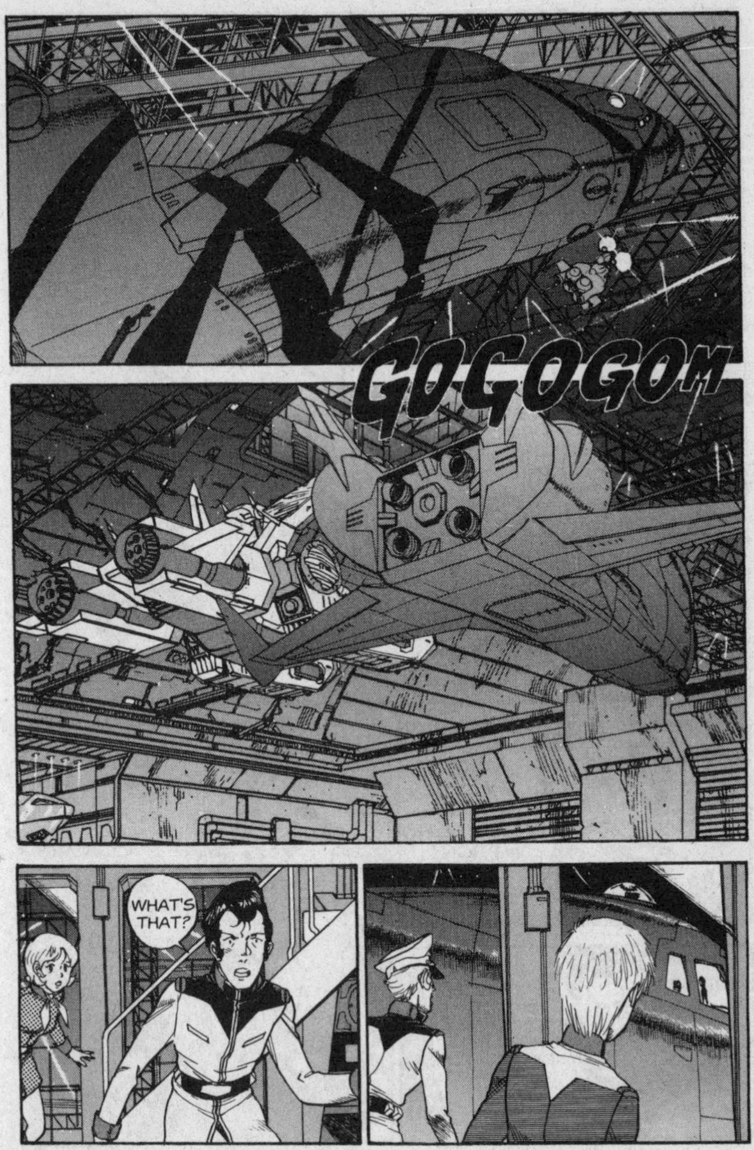
GOGOGOM
WHAT'S THAT?

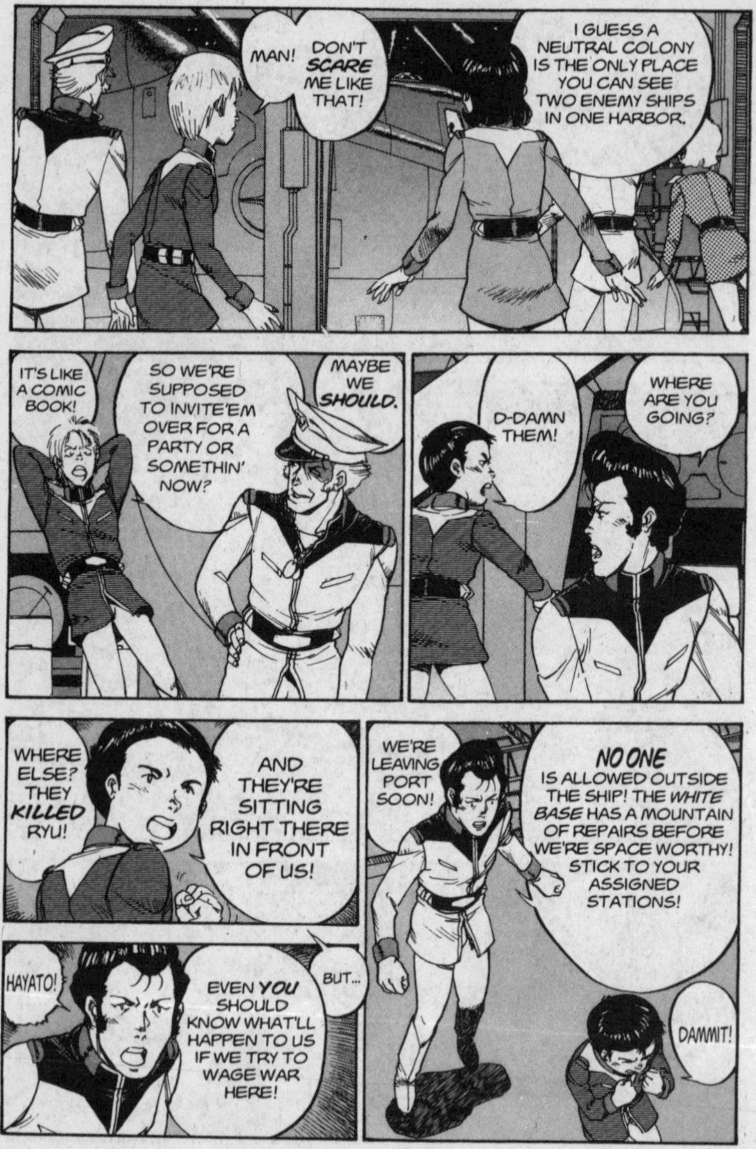

MAN!
DON'T SCARE ME LIKE THAT!
I GUESS A NEUTRAL COLONY IS THE ONLY PLACE YOU CAN SEE TWO ENEMY SHIPS IN ONE HARBOR.
IT'S LIKE A COMIC BOOK!
SO WE'RE SUPPOSED TO INVITE'EM OVER FOR A PARTY OR SOMETHIN' NOW?
MAYBE WE SHOULD.
D-DAMN THEM!
WHERE ARE YOU GOING?
WHERE ELSE? THEY KILLED RYU!
AND THEY'RE SITTING RIGHT THERE IN FRONT OF US!
HAYATO!
BUT...
EVEN YOU SHOULD KNOW WHAT'LL HAPPEN TO US IF WE TRY TO WAGE WAR HERE!
WE'RE LEAVING PORT SOON!
NO ONE IS ALLOWED OUTSIDE THE SHIP! THE WHITE BASE HAS A MOUNTAIN OF REPAIRS BEFORE WE'RE SPACE WORTHY! STICK TO YOUR ASSIGNED STATIONS!
DAMMIT!

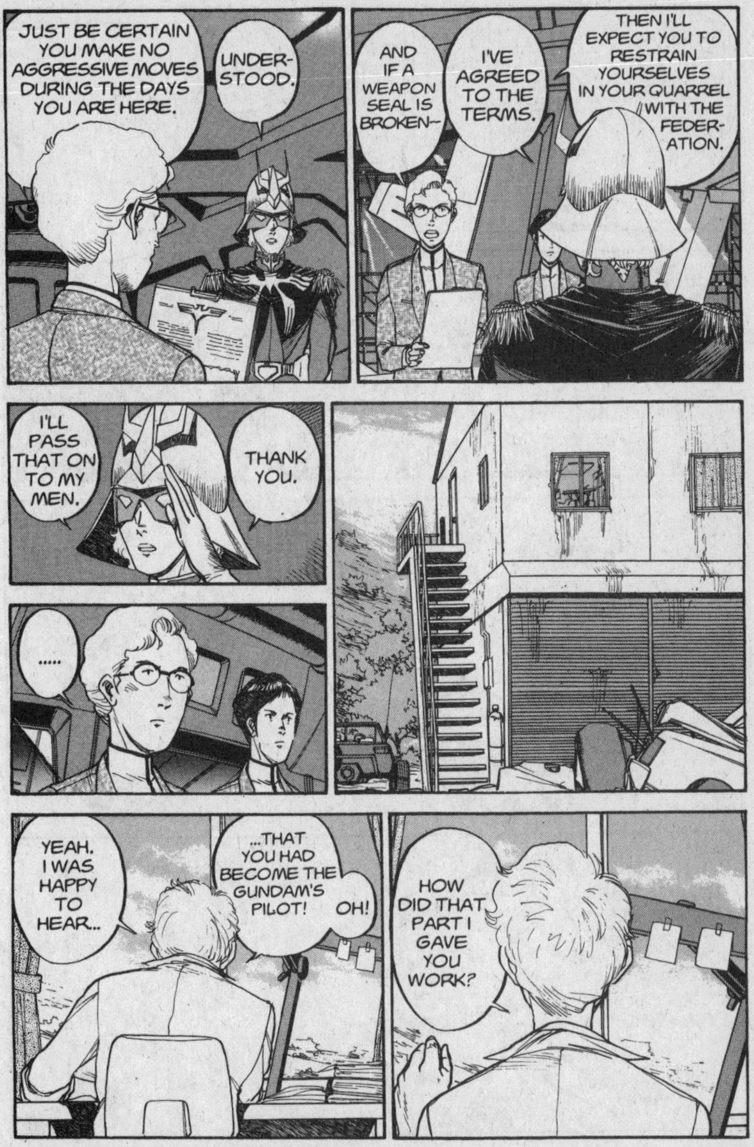
JUST BE CERTAIN YOU MAKE NO AGGRESSIVE MOVES DURING THE DAYS YOU ARE HERE.
UNDER-STOOD.
AND IF A WEAPON SEAL IS BROKEN--
I'VE AGREED TO THE TERMS.
THEN I'LL EXPECT YOU TO RESTRAIN YOURSELVES IN YOUR QUARREL WITH THE FEDER-ATION.
I'LL PASS THAT ON TO MY MEN.
THANK YOU.
.....
YEAH. I WAS HAPPY TO HEAR...
...THAT YOU HAD BECOME THE GUNDAM'S PILOT!
OH!
HOW DID THAT PART I GAVE YOU WORK?

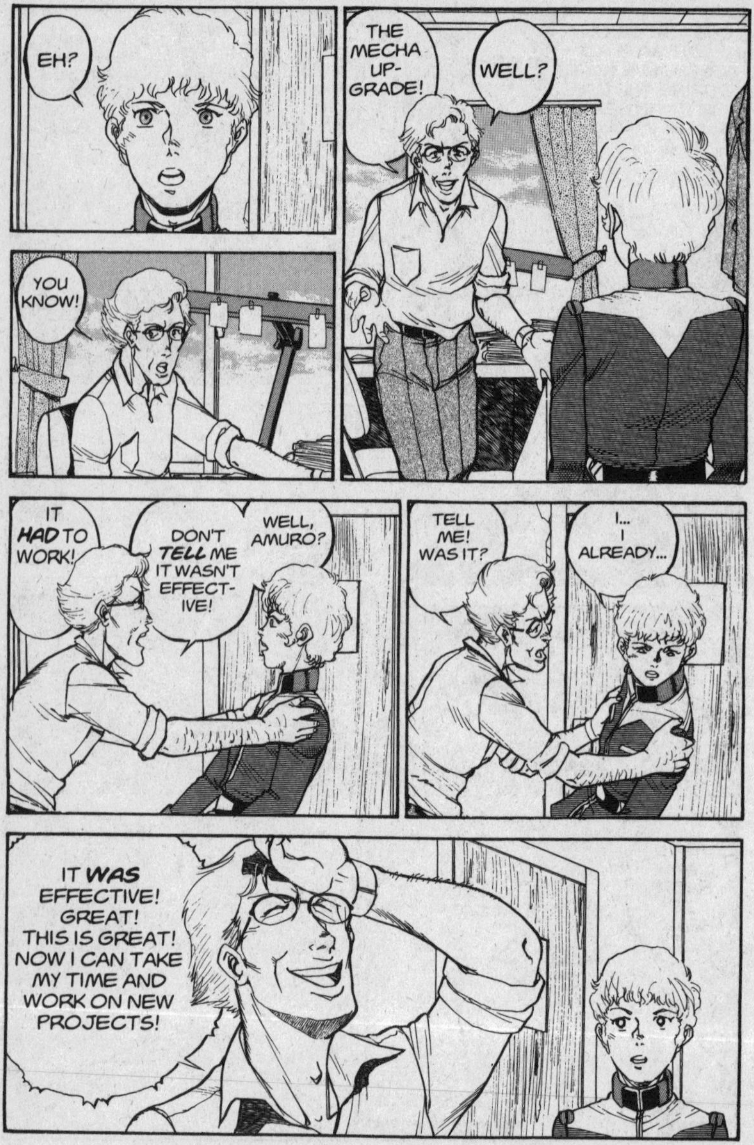
EH?
YOU KNOW!
THE MECHA UP-GRADE!
WELL?
IT HAD TO WORK!
DON'T TELL ME IT WASN'T EFFECT-IVE!
WELL, AMURO?
TELL ME! WAS IT?
I... I ALREADY...
IT WAS EFFECTIVE! GREAT! THIS IS GREAT! NOW I CAN TAKE MY TIME AND WORK ON NEW PROJECTS!

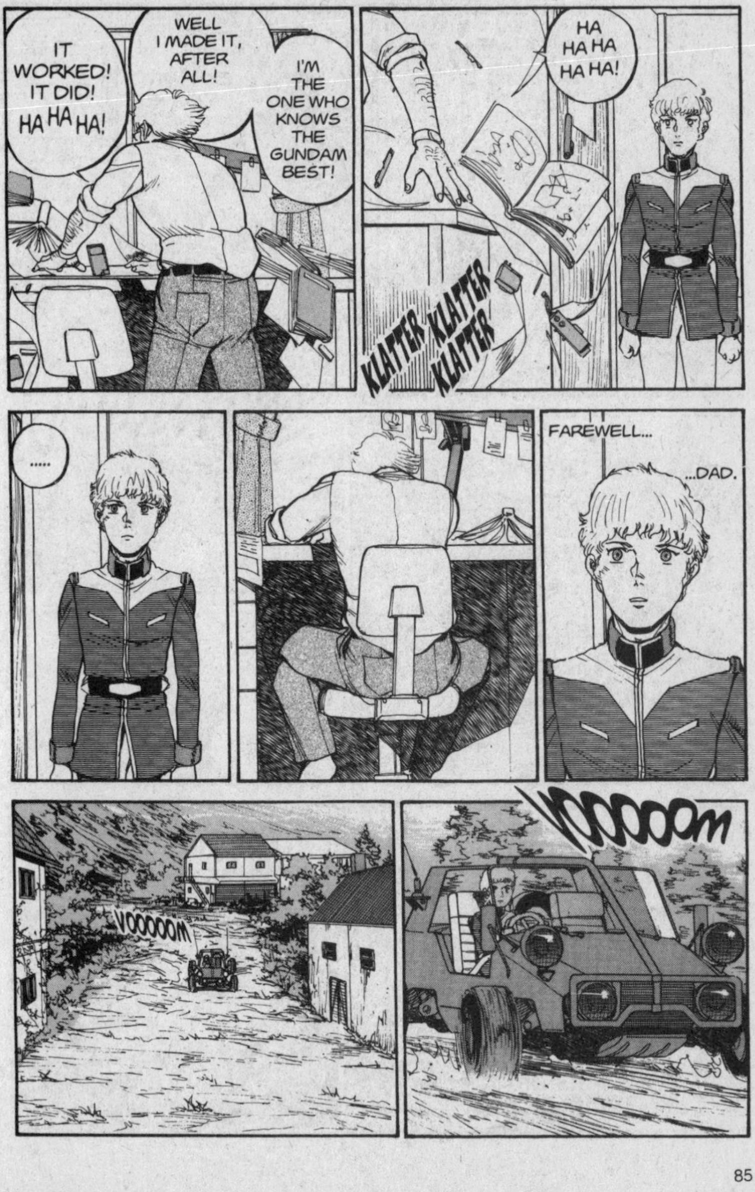

IT WORKED! IT DID! HA HA HA!
WELL I MADE IT, AFTER ALL!
I'M THE ONE WHO KNOWS THE GUNDAM BEST!
HA HA HA HA HA!
KLATTER KLATTER KLATTER
......
FAREWELL...
...DAD.
VOOOOOM
VOOOOOM

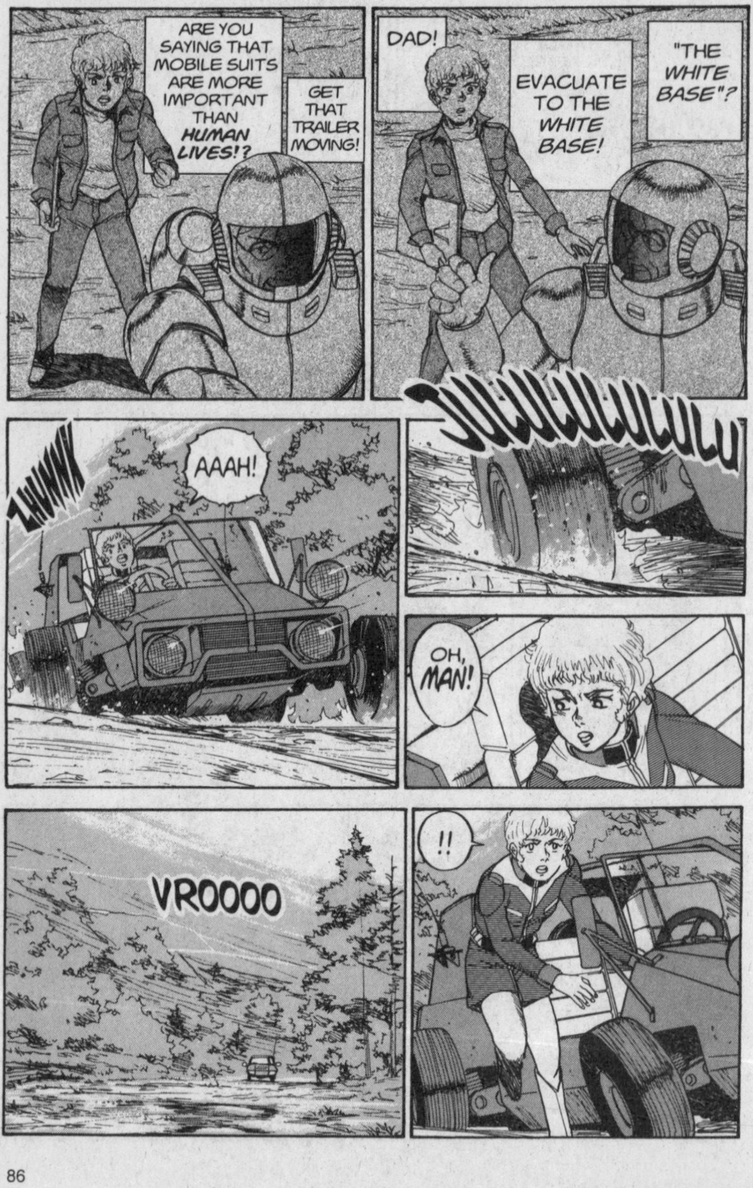
ARE YOU SAYING THAT MOBILE SUITS ARE MORE IMPORTANT THAN *HUMAN LIVES!?*
GET THAT TRAILER MOVING!
DAD!
EVACUATE TO THE *WHITE BASE!*
"THE *WHITE BASE*"?
AAAH!
JULULULULULU
OH, *MAN!*
VROOOO
!!

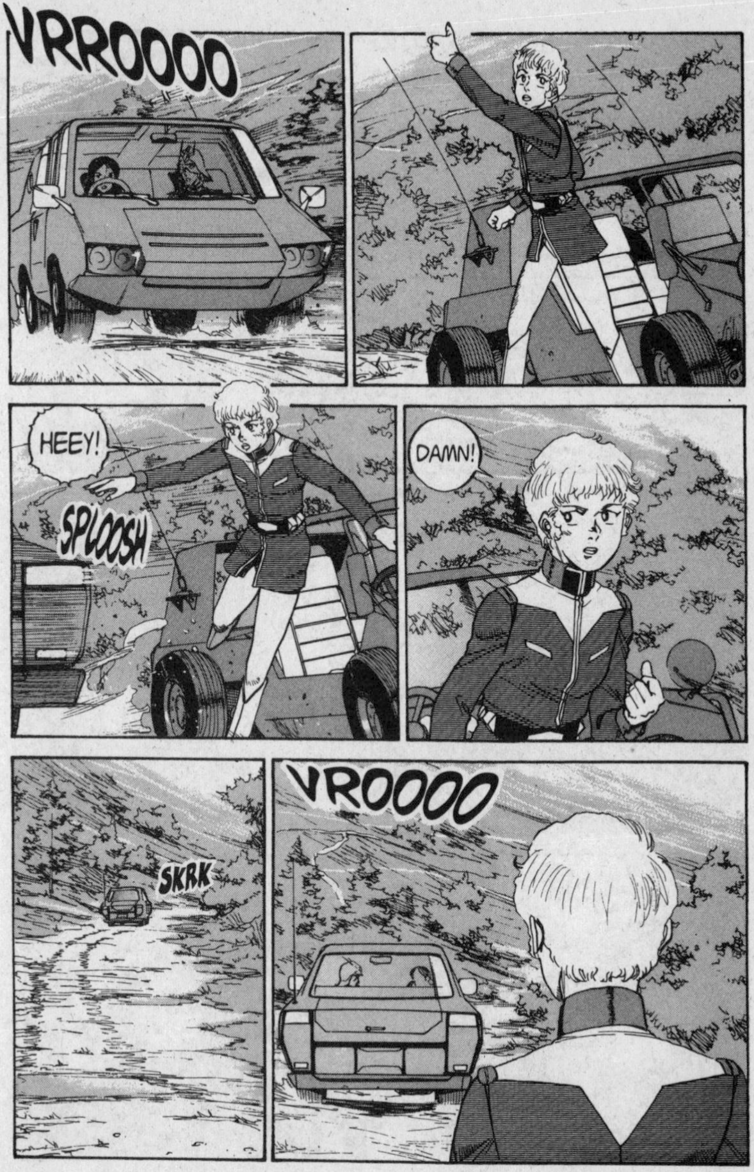
VRROOOO
HEEY!
SPLOOSH
DAMN!
SKRK
VROOOO

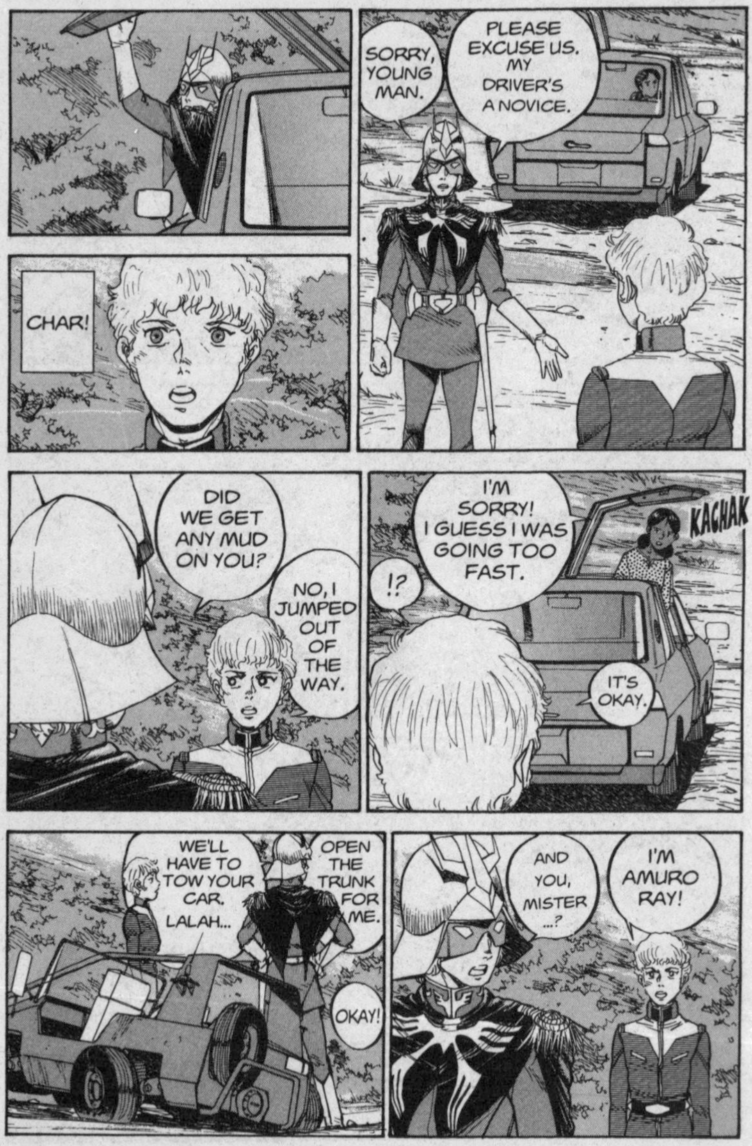
SORRY, YOUNG MAN.
PLEASE EXCUSE US. MY DRIVER'S A NOVICE.
CHAR!
DID WE GET ANY MUD ON YOU?
NO, I JUMPED OUT OF THE WAY.
I'M SORRY! I GUESS I WAS GOING TOO FAST.
KACHAK
!?
IT'S OKAY.
WE'LL HAVE TO TOW YOUR CAR. LALAH...
OPEN THE TRUNK FOR ME.
OKAY!
I'M AMURO RAY!
AND YOU, MISTER ...?

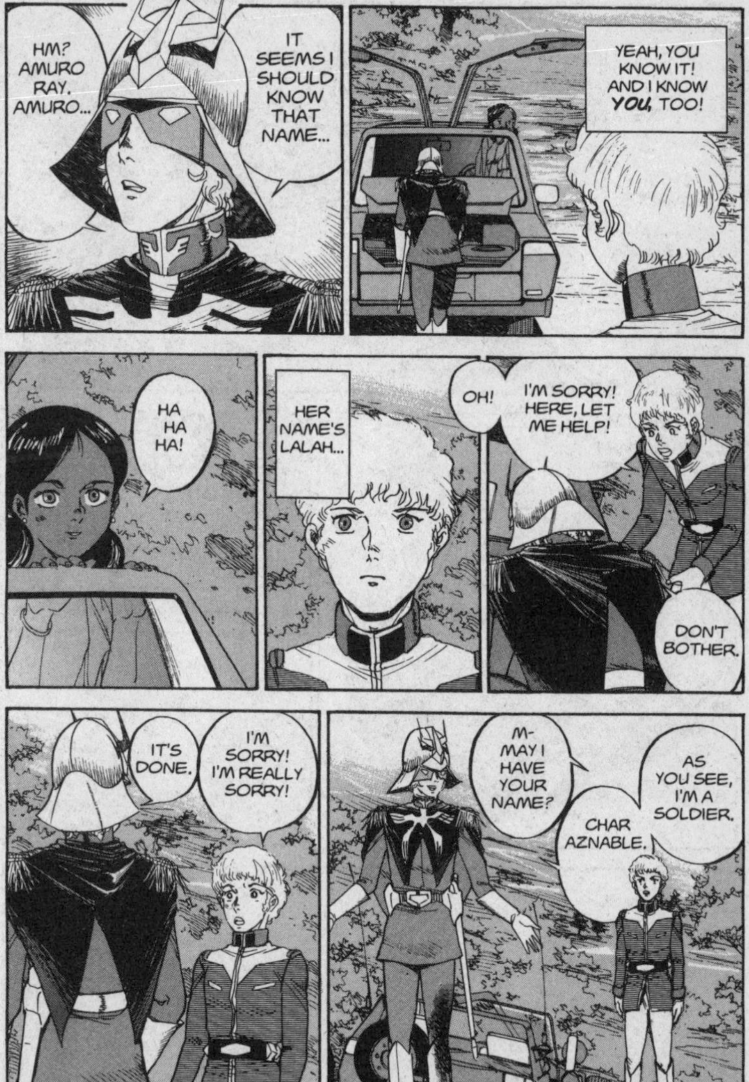
HM? AMURO RAY. AMURO...
IT SEEMS I SHOULD KNOW THAT NAME...
YEAH, YOU KNOW IT! AND I KNOW **YOU,** TOO!
HA HA HA!
HER NAME'S LALAH...
OH!
I'M SORRY! HERE, LET ME HELP!
DON'T BOTHER.
IT'S DONE.
I'M SORRY! I'M REALLY SORRY!
M-MAY I HAVE YOUR NAME?
AS YOU SEE, I'M A SOLDIER.
CHAR AZNABLE.

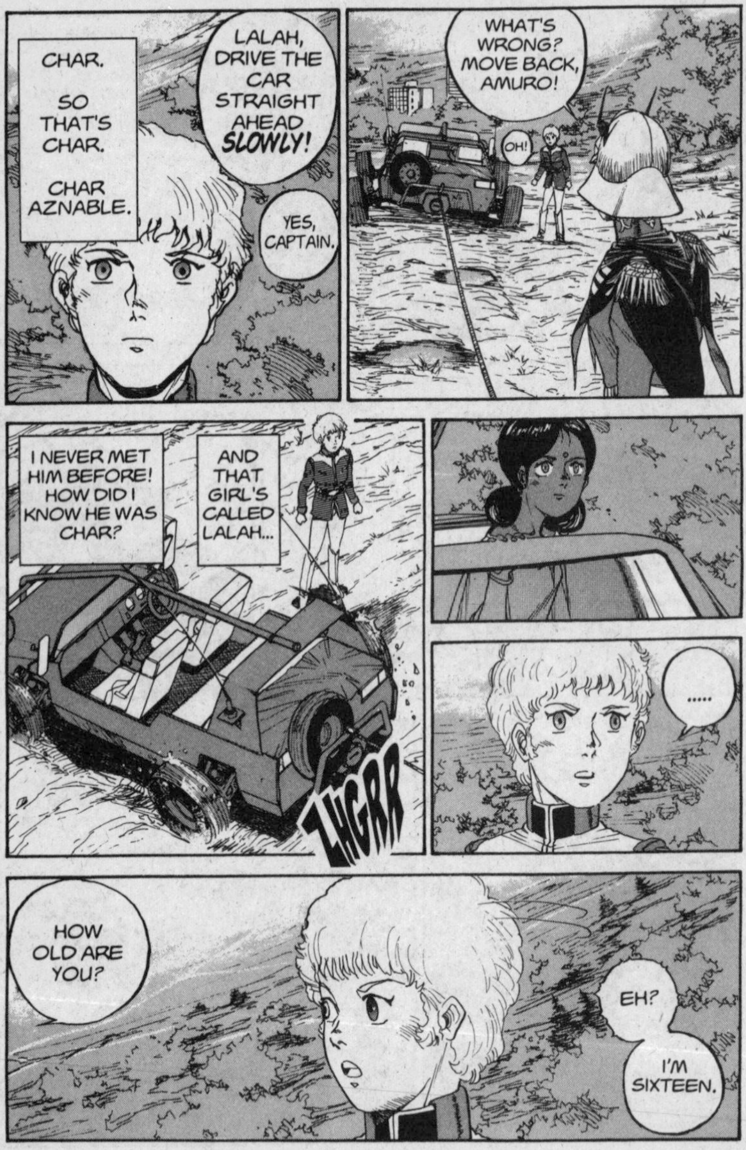
CHAR.
SO THAT'S CHAR.
CHAR AZNABLE.
LALAH, DRIVE THE CAR STRAIGHT AHEAD SLOWLY!
YES, CAPTAIN.
WHAT'S WRONG? MOVE BACK, AMURO!
OH!
I NEVER MET HIM BEFORE! HOW DID I KNOW HE WAS CHAR?
AND THAT GIRL'S CALLED LALAH...
LHGRR
.....
HOW OLD ARE YOU?
EH?
I'M SIXTEEN.

REALLY? THAT'S PRETTY YOUNG.

I UNDERSTAND YOUR FREEZING UP IN THE FACE OF AN ENEMY OFFICER, BUT I RATHER EXPECTED A WORD OF THANKS...

AH! I'M SORRY!

THANK YOU VERY MUCH!

IT'S ALL RIGHT.

BUT YOU SHOULD HAVE LEFT THE DIRTY WORK TO ME.

OH, THIS? THIS IS NO-THING!

I MEAN IT! TH... TH...

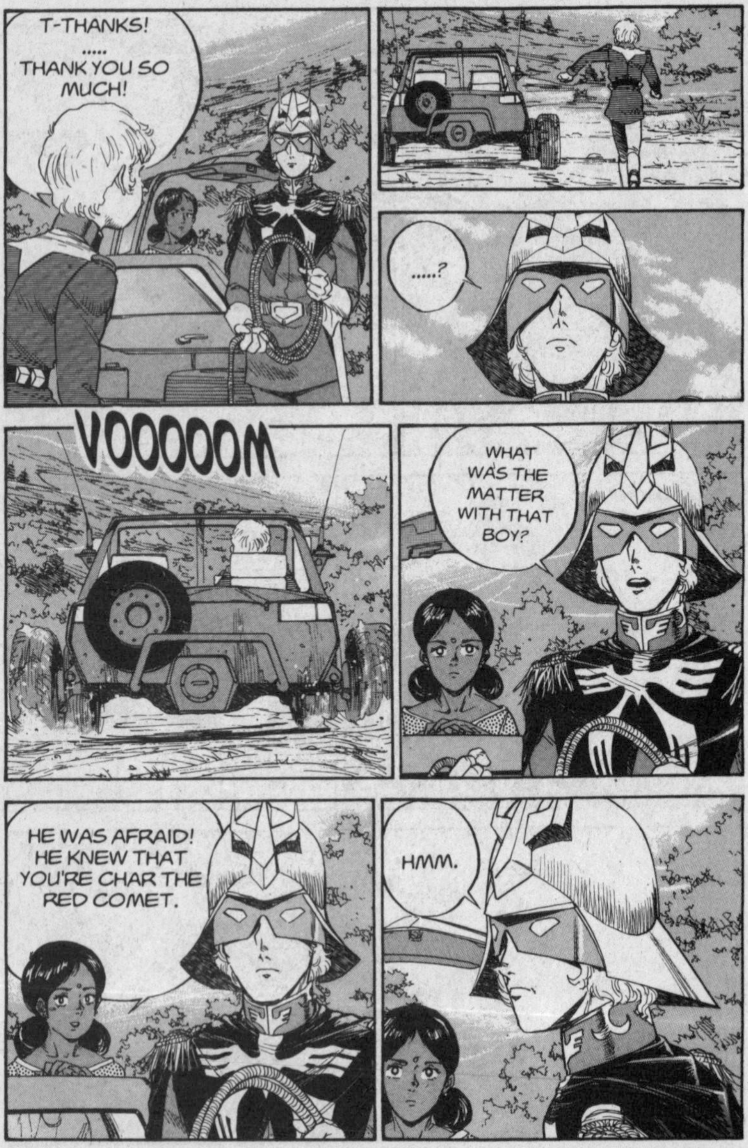
T-THANKS!
.....
THANK YOU SO MUCH!
.....?
VOOOOOM
WHAT WAS THE MATTER WITH THAT BOY?
HE WAS AFRAID! HE KNEW THAT YOU'RE CHAR THE RED COMET.
HMM.

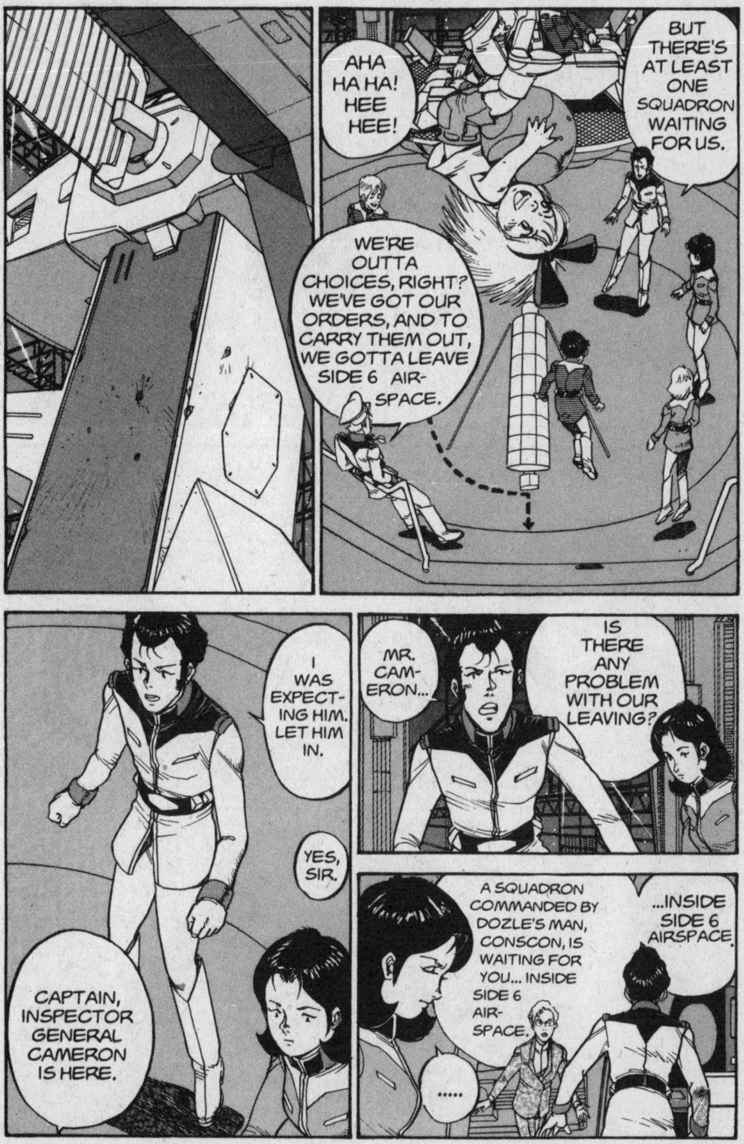
AHA HA HA! HEE HEE!
BUT THERE'S AT LEAST ONE SQUADRON WAITING FOR US.
WE'RE OUTTA CHOICES, RIGHT? WE'VE GOT OUR ORDERS, AND TO CARRY THEM OUT, WE GOTTA LEAVE SIDE 6 AIR-SPACE.
I WAS EXPECTING HIM. LET HIM IN.
YES, SIR.
CAPTAIN, INSPECTOR GENERAL CAMERON IS HERE.
MR. CAMERON...
IS THERE ANY PROBLEM WITH OUR LEAVING?
A SQUADRON COMMANDED BY DOZLE'S MAN, CONSCON, IS WAITING FOR YOU... INSIDE SIDE 6 AIR-SPACE.
...INSIDE SIDE 6 AIRSPACE.
.....

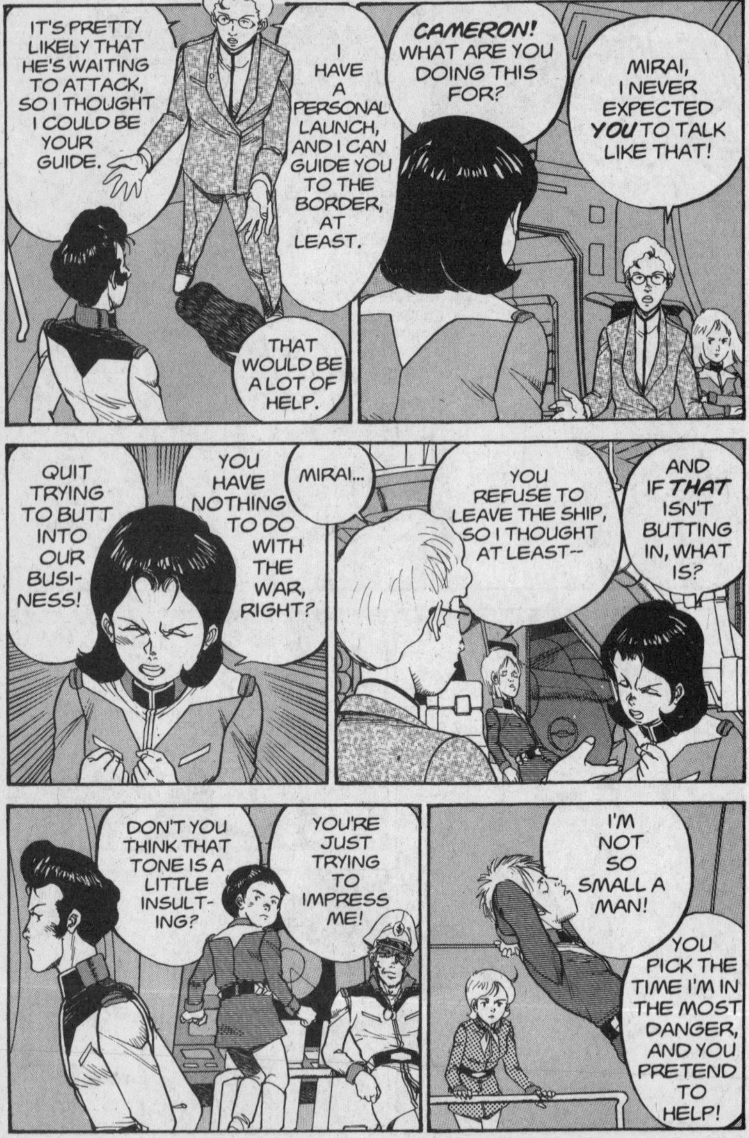
IT'S PRETTY LIKELY THAT HE'S WAITING TO ATTACK, SO I THOUGHT I COULD BE YOUR GUIDE.
I HAVE A PERSONAL LAUNCH, AND I CAN GUIDE YOU TO THE BORDER, AT LEAST.
THAT WOULD BE A LOT OF HELP.
CAMERON! WHAT ARE YOU DOING THIS FOR?
MIRAI, I NEVER EXPECTED YOU TO TALK LIKE THAT!
QUIT TRYING TO BUTT INTO OUR BUSI- NESS!
YOU HAVE NOTHING TO DO WITH THE WAR, RIGHT?
MIRAI...
YOU REFUSE TO LEAVE THE SHIP, SO I THOUGHT AT LEAST--
AND IF THAT ISN'T BUTTING IN, WHAT IS?
DON'T YOU THINK THAT TONE IS A LITTLE INSULT- ING?
YOU'RE JUST TRYING TO IMPRESS ME!
I'M NOT SO SMALL A MAN!
YOU PICK THE TIME I'M IN THE MOST DANGER, AND YOU PRETEND TO HELP!

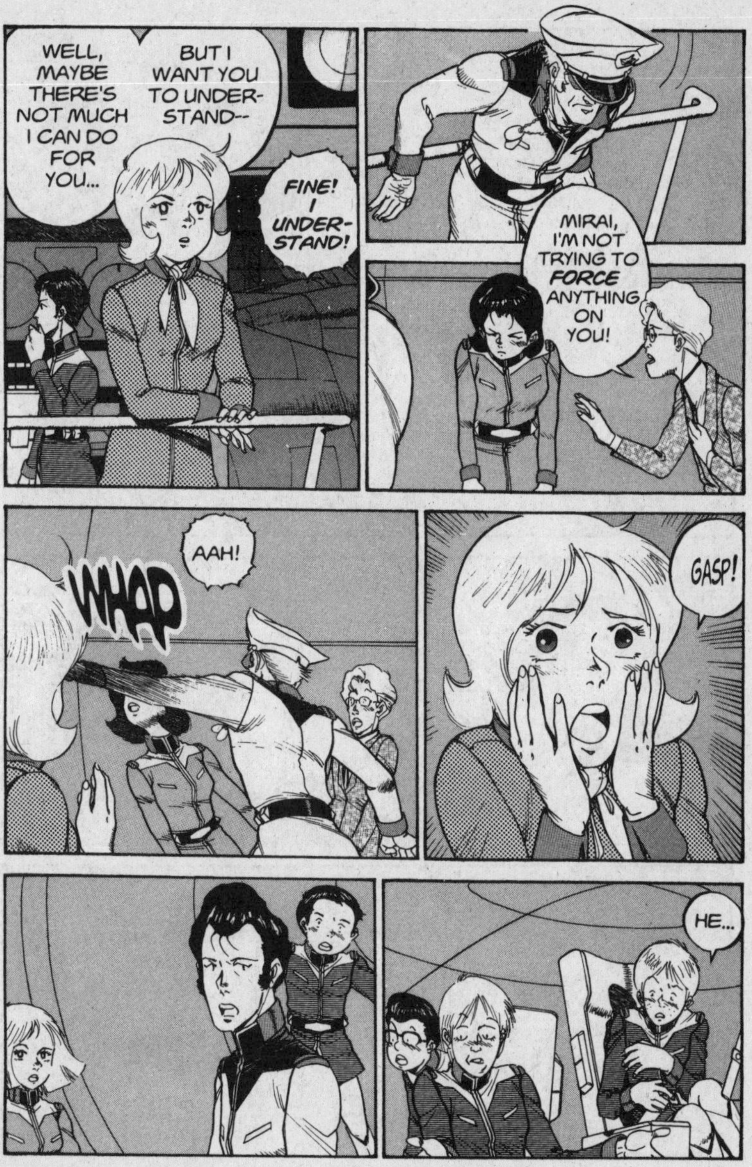

WELL, MAYBE THERE'S NOT MUCH I CAN DO FOR YOU...
BUT I WANT YOU TO UNDER-STAND--
FINE! I UNDER-STAND!
MIRAI, I'M NOT TRYING TO FORCE ANYTHING ON YOU!
WHAP
AAH!
GASP!
HE...

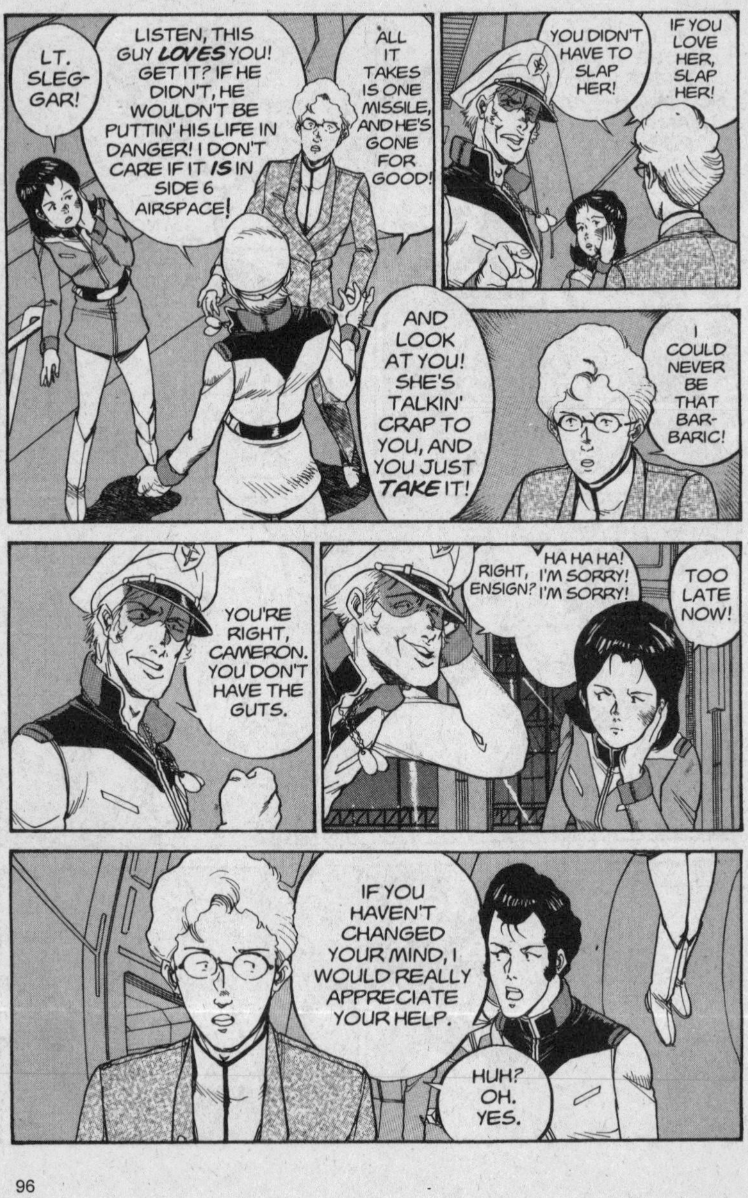

LT. SLEGGAR!
LISTEN, THIS GUY **LOVES** YOU! GET IT? IF HE DIDN'T, HE WOULDN'T BE PUTTIN' HIS LIFE IN DANGER! I DON'T CARE IF IT **IS** IN SIDE 6 AIRSPACE!
ALL IT TAKES IS ONE MISSILE, AND HE'S GONE FOR GOOD!
YOU DIDN'T HAVE TO SLAP HER!
IF YOU LOVE HER, SLAP HER!
AND LOOK AT YOU! SHE'S TALKIN' CRAP TO YOU, AND YOU JUST **TAKE** IT!
I COULD NEVER BE THAT BARBARIC!
YOU'RE RIGHT, CAMERON. YOU DON'T HAVE THE GUTS.
RIGHT, ENSIGN?
HA HA HA! I'M SORRY! I'M SORRY!
TOO LATE NOW!
IF YOU HAVEN'T CHANGED YOUR MIND, I WOULD REALLY APPRECIATE YOUR HELP.
HUH? OH. YES.

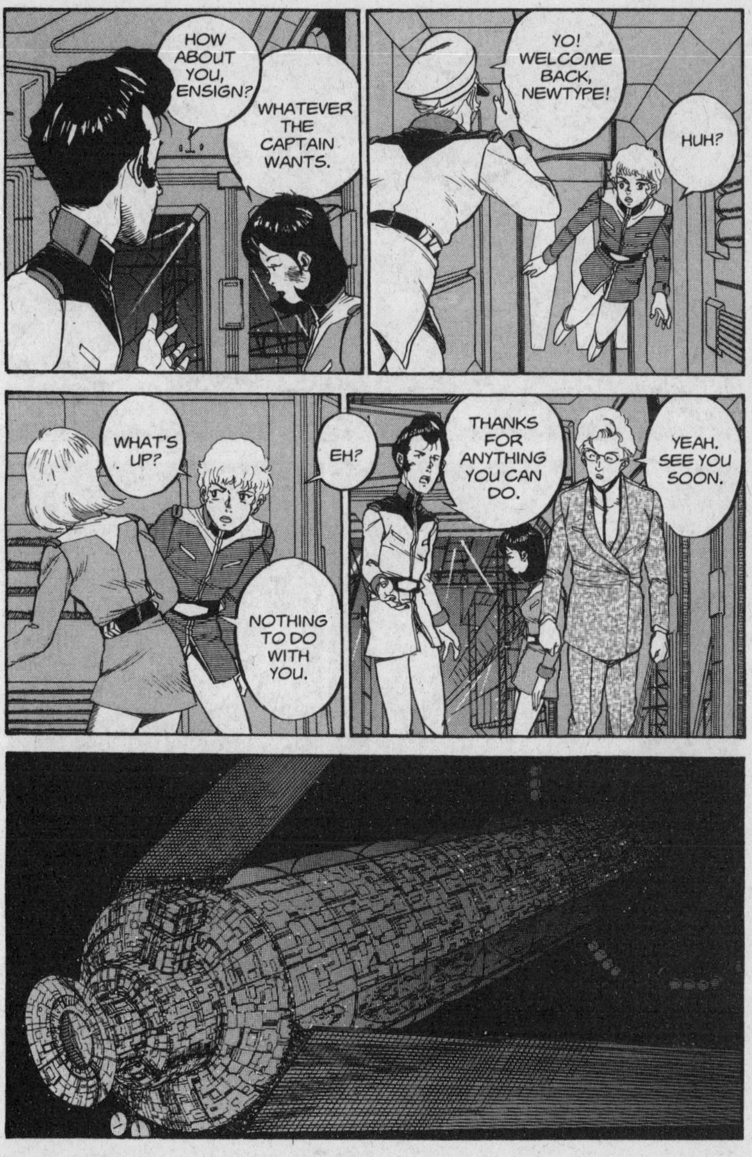
HOW ABOUT YOU, ENSIGN?
WHATEVER THE CAPTAIN WANTS.
YO! WELCOME BACK, NEWTYPE!
HUH?
WHAT'S UP?
NOTHING TO DO WITH YOU.
EH?
THANKS FOR ANYTHING YOU CAN DO.
YEAH. SEE YOU SOON.

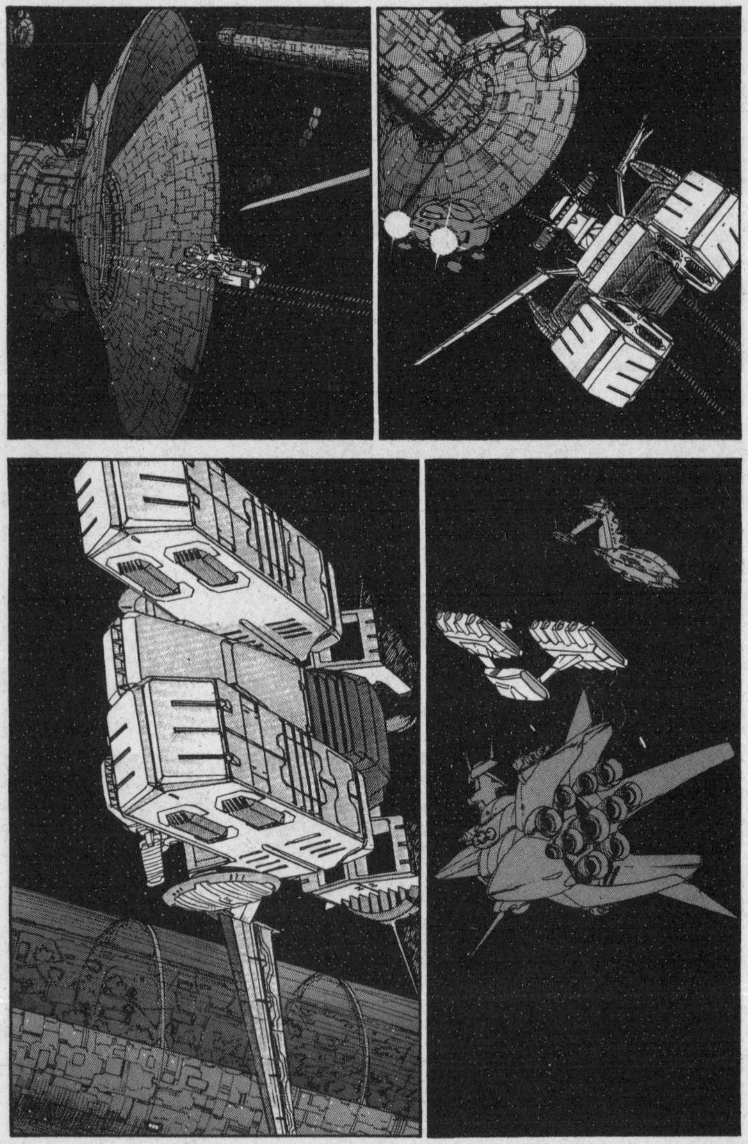

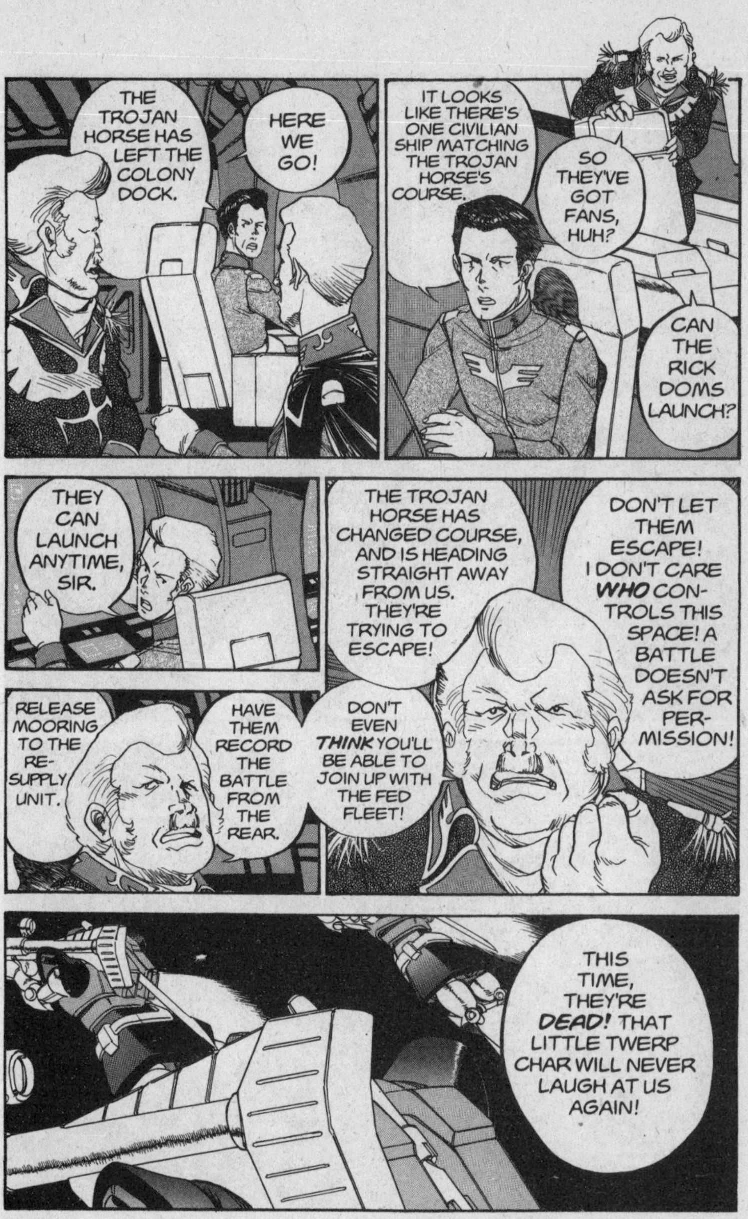

THE TROJAN HORSE HAS LEFT THE COLONY DOCK.
HERE WE GO!
IT LOOKS LIKE THERE'S ONE CIVILIAN SHIP MATCHING THE TROJAN HORSE'S COURSE.
SO THEY'VE GOT FANS, HUH?
CAN THE RICK DOMS LAUNCH?
THEY CAN LAUNCH ANYTIME, SIR.
RELEASE MOORING TO THE RE-SUPPLY UNIT.
HAVE THEM RECORD THE BATTLE FROM THE REAR.
THE TROJAN HORSE HAS CHANGED COURSE, AND IS HEADING STRAIGHT AWAY FROM US. THEY'RE TRYING TO ESCAPE!
DON'T LET THEM ESCAPE! I DON'T CARE ***WHO*** CON-TROLS THIS SPACE! A BATTLE DOESN'T ASK FOR PER-MISSION!
DON'T EVEN ***THINK*** YOU'LL BE ABLE TO JOIN UP WITH THE FED FLEET!
THIS TIME, THEY'RE ***DEAD!*** THAT LITTLE TWERP CHAR WILL NEVER LAUGH AT US AGAIN!

TO ALL CREW! NOT ONE SHOT IS TO BE FIRED WHILE IN SIDE 6 CONTROLLED AIRSPACE! GOT THAT?

DO NOT FIRE, EVEN IF FIRED UPON!

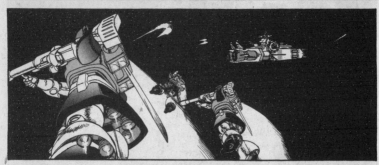

HEH! YOU'VE GOT A LOTTA NERVE, BRINGIN' YER SKIRTS THIS CLOSE!

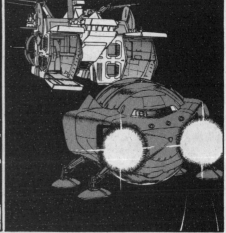

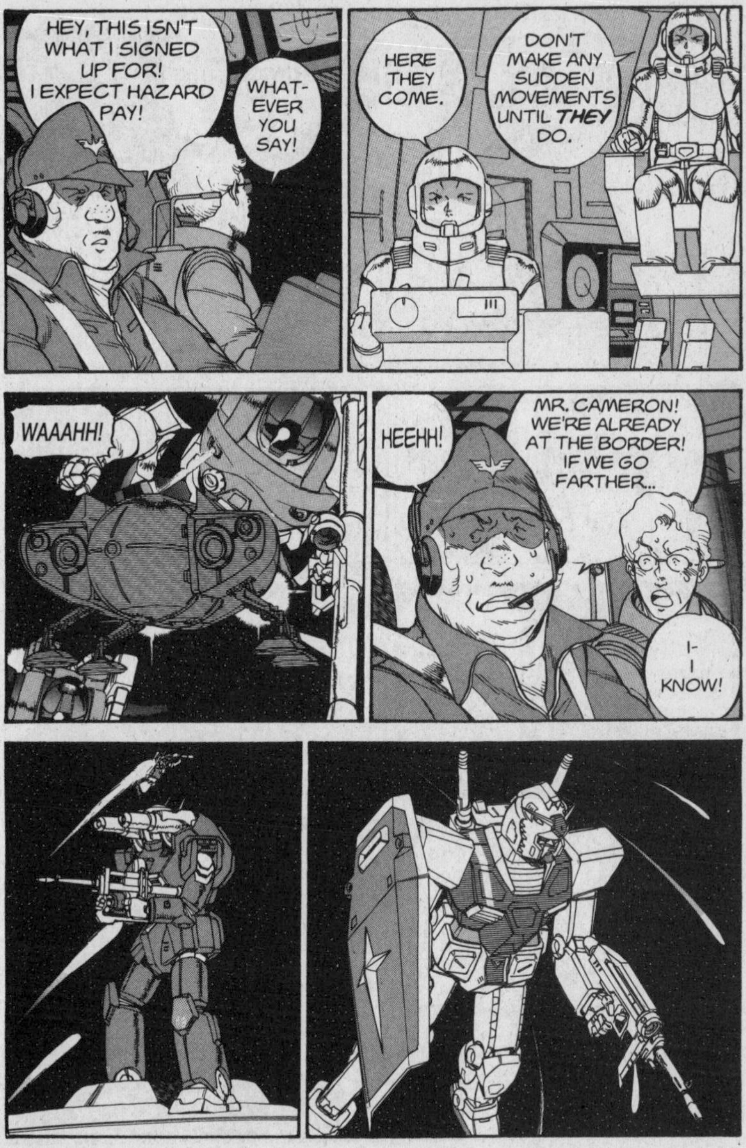

HEY, THIS ISN'T WHAT I SIGNED UP FOR! I EXPECT HAZARD PAY!
WHAT-EVER YOU SAY!
HERE THEY COME.
DON'T MAKE ANY SUDDEN MOVEMENTS UNTIL **THEY** DO.
WAAAHH!
HEEHH!
MR. CAMERON! WE'RE ALREADY AT THE BORDER! IF WE GO FARTHER...
I- I KNOW!

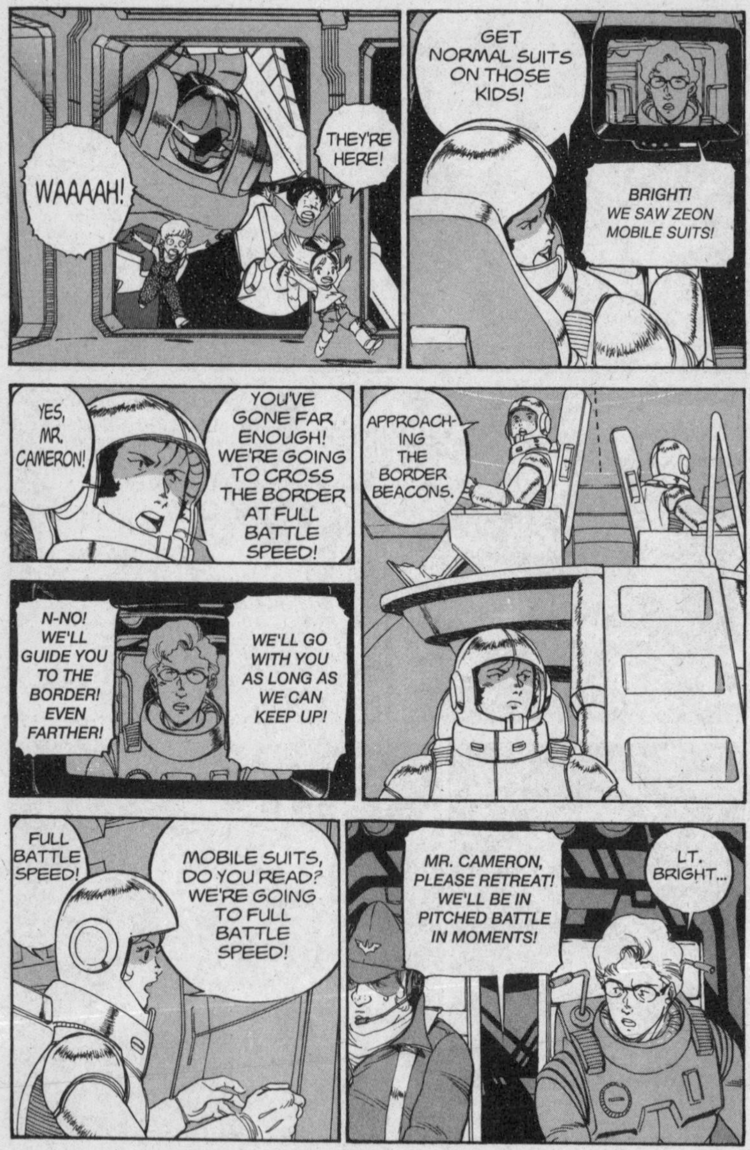
WAAAAH!
THEY'RE HERE!
GET NORMAL SUITS ON THOSE KIDS!
BRIGHT! WE SAW ZEON MOBILE SUITS!
YES, MR. CAMERON!
YOU'VE GONE FAR ENOUGH! WE'RE GOING TO CROSS THE BORDER AT FULL BATTLE SPEED!
N-NO! WE'LL GUIDE YOU TO THE BORDER! EVEN FARTHER!
WE'LL GO WITH YOU AS LONG AS WE CAN KEEP UP!
APPROACH-ING THE BORDER BEACONS.
FULL BATTLE SPEED!
MOBILE SUITS, DO YOU READ? WE'RE GOING TO FULL BATTLE SPEED!
MR. CAMERON, PLEASE RETREAT! WE'LL BE IN PITCHED BATTLE IN MOMENTS!
LT. BRIGHT...

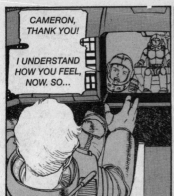

CAMERON, THANK YOU!

I UNDERSTAND HOW YOU FEEL, NOW. SO...

THANK YOU, CAMERON. PLEASE GO BACK.

AND PASS ON MY LOVE TO YOUR FATHER AND MOTHER.

M-MIRAI...

I'M PULLING BACK!

AH!

PLEASE! PASS THE BRIDGE!

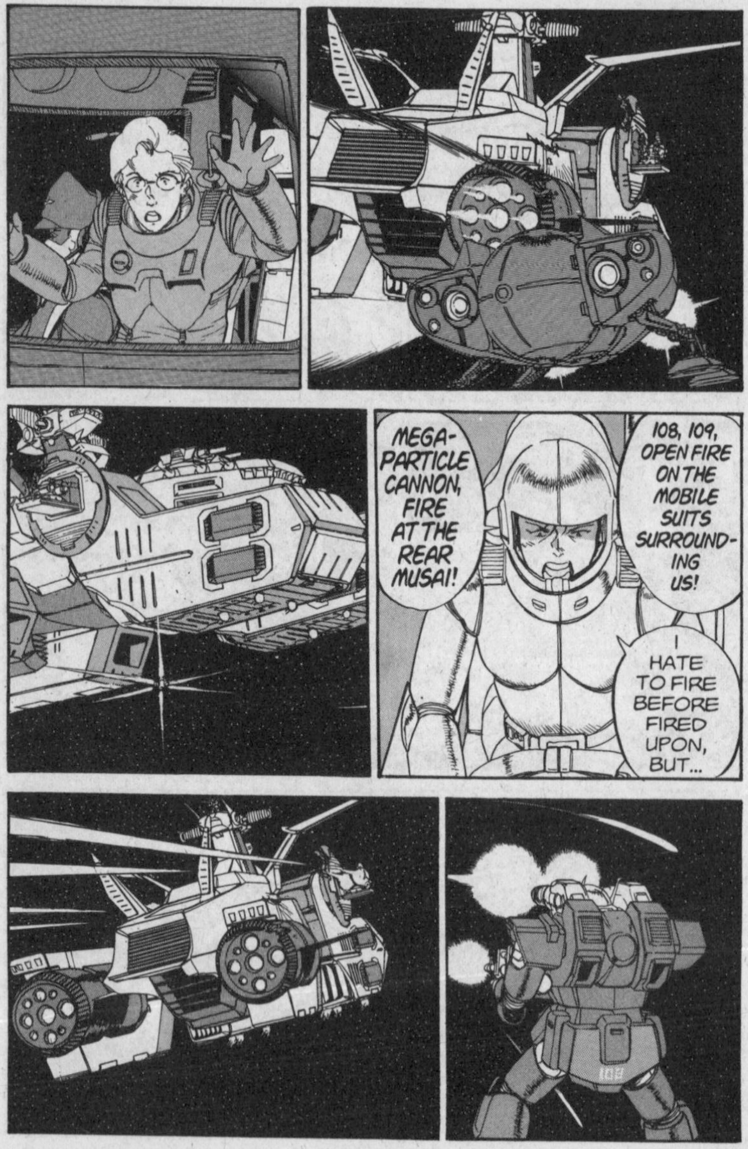
MEGA-PARTICLE CANNON, FIRE AT THE REAR MUSAI!
108, 109, OPEN FIRE ON THE MOBILE SUITS SURROUNDING US!
I HATE TO FIRE BEFORE FIRED UPON, BUT...

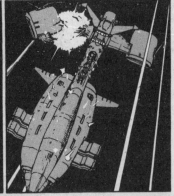

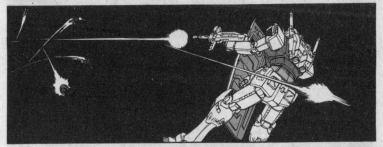

FIRING ON US WHILE HE KNOWS...

...THAT WE CAN'T FIRE BACK! THAT'S *DIRTY*!

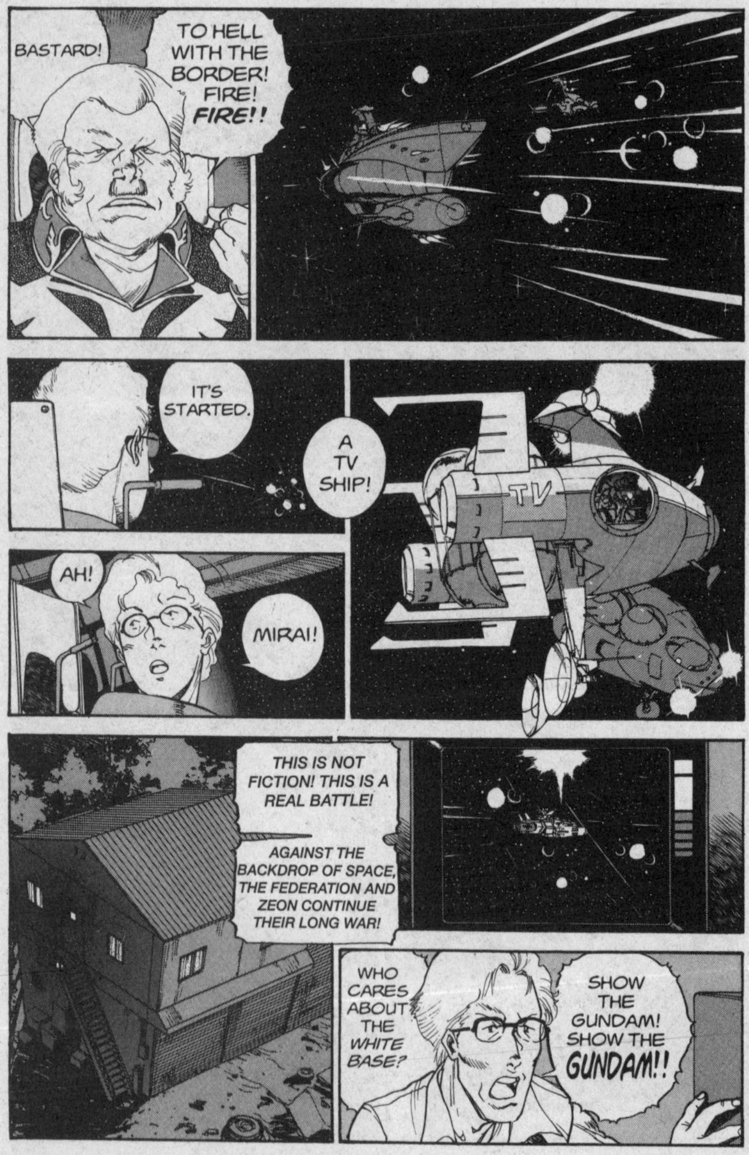
BASTARD!
TO HELL WITH THE BORDER! FIRE! FIRE!!
IT'S STARTED.
AH!
MIRAI!
A TV SHIP!
THIS IS NOT FICTION! THIS IS A REAL BATTLE!
AGAINST THE BACKDROP OF SPACE, THE FEDERATION AND ZEON CONTINUE THEIR LONG WAR!
TV
WHO CARES ABOUT THE WHITE BASE?
SHOW THE GUNDAM! SHOW THE GUNDAM!!

I WANT TO SEE HOW THE GUNDAM FIGHTS!

THERE! THERE YOU GO!

OH, AMURO, WHAT ARE YOU *DOING!?*

HARD ABOUT, 90 DEGREES! WE'LL TAKE UP A T FORMATION!

ALL GUNS, CONCENTRATE FIRE ON THE MUSAI!

HAVE HAYATO'S 109 PROVIDE SUPPORT FOR THE GUNDAM!

DAMN! I DON'T WANT TO DIE TRAPPED IN THIS COFFIN!

BRIDGE! CAN'T YOU SEND THE CORE BOOSTER OUT?

I GUESS YOU GET USED TO IT.

I USED TO FEEL THAT WAY.

107

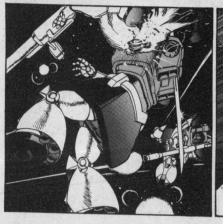

I SEE YOU!
I SEE YOU!

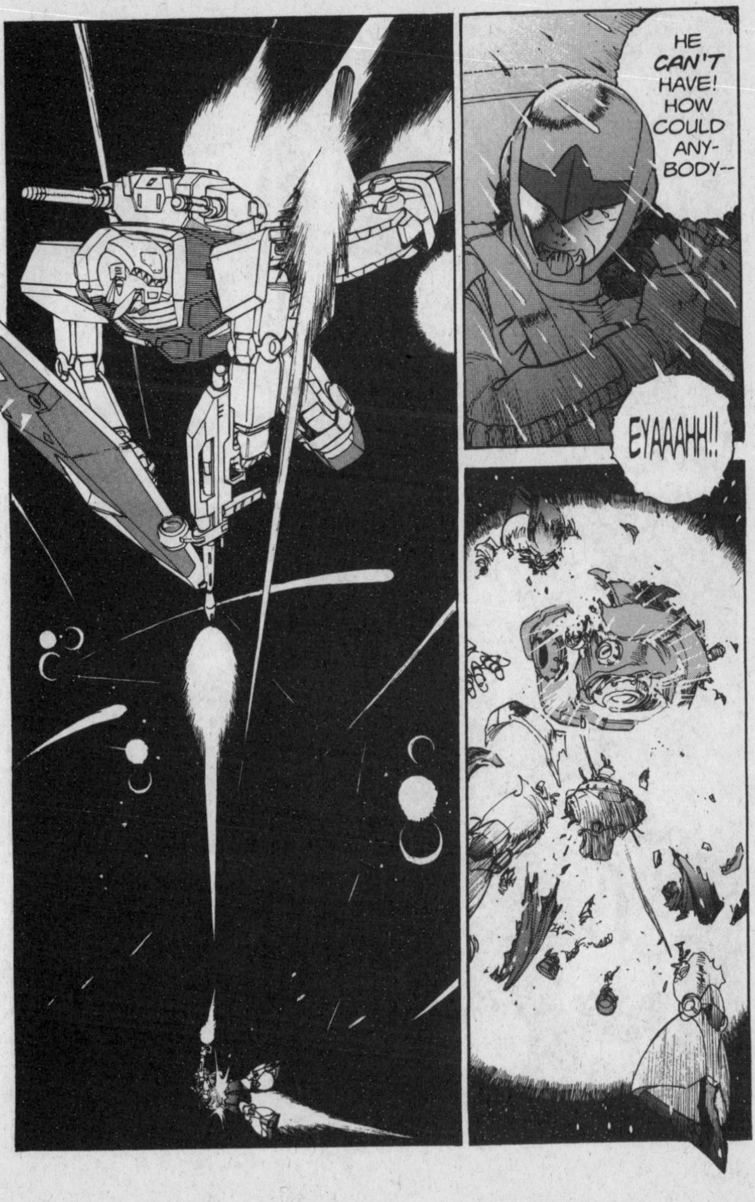
HE CAN'T HAVE! HOW COULD ANY-BODY--
EYAAAHH!!

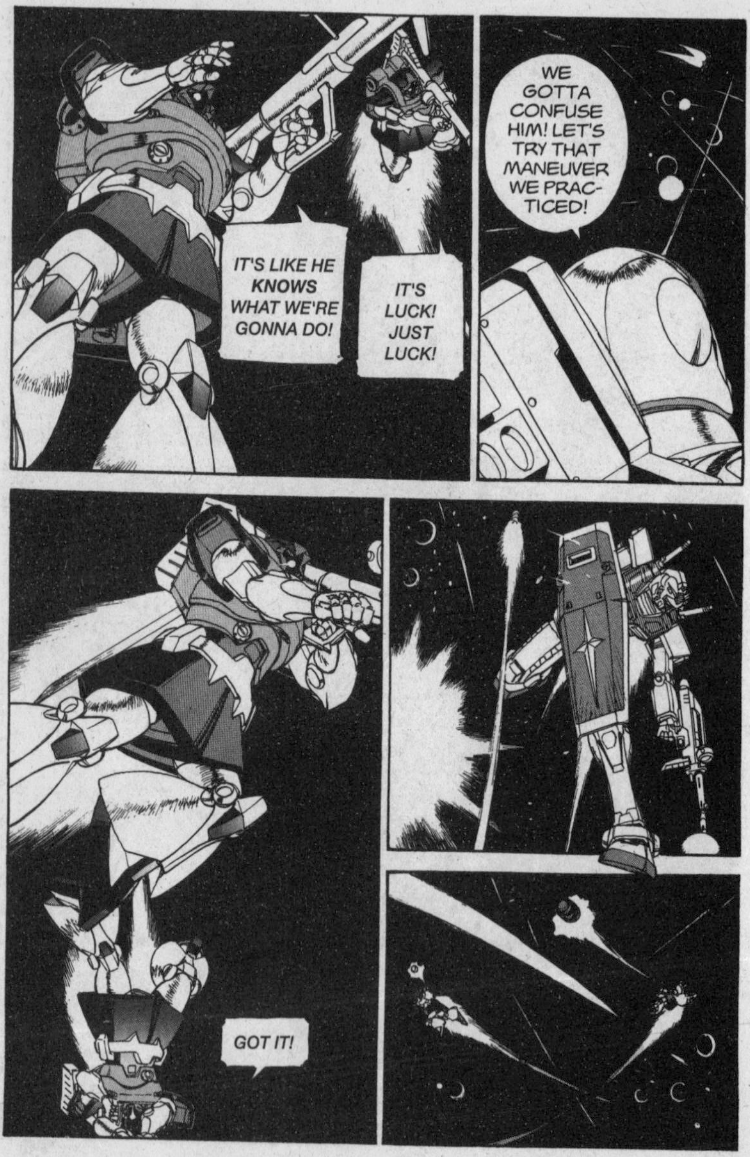
IT'S LIKE HE KNOWS WHAT WE'RE GONNA DO!
IT'S LUCK! JUST LUCK!
WE GOTTA CONFUSE HIM! LET'S TRY THAT MANEUVER WE PRACTICED!
GOT IT!

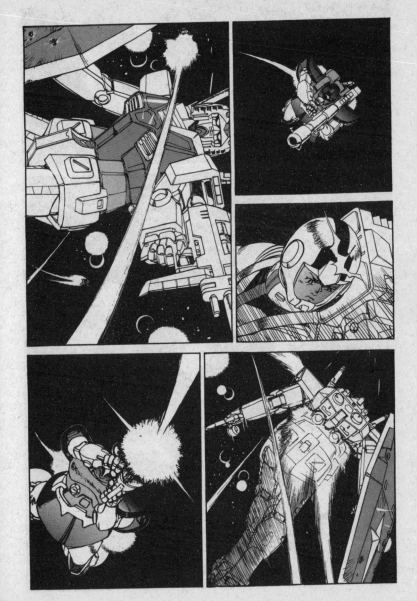

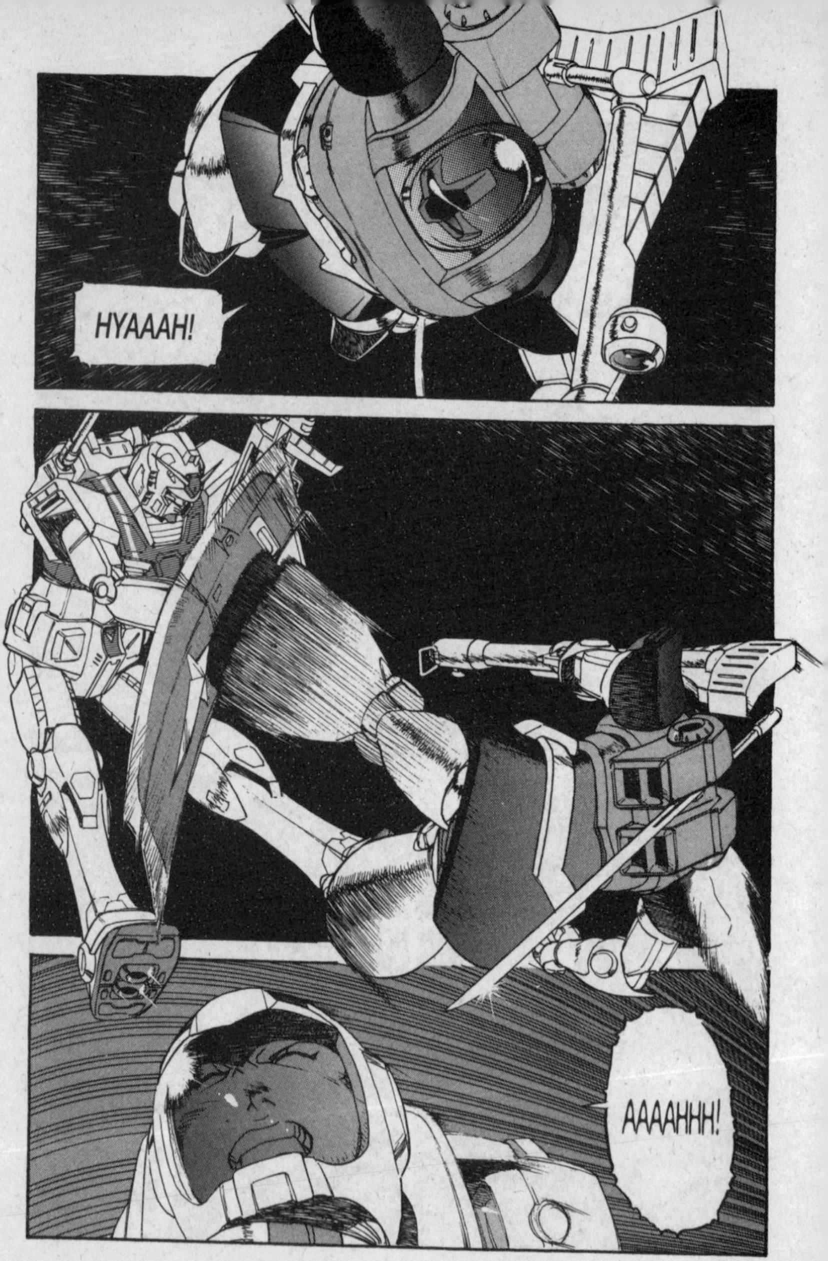
HYAAAH!
AAAAHHH!

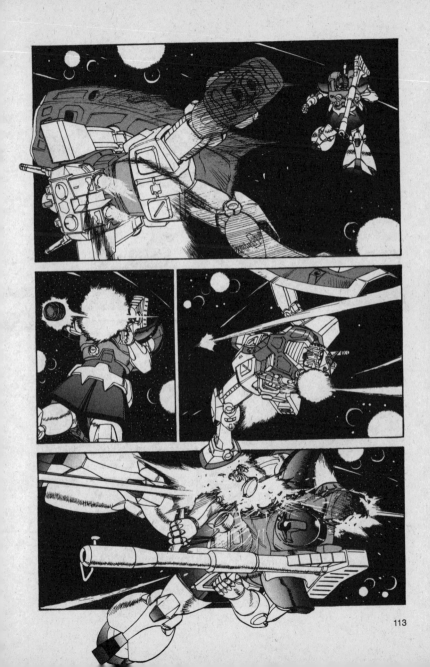

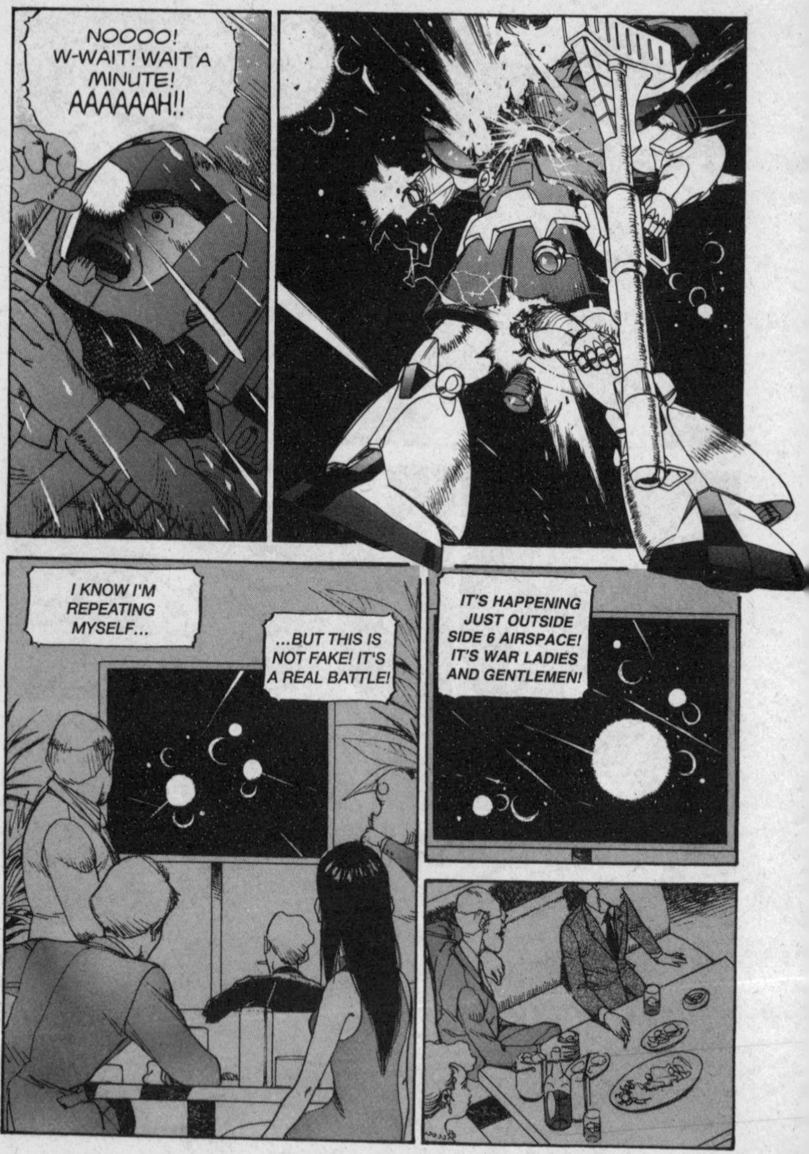
NOOOO! W-WAIT! WAIT A MINUTE! AAAAAAH!!
I KNOW I'M REPEATING MYSELF...
...BUT THIS IS NOT FAKE! IT'S A REAL BATTLE!
IT'S HAPPENING JUST OUTSIDE SIDE 6 AIRSPACE! IT'S WAR LADIES AND GENTLEMEN!

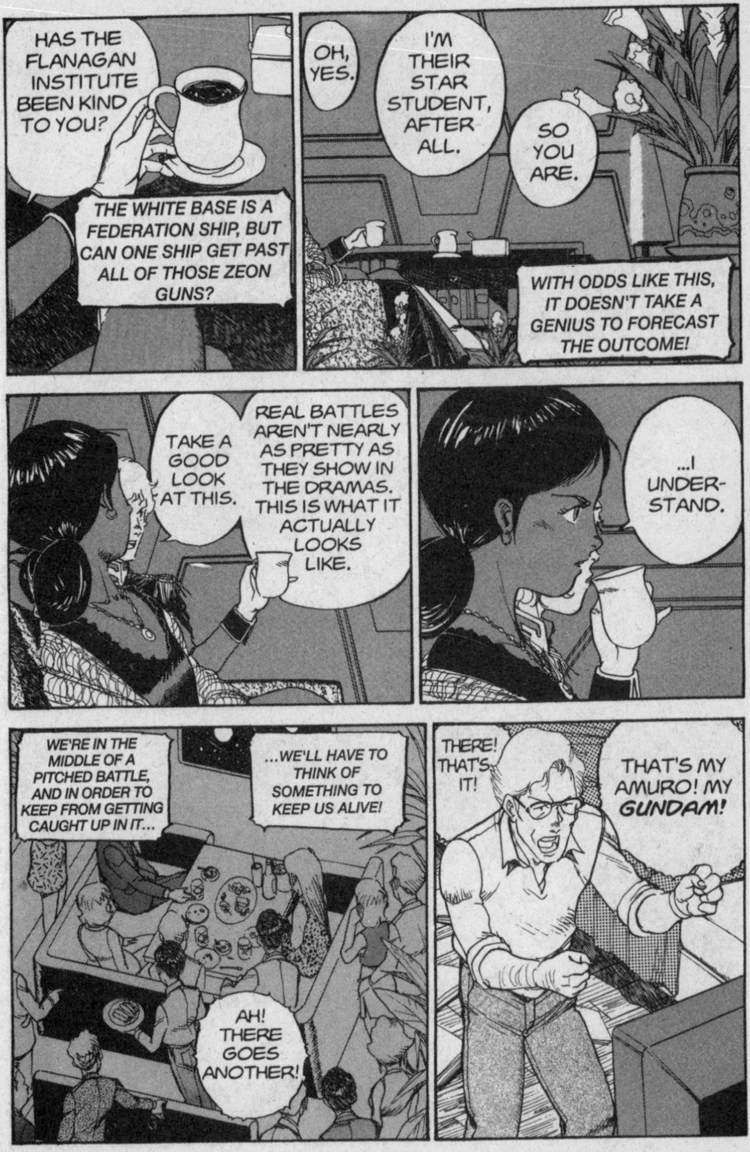
HAS THE FLANAGAN INSTITUTE BEEN KIND TO YOU?
THE WHITE BASE IS A FEDERATION SHIP, BUT CAN ONE SHIP GET PAST ALL OF THOSE ZEON GUNS?
OH, YES.
I'M THEIR STAR STUDENT, AFTER ALL.
SO YOU ARE.
WITH ODDS LIKE THIS, IT DOESN'T TAKE A GENIUS TO FORECAST THE OUTCOME!
TAKE A GOOD LOOK AT THIS.
REAL BATTLES AREN'T NEARLY AS PRETTY AS THEY SHOW IN THE DRAMAS. THIS IS WHAT IT ACTUALLY LOOKS LIKE.
...I UNDER-STAND.
WE'RE IN THE MIDDLE OF A PITCHED BATTLE, AND IN ORDER TO KEEP FROM GETTING CAUGHT UP IN IT...
...WE'LL HAVE TO THINK OF SOMETHING TO KEEP US ALIVE!
AH! THERE GOES ANOTHER!
THERE! THAT'S IT!
THAT'S MY AMURO! MY GUNDAM!

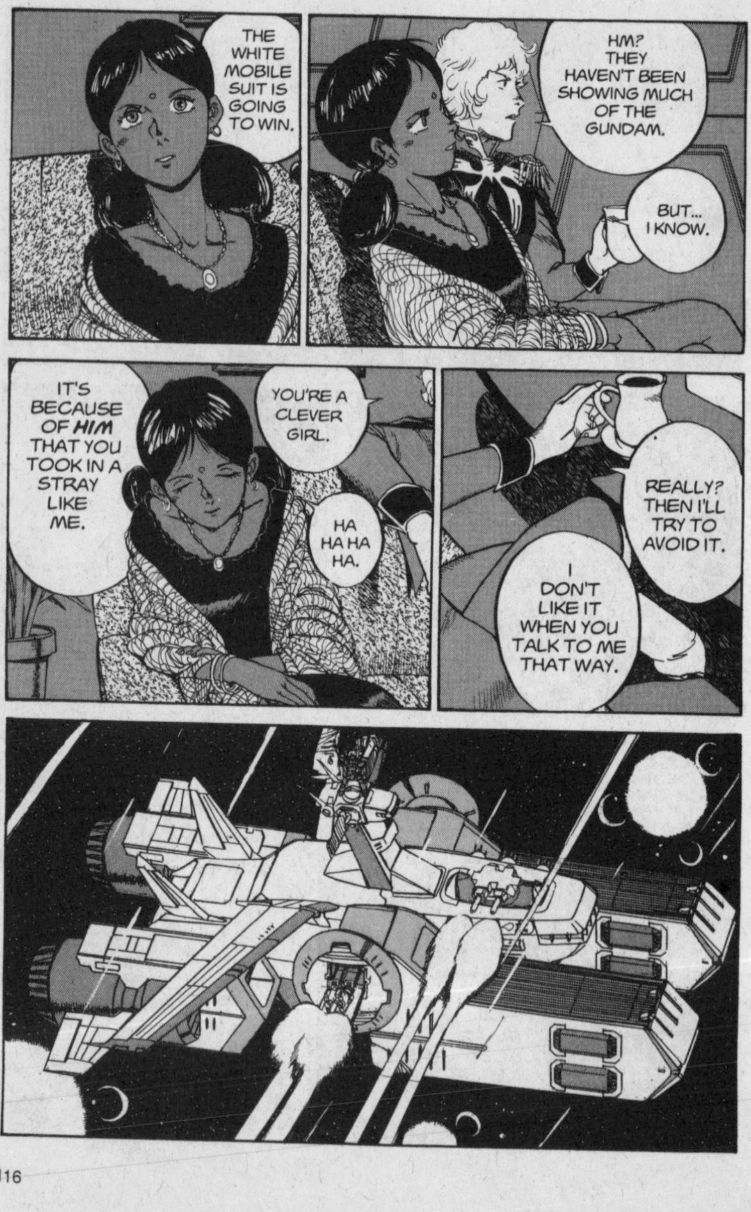
THE WHITE MOBILE SUIT IS GOING TO WIN.
HM? THEY HAVEN'T BEEN SHOWING MUCH OF THE GUNDAM.
BUT... I KNOW.
IT'S BECAUSE OF ***HIM*** THAT YOU TOOK IN A STRAY LIKE ME.
YOU'RE A CLEVER GIRL.
HA HA HA HA.
REALLY? THEN I'LL TRY TO AVOID IT.
I DON'T LIKE IT WHEN YOU TALK TO ME THAT WAY.

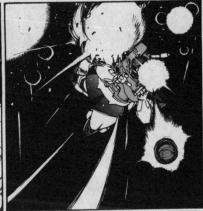

EYAAAH!

GET YOUR FREAKIN' HAND OFF ME!

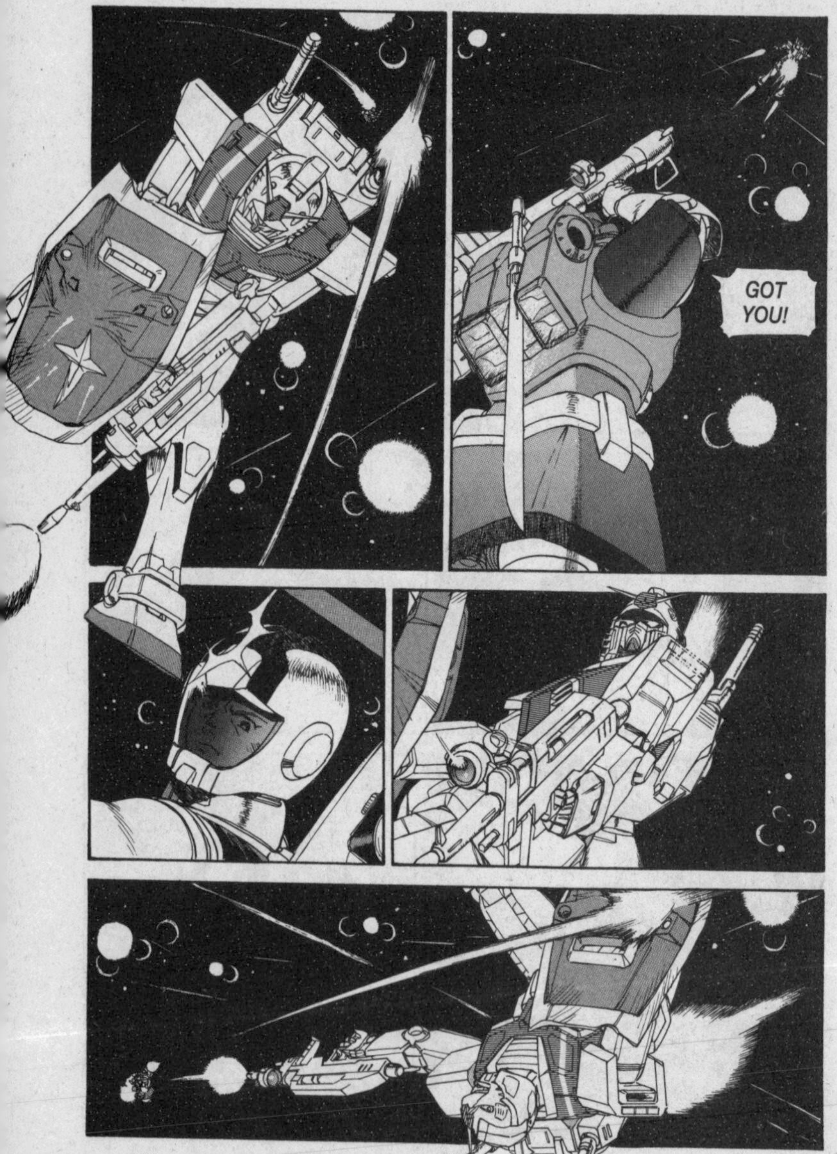
GOT YOU!

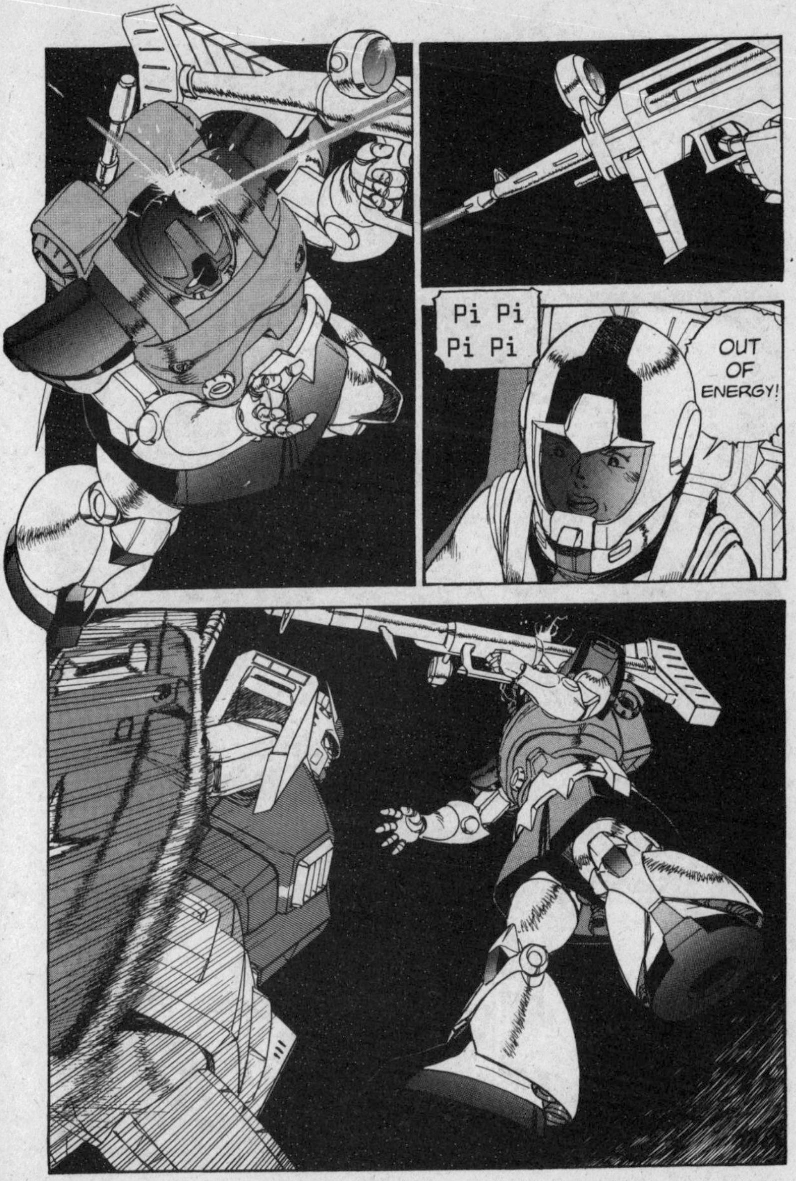
Pi Pi
Pi Pi
OUT OF ENERGY!

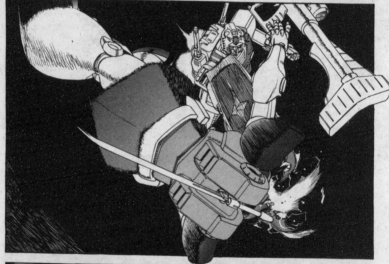

YAAAHH!

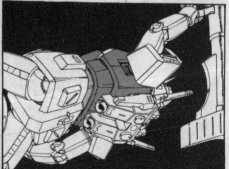

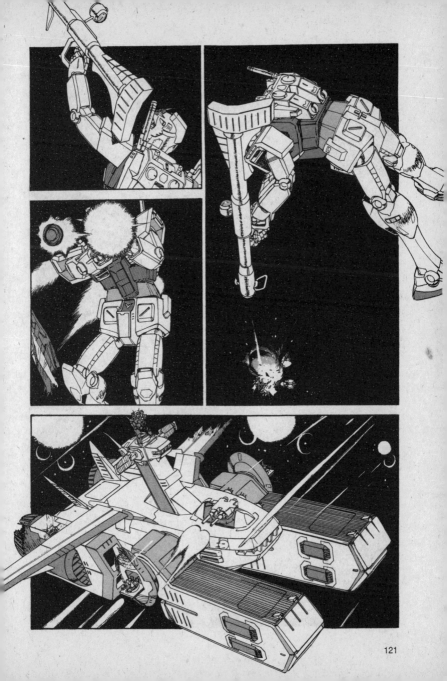

121

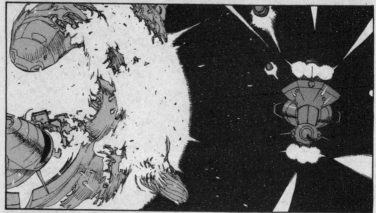

AAAHH!

I- I CAN'T REPORT *THIS!!*

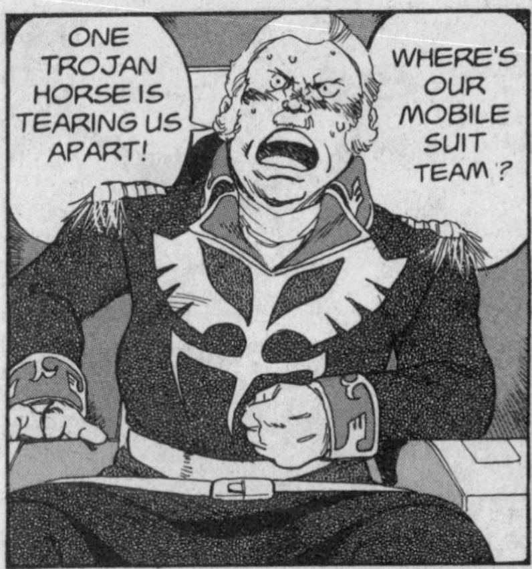
ONE TROJAN HORSE IS TEARING US APART!
WHERE'S OUR MOBILE SUIT TEAM?
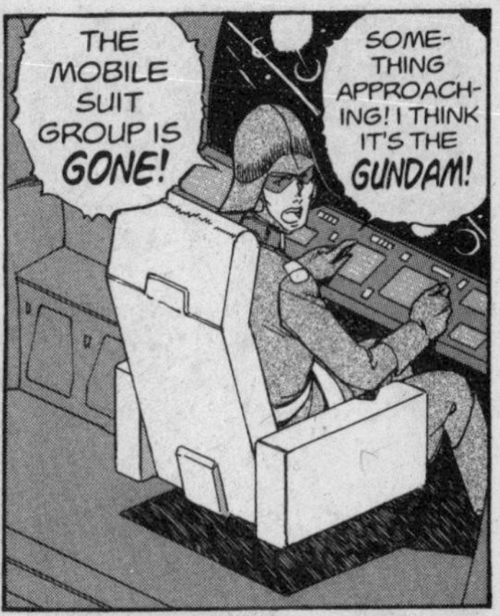
THE MOBILE SUIT GROUP IS GONE!
SOME-THING APPROACH-ING! I THINK IT'S THE GUNDAM!
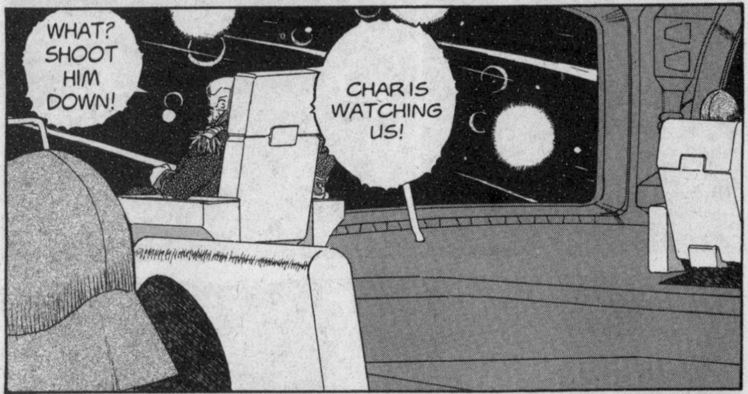
WHAT? SHOOT HIM DOWN!
CHAR IS WATCHING US!
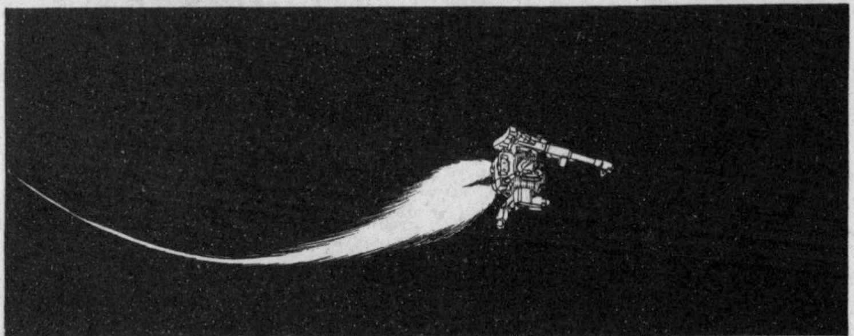

AMURO TO WHITE BASE...

HOLD YOUR FIRE!

I'LL TAKE THIS SHIP DOWN!

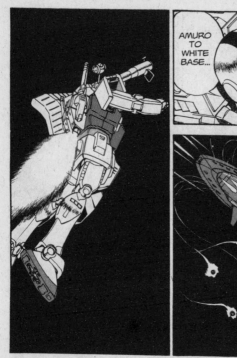

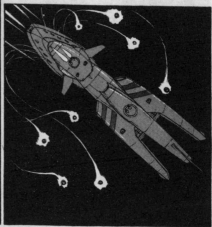

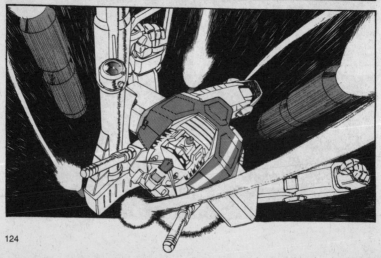

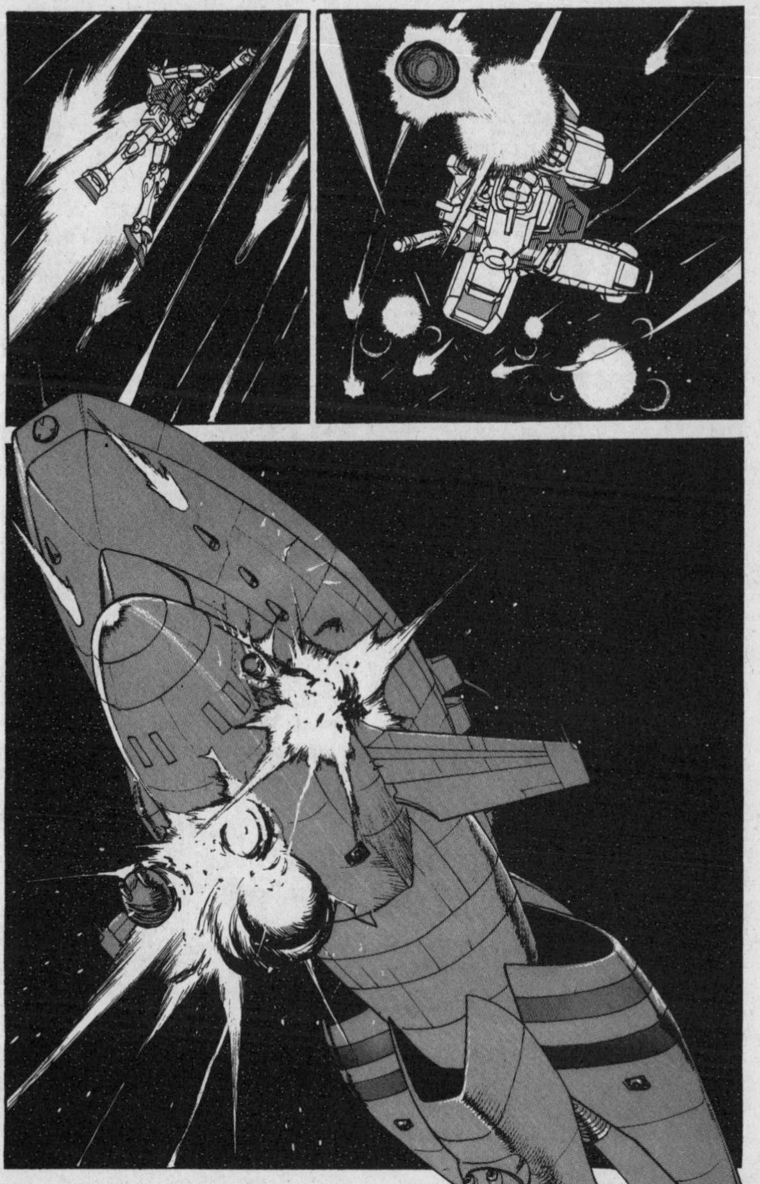

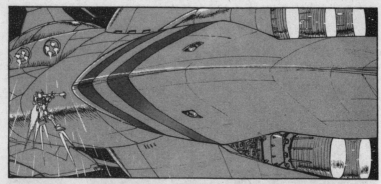

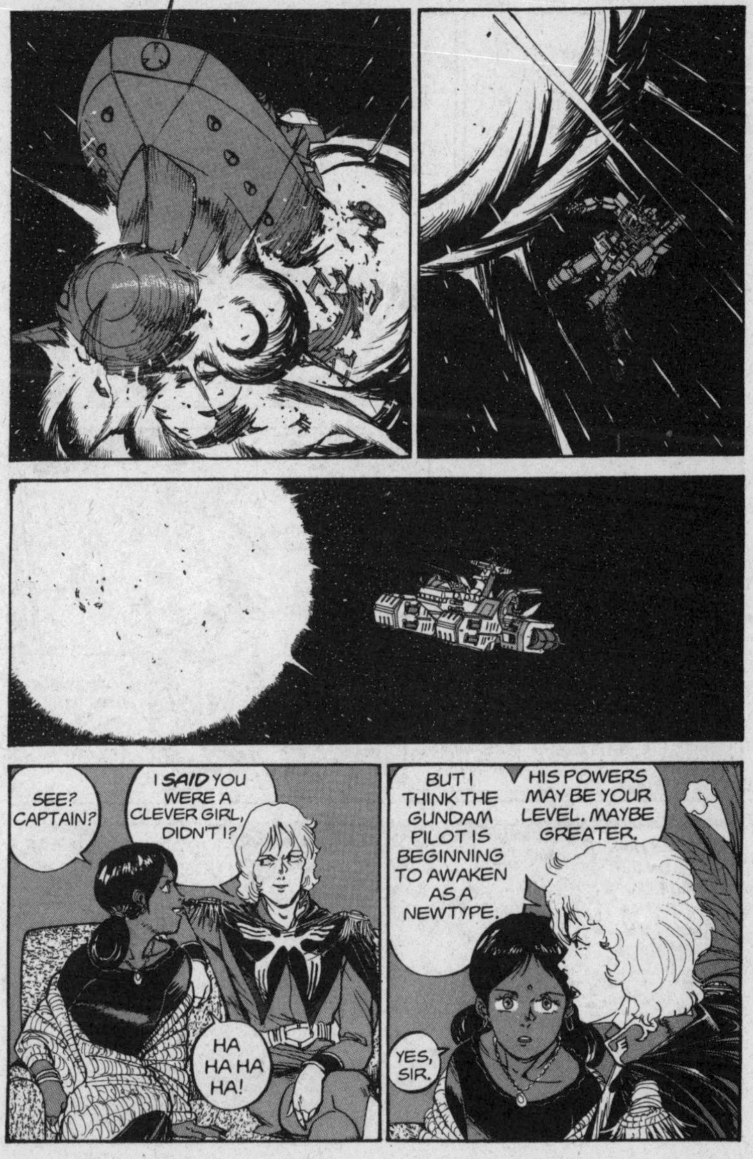
SEE? CAPTAIN?
I SAID YOU WERE A CLEVER GIRL, DIDN'T I?
HA HA HA HA!
BUT I THINK THE GUNDAM PILOT IS BEGINNING TO AWAKEN AS A NEWTYPE.
HIS POWERS MAY BE YOUR LEVEL. MAYBE GREATER.
YES, SIR.

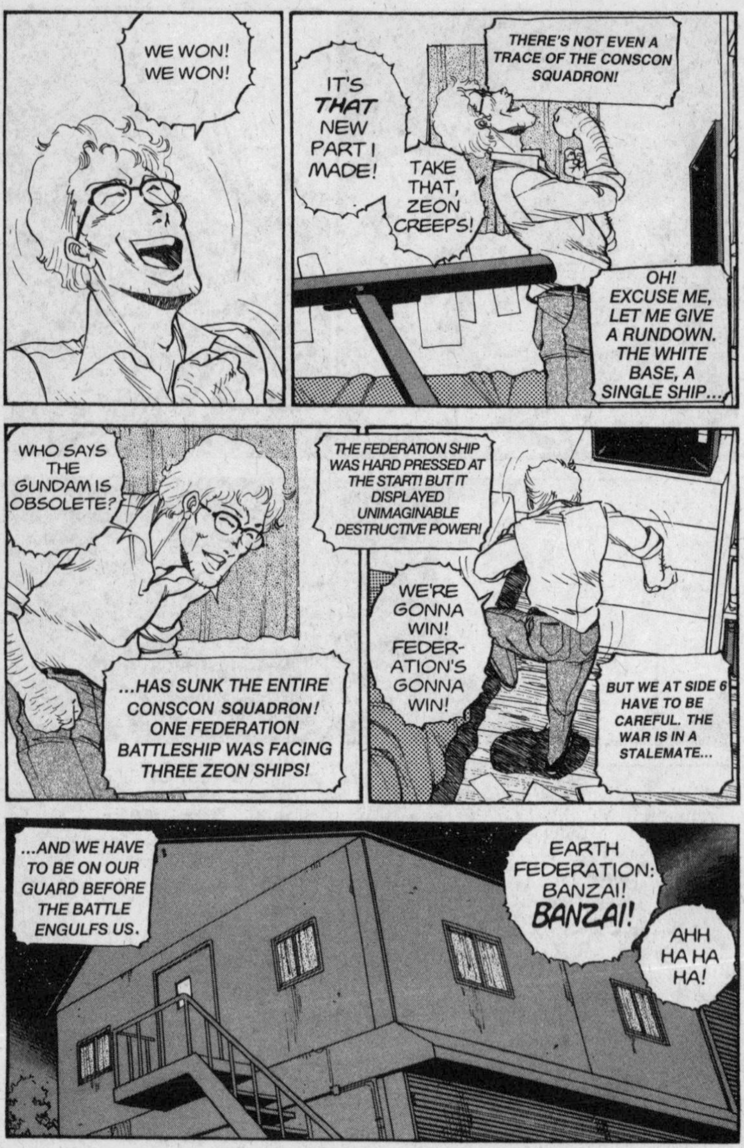
WE WON! WE WON!
THERE'S NOT EVEN A TRACE OF THE CONSCON SQUADRON!
IT'S *THAT* NEW PART I MADE!
TAKE THAT, ZEON CREEPS!
OH! EXCUSE ME, LET ME GIVE A RUNDOWN. THE WHITE BASE, A SINGLE SHIP...
WHO SAYS THE GUNDAM IS OBSOLETE?
...HAS SUNK THE ENTIRE CONSCON SQUADRON! ONE FEDERATION BATTLESHIP WAS FACING THREE ZEON SHIPS!
THE FEDERATION SHIP WAS HARD PRESSED AT THE START! BUT IT DISPLAYED UNIMAGINABLE DESTRUCTIVE POWER!
WE'RE GONNA WIN! FEDER-ATION'S GONNA WIN!
BUT WE AT SIDE 6 HAVE TO BE CAREFUL. THE WAR IS IN A STALEMATE...
...AND WE HAVE TO BE ON OUR GUARD BEFORE THE BATTLE ENGULFS US.
EARTH FEDERATION: BANZAI! **BANZAI!**
AHH HA HA HA!

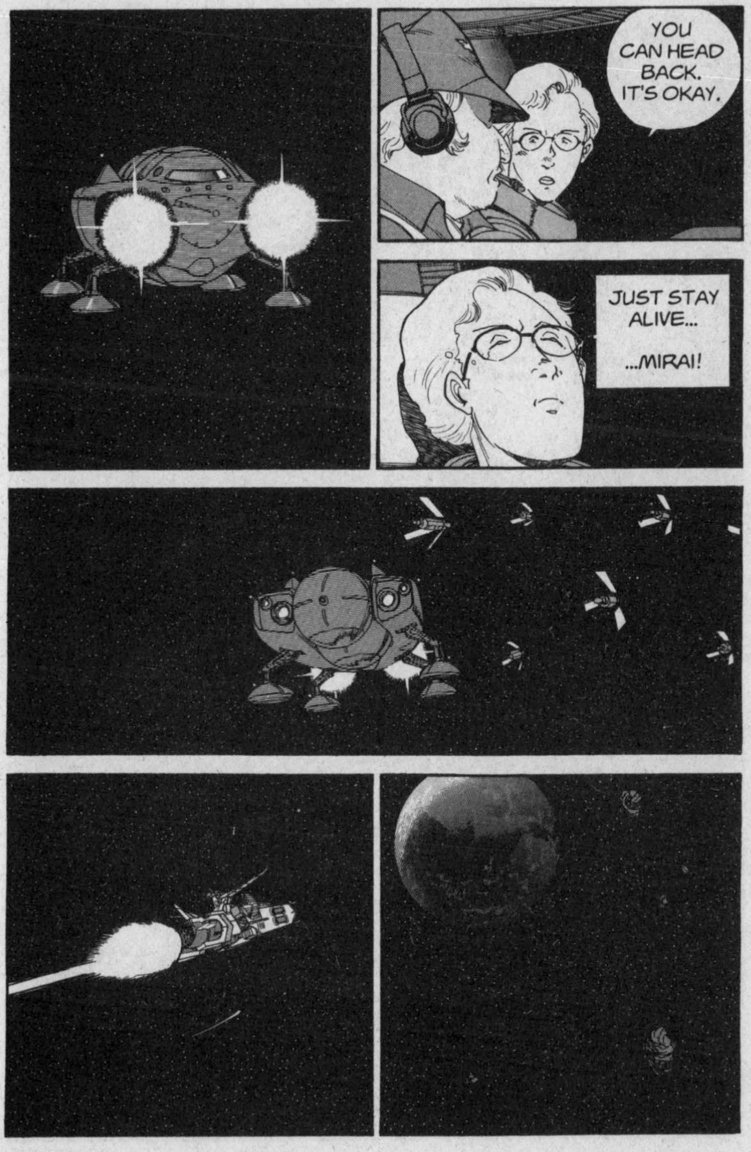
YOU CAN HEAD BACK. IT'S OKAY.
JUST STAY ALIVE...
...MIRAI!

SUPPLY SHIP DOCKED!

ADMIRAL DOZLE, SUPPLIES HAVE ARRIVED FROM A BAOA QU.

YES.

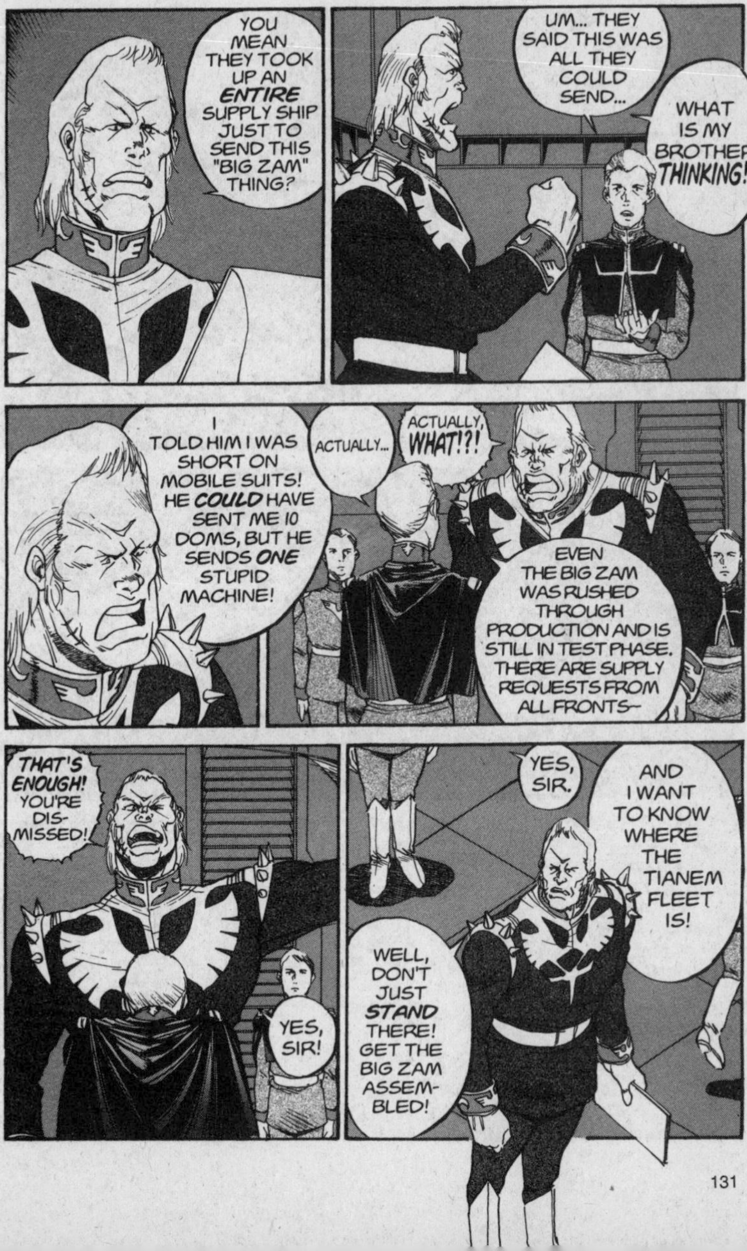
YOU MEAN THEY TOOK UP AN ENTIRE SUPPLY SHIP JUST TO SEND THIS "BIG ZAM" THING?
UM... THEY SAID THIS WAS ALL THEY COULD SEND...
WHAT IS MY BROTHER THINKING!?
I TOLD HIM I WAS SHORT ON MOBILE SUITS! HE COULD HAVE SENT ME 10 DOMS, BUT HE SENDS ONE STUPID MACHINE!
ACTUALLY...
ACTUALLY, WHAT!?!
EVEN THE BIG ZAM WAS RUSHED THROUGH PRODUCTION AND IS STILL IN TEST PHASE. THERE ARE SUPPLY REQUESTS FROM ALL FRONTS~
THAT'S ENOUGH! YOU'RE DIS-MISSED!
YES, SIR!
AND I WANT TO KNOW WHERE THE TIANEM FLEET IS!
YES, SIR.
WELL, DON'T JUST STAND THERE! GET THE BIG ZAM ASSEM-BLED!

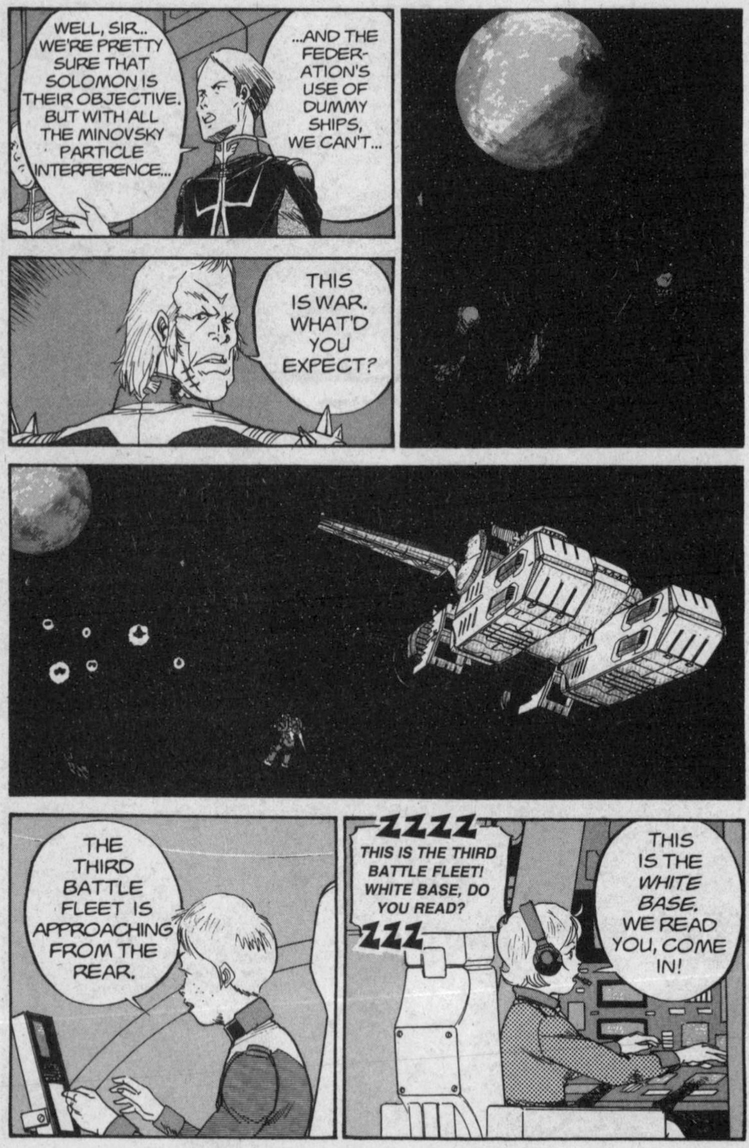
WELL, SIR... WE'RE PRETTY SURE THAT SOLOMON IS THEIR OBJECTIVE. BUT WITH ALL THE MINOVSKY PARTICLE INTERFERENCE...
...AND THE FEDERATION'S USE OF DUMMY SHIPS, WE CAN'T...
THIS IS WAR. WHAT'D YOU EXPECT?
THE THIRD BATTLE FLEET IS APPROACHING FROM THE REAR.
ZZZZ
THIS IS THE THIRD BATTLE FLEET! WHITE BASE, DO YOU READ?
ZZZ
THIS IS THE WHITE BASE. WE READ YOU, COME IN!

CHANGE COURSE TO ENTER FORMATION. YOU ARE ASSIGNED TO OUR GROUP! STANDBY TO BE RESUPPLIED.

ZZ ZZ

ZZZ

SEND THEM A "WILL COMPLY."

Y-YES, SIR!

THERE'S A COLUMBUS-CLASS SUPPLY SHIP MOVING FROM PORT TO OUR PROW.

GOOD. TELL SUPPLY CREWS TO HURRY!

I'M GOING TO PAY MY RESPECTS TO OUR FLEET COMMANDER.

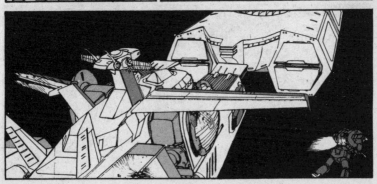

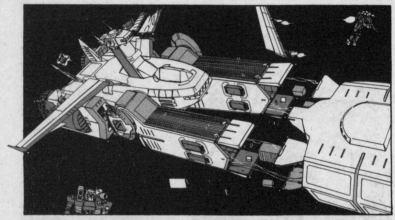

WHAT ARE ALL THOSE G-FIGHTER LOOKIN' THINGS FLYIN' AROUND OUT THERE?

THOSE ARE PUBLIC ASSAULT SHIPS.

ASSAULT!?

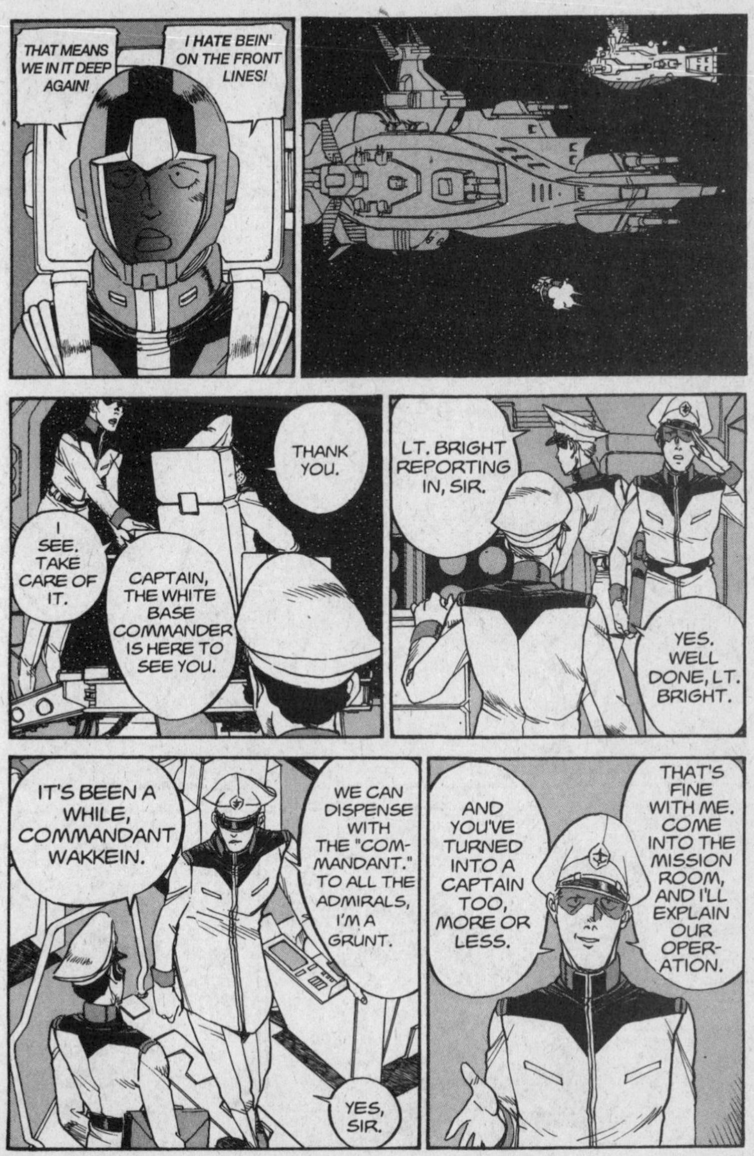
THAT MEANS WE IN IT DEEP AGAIN!
I HATE BEIN' ON THE FRONT LINES!
CAPTAIN, THE WHITE BASE COMMANDER IS HERE TO SEE YOU.
I SEE. TAKE CARE OF IT.
THANK YOU.
LT. BRIGHT REPORTING IN, SIR.
YES. WELL DONE, LT. BRIGHT.
IT'S BEEN A WHILE, COMMANDANT WAKKEIN.
WE CAN DISPENSE WITH THE "COMMANDANT." TO ALL THE ADMIRALS, I'M A GRUNT.
YES, SIR.
AND YOU'VE TURNED INTO A CAPTAIN TOO, MORE OR LESS.
THAT'S FINE WITH ME. COME INTO THE MISSION ROOM, AND I'LL EXPLAIN OUR OPERATION.

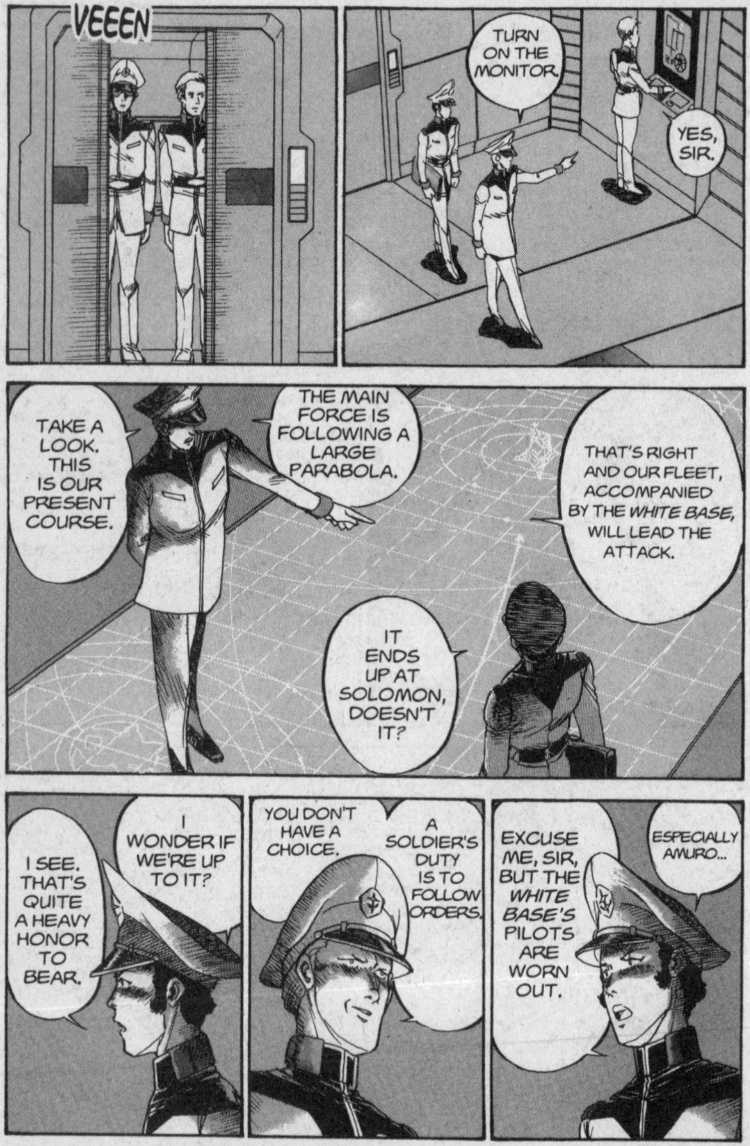
VEEEN
TURN ON THE MONITOR.
YES, SIR.
TAKE A LOOK. THIS IS OUR PRESENT COURSE.
THE MAIN FORCE IS FOLLOWING A LARGE PARABOLA.
IT ENDS UP AT SOLOMON, DOESN'T IT?
THAT'S RIGHT AND OUR FLEET, ACCOMPANIED BY THE *WHITE BASE*, WILL LEAD THE ATTACK.
I SEE. THAT'S QUITE A HEAVY HONOR TO BEAR.
I WONDER IF WE'RE UP TO IT?
YOU DON'T HAVE A CHOICE.
A SOLDIER'S DUTY IS TO FOLLOW ORDERS.
EXCUSE ME, SIR, BUT THE *WHITE BASE'S* PILOTS ARE WORN OUT.
ESPECIALLY AMURO...

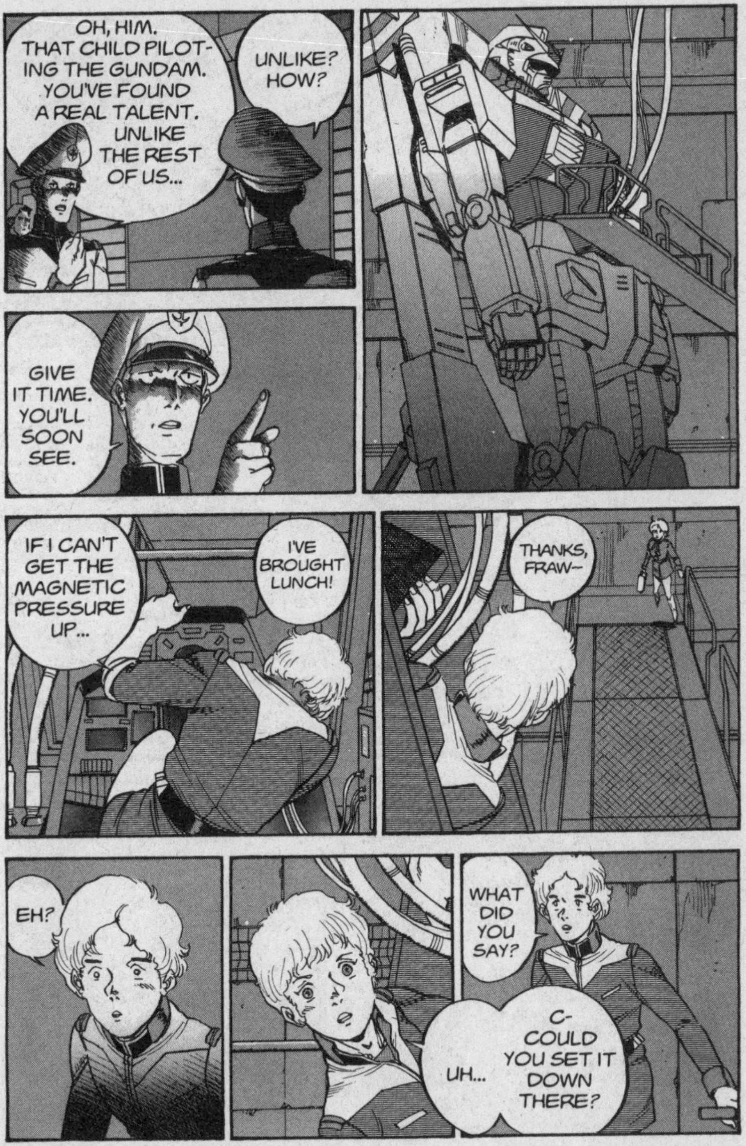
OH, HIM. THAT CHILD PILOTING THE GUNDAM. YOU'VE FOUND A REAL TALENT.
UNLIKE THE REST OF US...
UNLIKE? HOW?
GIVE IT TIME. YOU'LL SOON SEE.
IF I CAN'T GET THE MAGNETIC PRESSURE UP...
I'VE BROUGHT LUNCH!
THANKS, FRAW–
EH?
WHAT DID YOU SAY?
C- COULD YOU SET IT DOWN THERE?
UH...

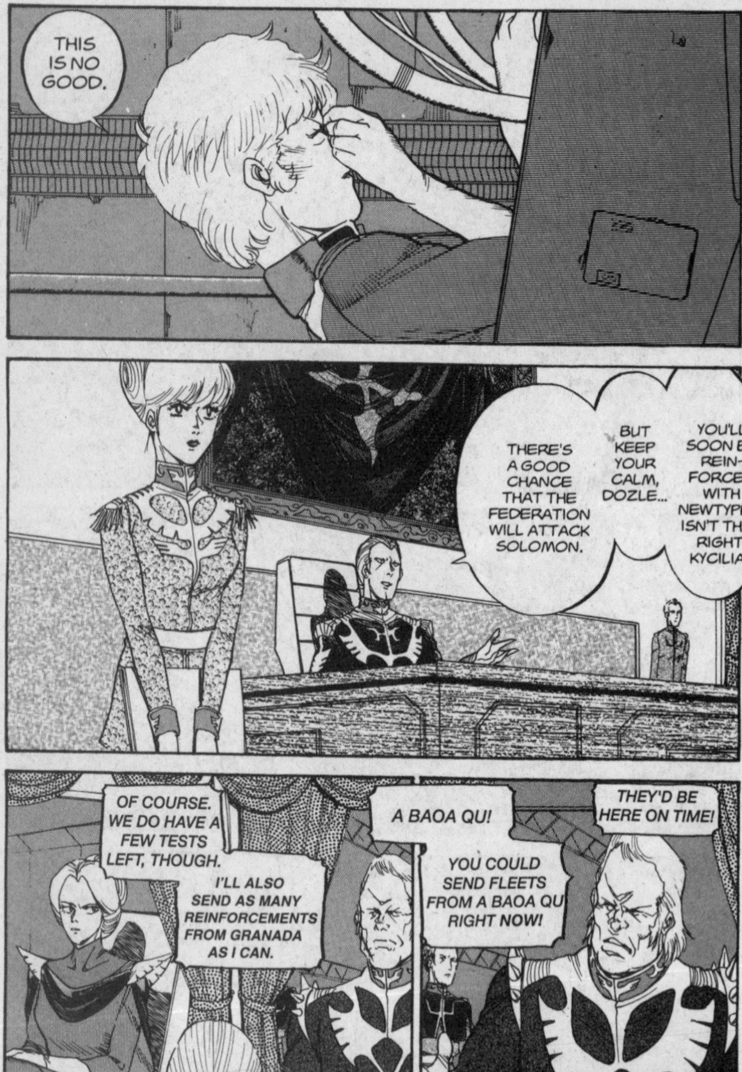
THIS IS NO GOOD.
THERE'S A GOOD CHANCE THAT THE FEDERATION WILL ATTACK SOLOMON.
BUT KEEP YOUR CALM, DOZLE...
YOU'LL SOON BE REIN-FORCED WITH NEWTYPES. ISN'T THAT RIGHT, KYCILIA?
OF COURSE. WE DO HAVE A FEW TESTS LEFT, THOUGH.
I'LL ALSO SEND AS MANY REINFORCEMENTS FROM GRANADA AS I CAN.
A BAOA QU!
YOU COULD SEND FLEETS FROM A BAOA QU RIGHT NOW!
THEY'D BE HERE ON TIME!

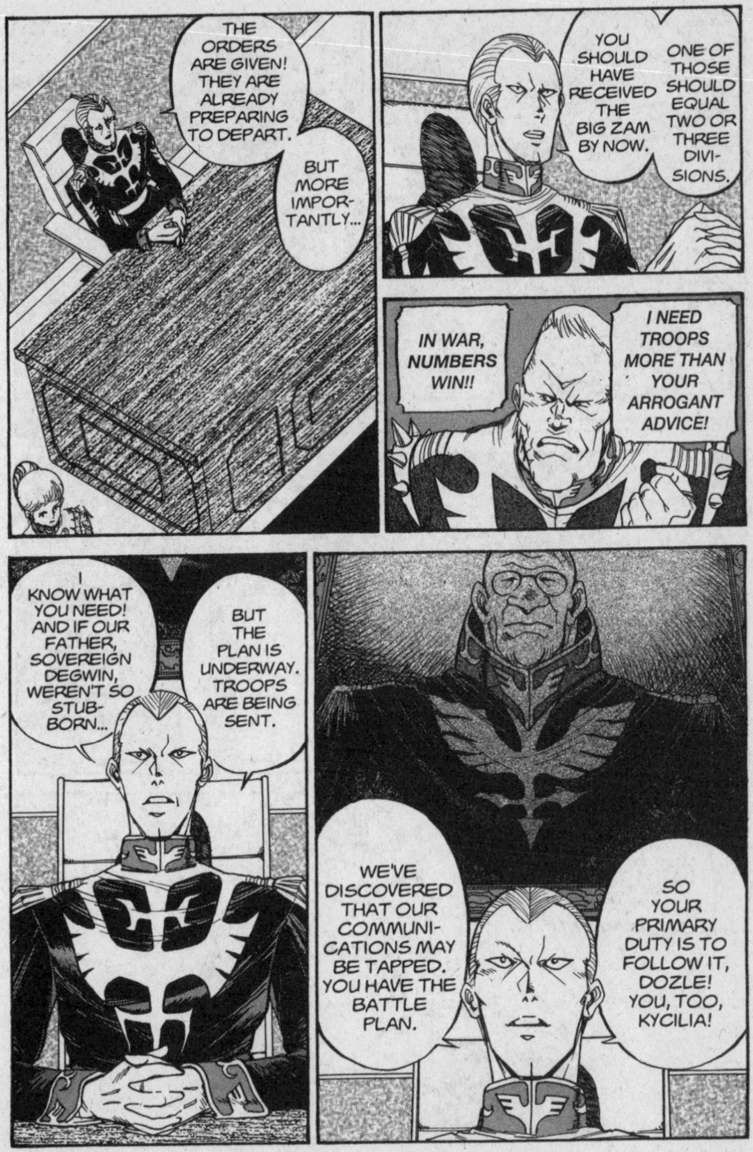
THE ORDERS ARE GIVEN! THEY ARE ALREADY PREPARING TO DEPART.
BUT MORE IMPORTANTLY...
YOU SHOULD HAVE RECEIVED THE BIG ZAM BY NOW.
ONE OF THOSE SHOULD EQUAL TWO OR THREE DIVISIONS.
IN WAR, NUMBERS WIN!!
I NEED TROOPS MORE THAN YOUR ARROGANT ADVICE!
I KNOW WHAT YOU NEED! AND IF OUR FATHER, SOVEREIGN DEGWIN, WEREN'T SO STUBBORN...
BUT THE PLAN IS UNDERWAY. TROOPS ARE BEING SENT.
WE'VE DISCOVERED THAT OUR COMMUNICATIONS MAY BE TAPPED. YOU HAVE THE BATTLE PLAN.
SO YOUR PRIMARY DUTY IS TO FOLLOW IT, DOZLE! YOU, TOO, KYCILIA!

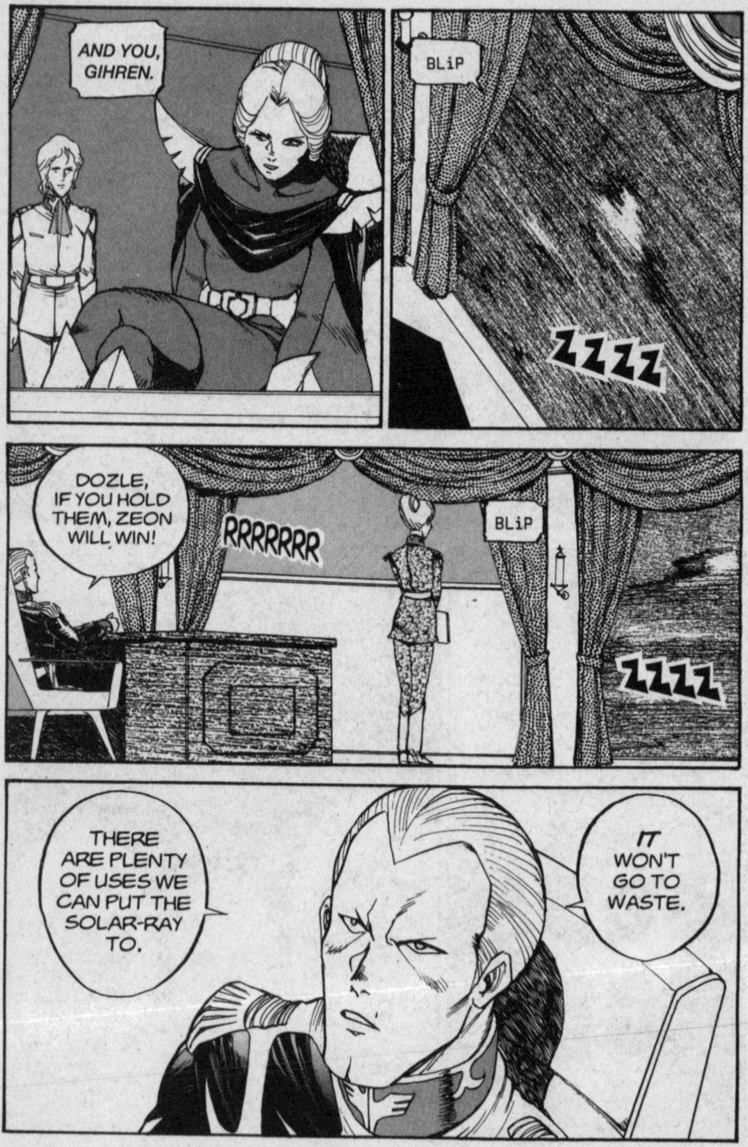
AND YOU, GIHREN.
BLiP
ZZZZ
DOZLE, IF YOU HOLD THEM, ZEON WILL WIN!
RRRRRRR
BLiP
ZZZZ
THERE ARE PLENTY OF USES WE CAN PUT THE SOLAR-RAY TO.
IT WON'T GO TO WASTE.

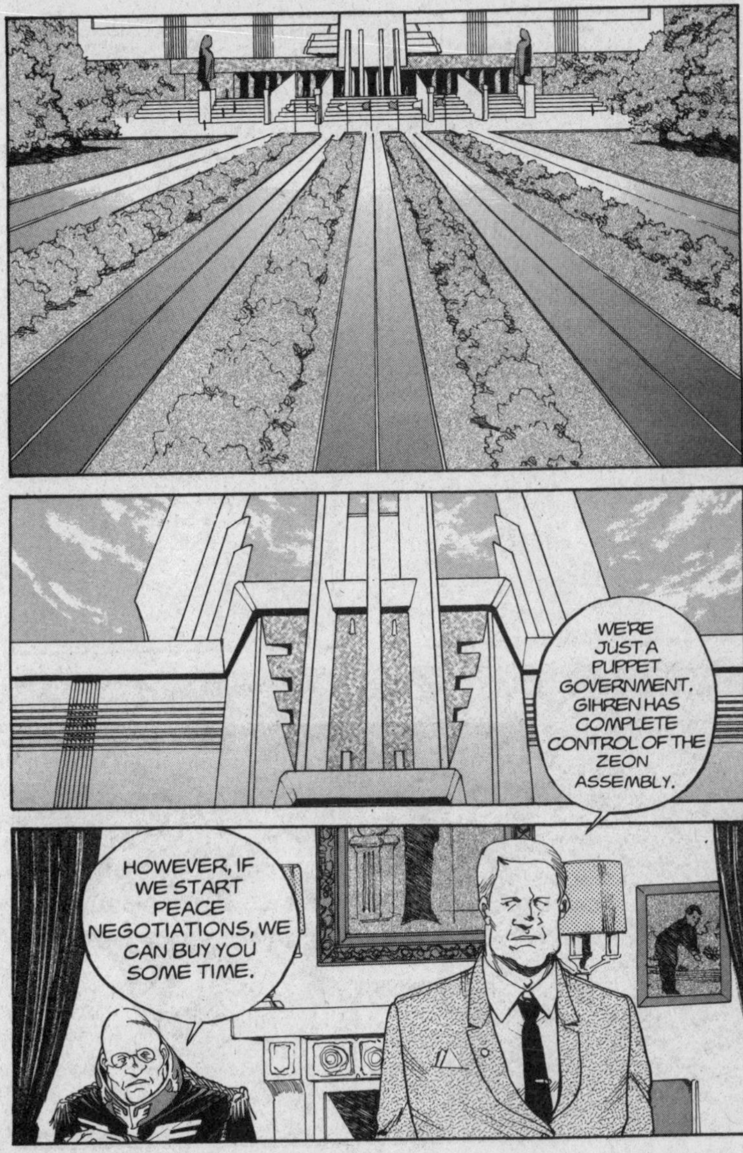
WE'RE JUST A PUPPET GOVERNMENT. GIHREN HAS COMPLETE CONTROL OF THE ZEON ASSEMBLY.
HOWEVER, IF WE START PEACE NEGOTIATIONS, WE CAN BUY YOU SOME TIME.

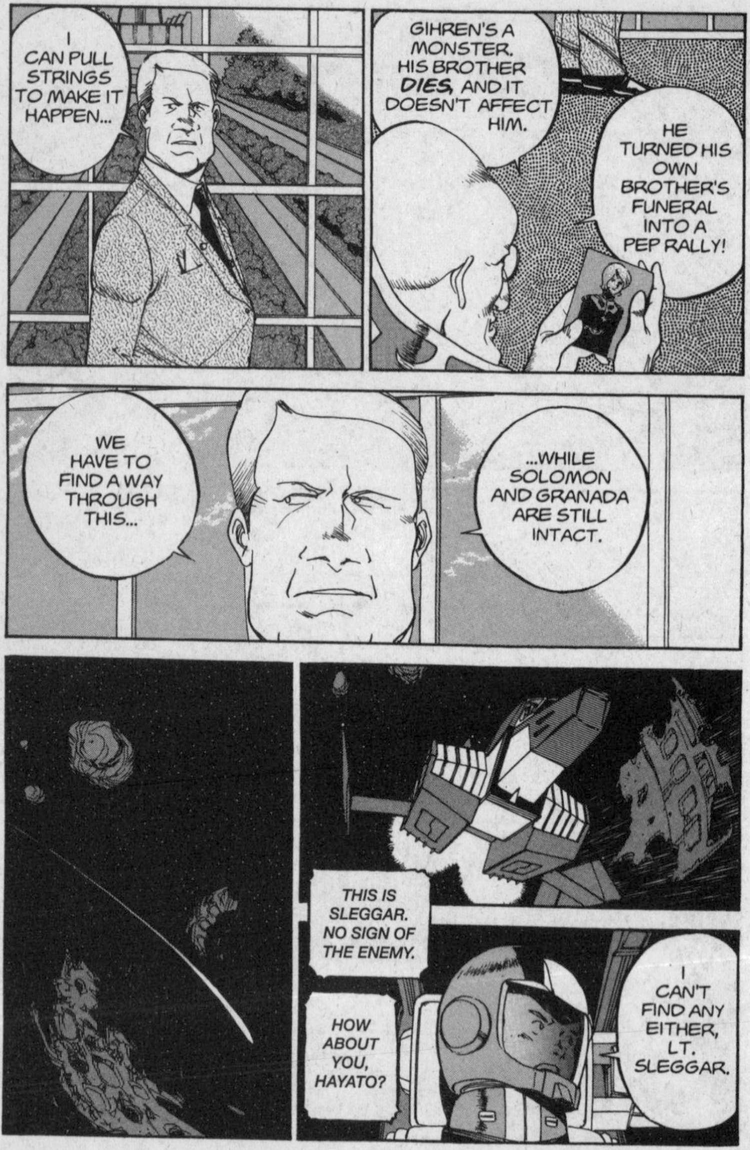
I CAN PULL STRINGS TO MAKE IT HAPPEN...
GIHREN'S A MONSTER. HIS BROTHER DIES, AND IT DOESN'T AFFECT HIM.
HE TURNED HIS OWN BROTHER'S FUNERAL INTO A PEP RALLY!
WE HAVE TO FIND A WAY THROUGH THIS...
...WHILE SOLOMON AND GRANADA ARE STILL INTACT.
THIS IS SLEGGAR. NO SIGN OF THE ENEMY.
HOW ABOUT YOU, HAYATO?
I CAN'T FIND ANY EITHER, LT. SLEGGAR.

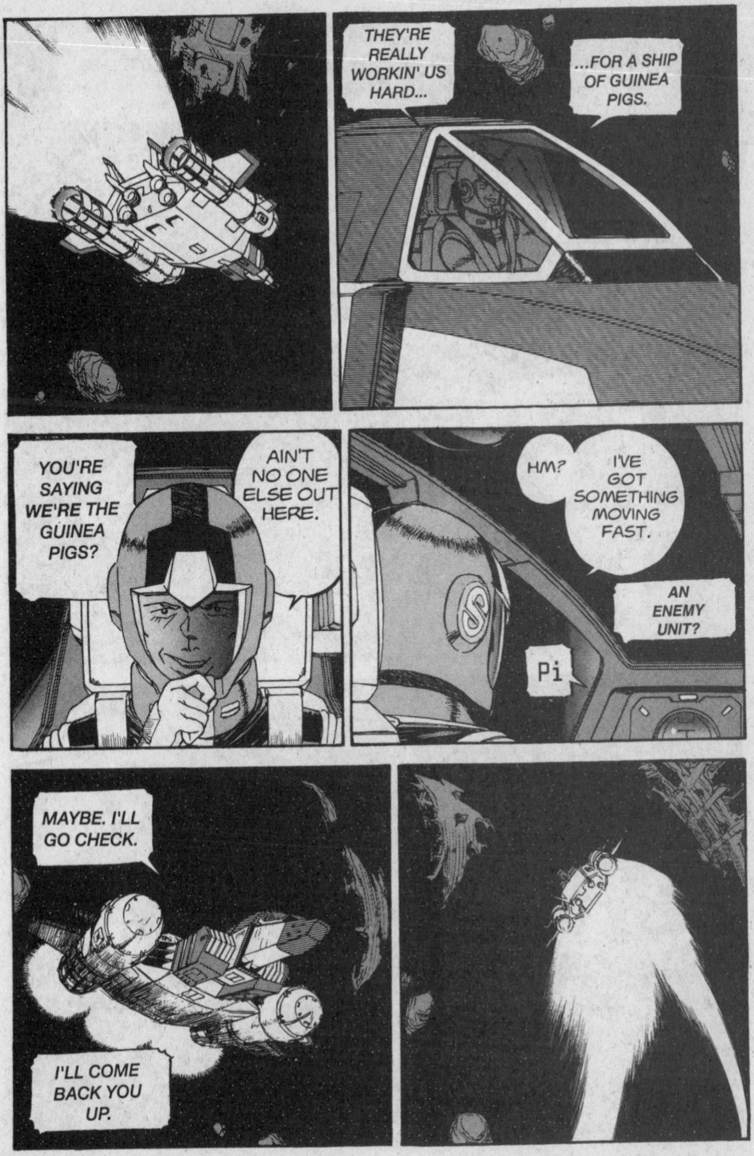
THEY'RE REALLY WORKIN' US HARD...
...FOR A SHIP OF GUINEA PIGS.
YOU'RE SAYING WE'RE THE GUINEA PIGS?
AIN'T NO ONE ELSE OUT HERE.
HM?
I'VE GOT SOMETHING MOVING FAST.
AN ENEMY UNIT?
Pi
MAYBE. I'LL GO CHECK.
I'LL COME BACK YOU UP.

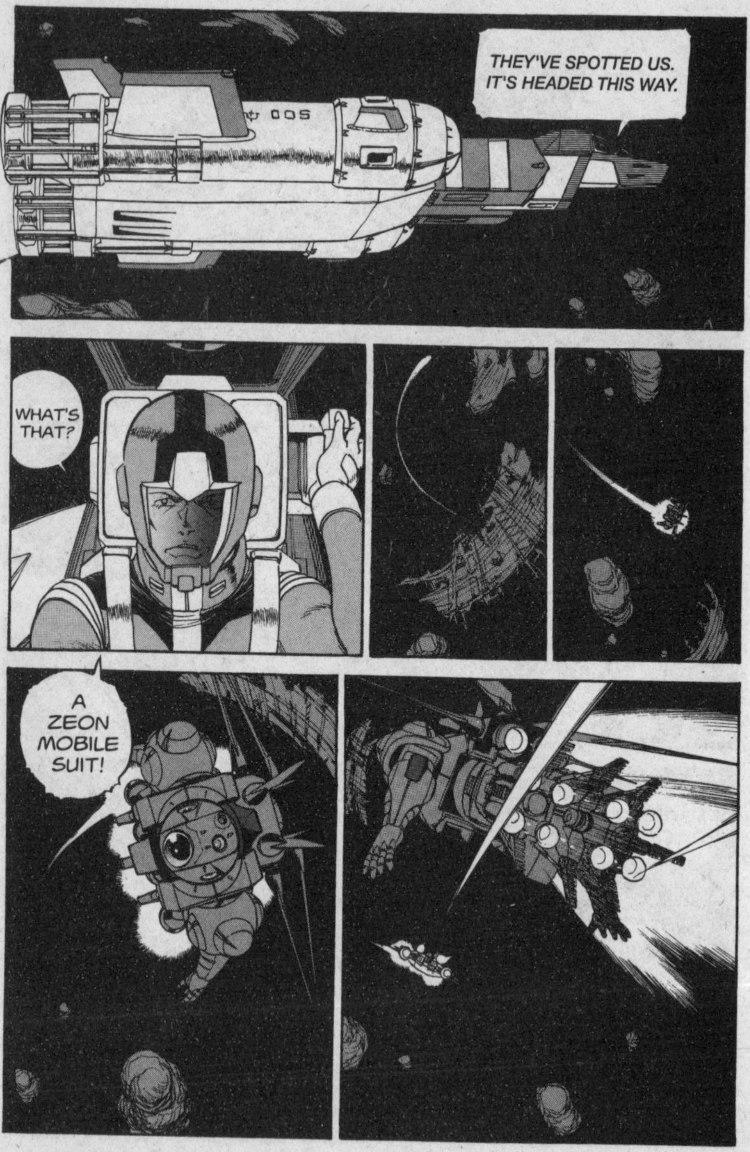
THEY'VE SPOTTED US. IT'S HEADED THIS WAY.
WHAT'S THAT?
A ZEON MOBILE SUIT!

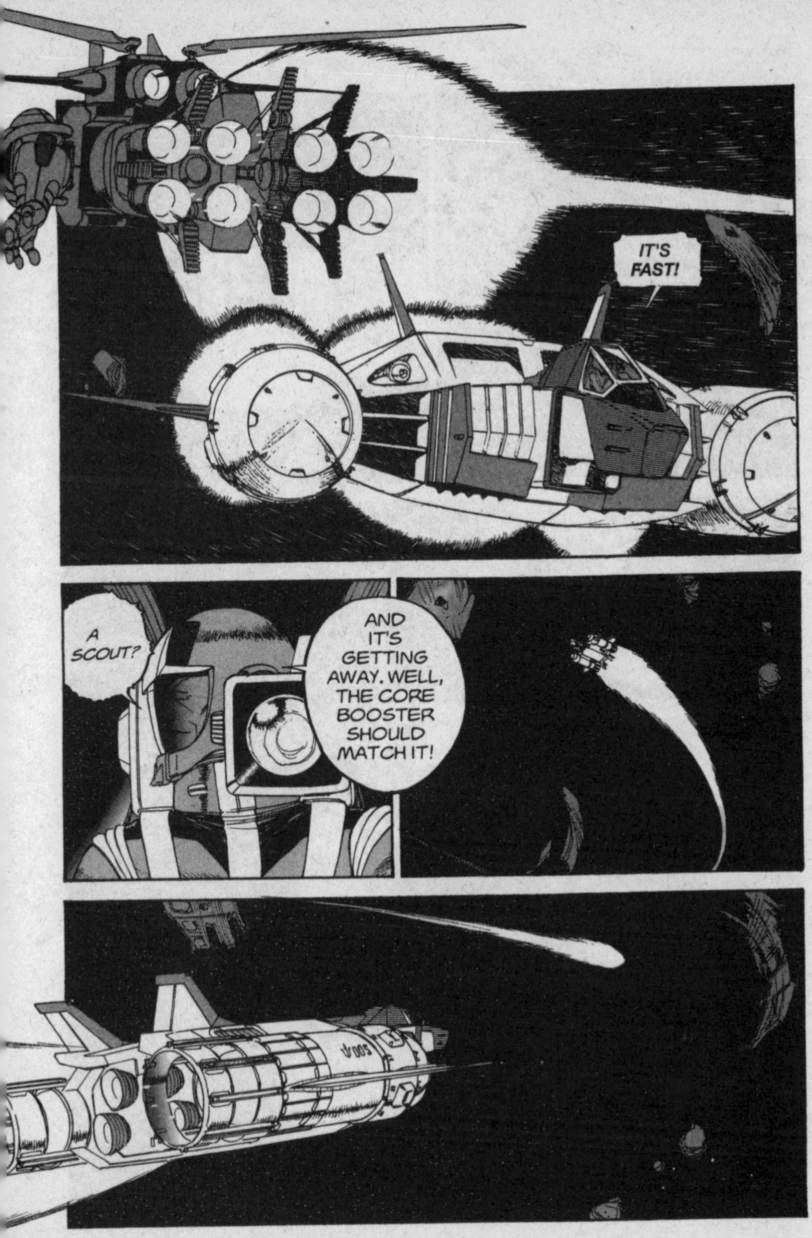
IT'S FAST!
A SCOUT?
AND IT'S GETTING AWAY. WELL, THE CORE BOOSTER SHOULD MATCH IT!

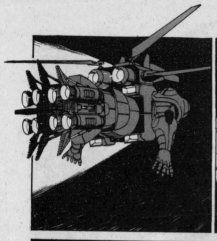

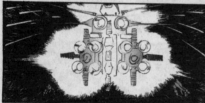

EH? WHAT'S THAT?

MINES!!

HYAAAAH!!

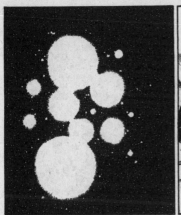

Beeeee

THAT'S NOT GOOD.

KACHAK

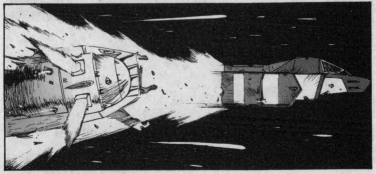

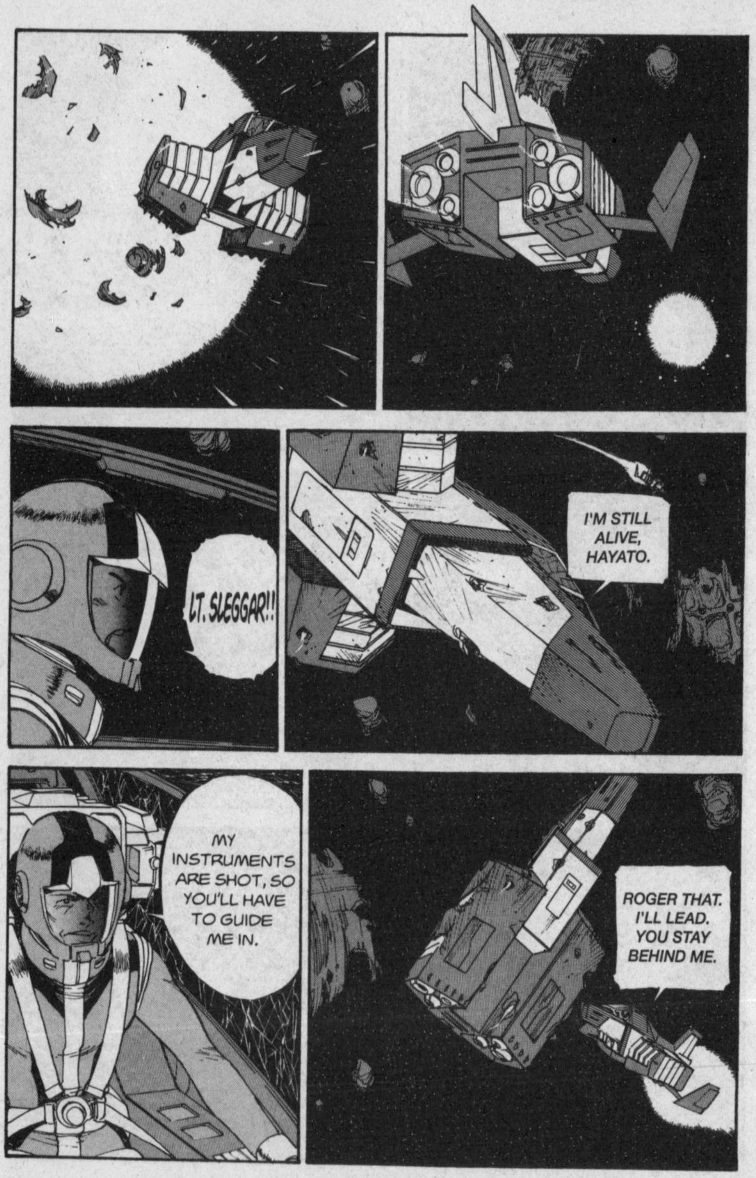
LT. SLEGGAR!!
I'M STILL ALIVE, HAYATO.
MY INSTRUMENTS ARE SHOT, SO YOU'LL HAVE TO GUIDE ME IN.
ROGER THAT. I'LL LEAD. YOU STAY BEHIND ME.

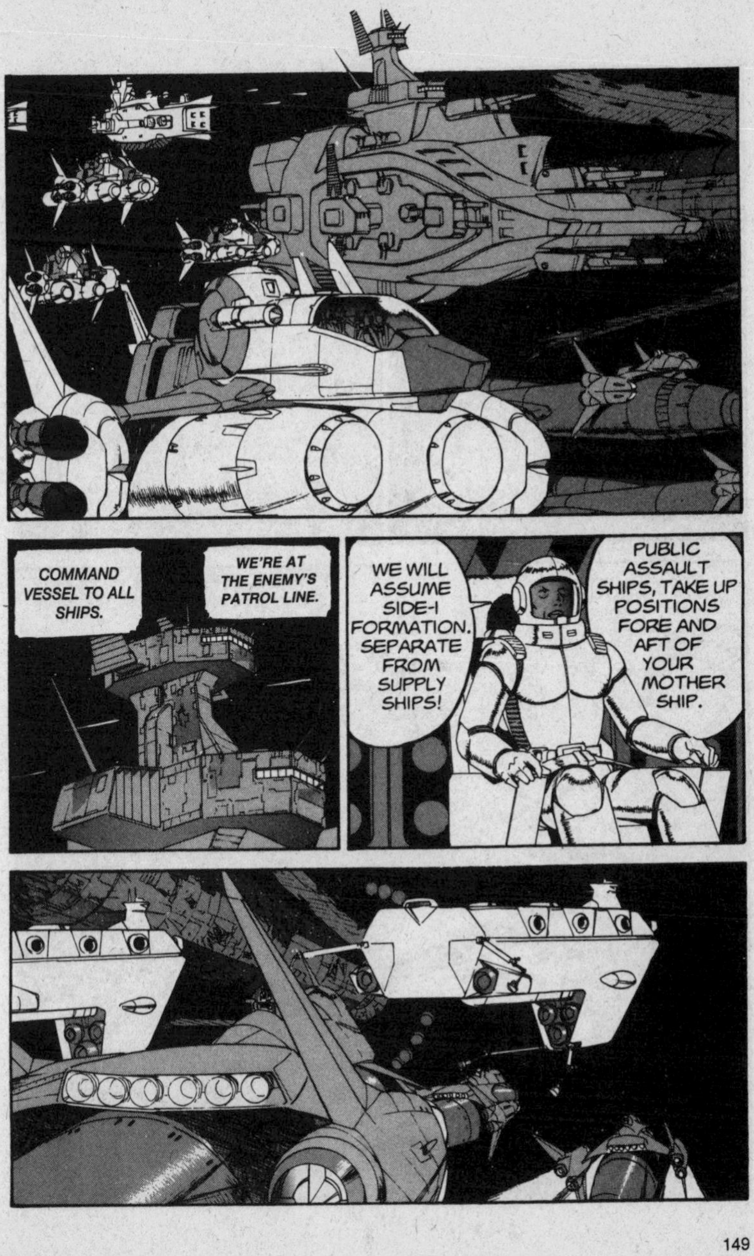
COMMAND VESSEL TO ALL SHIPS.
WE'RE AT THE ENEMY'S PATROL LINE.
WE WILL ASSUME SIDE-1 FORMATION. SEPARATE FROM SUPPLY SHIPS!
PUBLIC ASSAULT SHIPS, TAKE UP POSITIONS FORE AND AFT OF YOUR MOTHER SHIP.

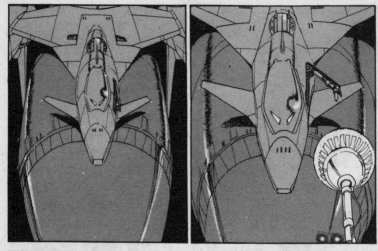

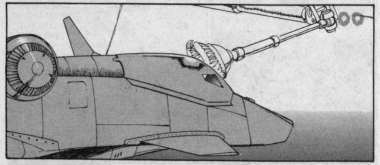

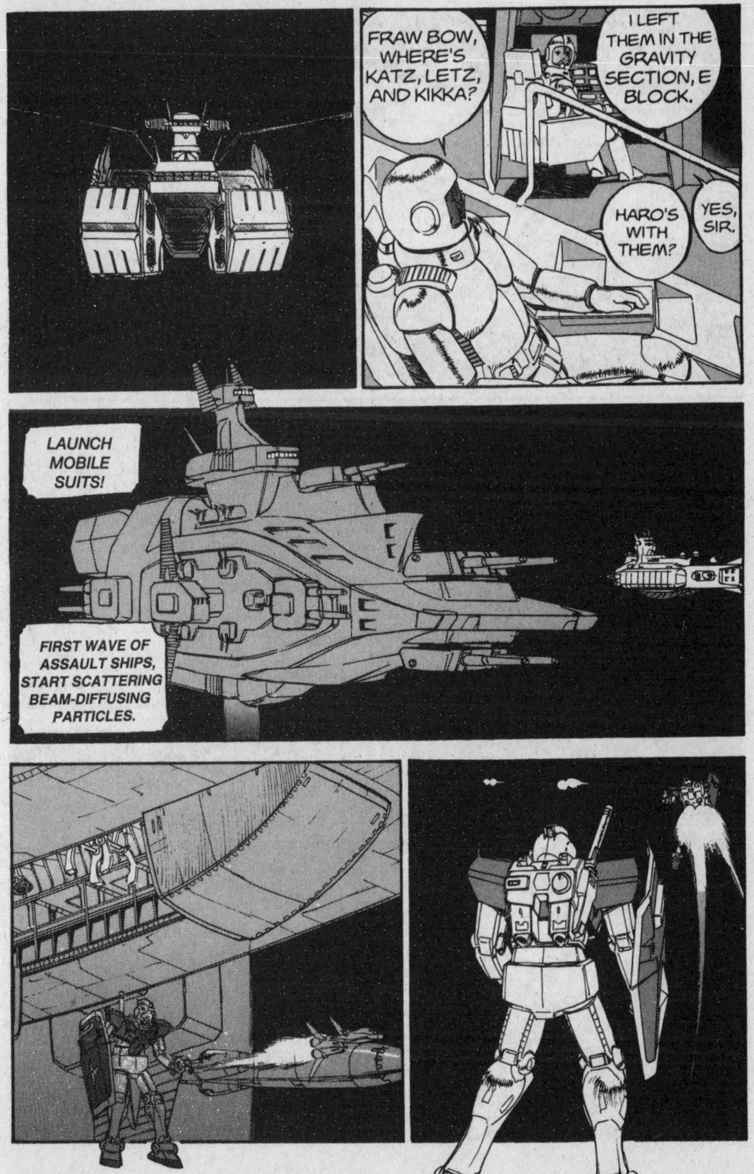
FRAW BOW, WHERE'S KATZ, LETZ, AND KIKKA?
I LEFT THEM IN THE GRAVITY SECTION, E BLOCK.
HARO'S WITH THEM?
YES, SIR.
LAUNCH MOBILE SUITS!
FIRST WAVE OF ASSAULT SHIPS, START SCATTERING BEAM-DIFFUSING PARTICLES.

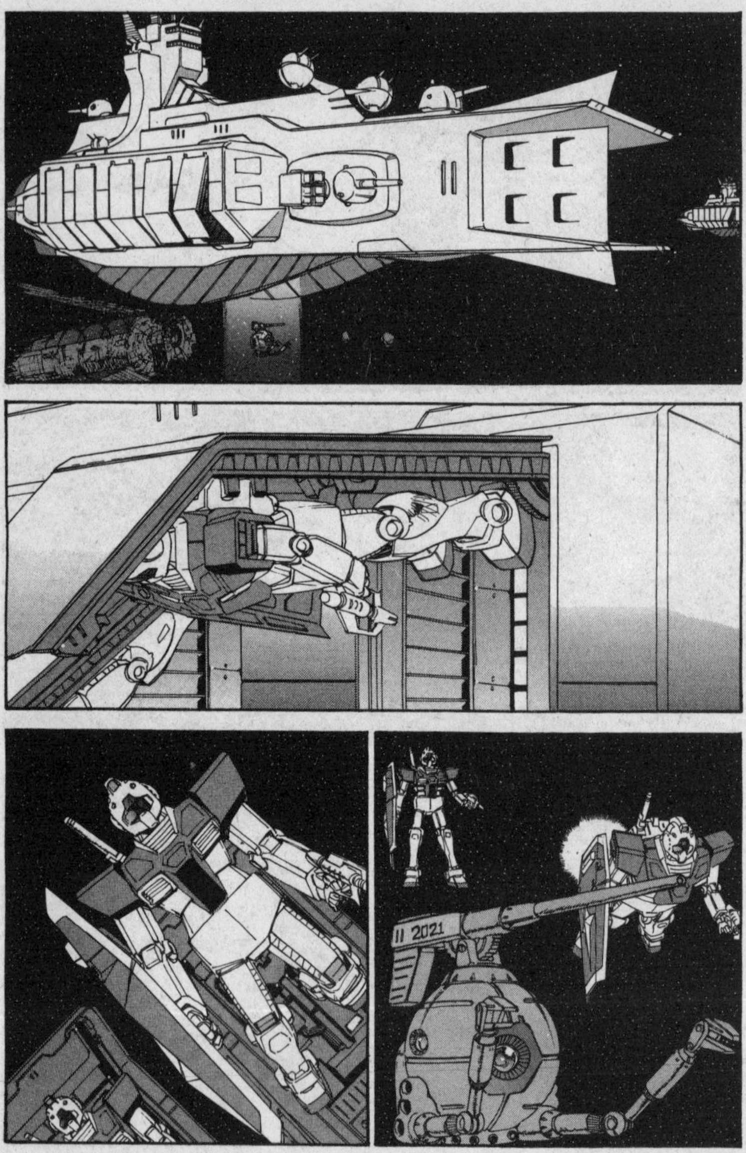
2021

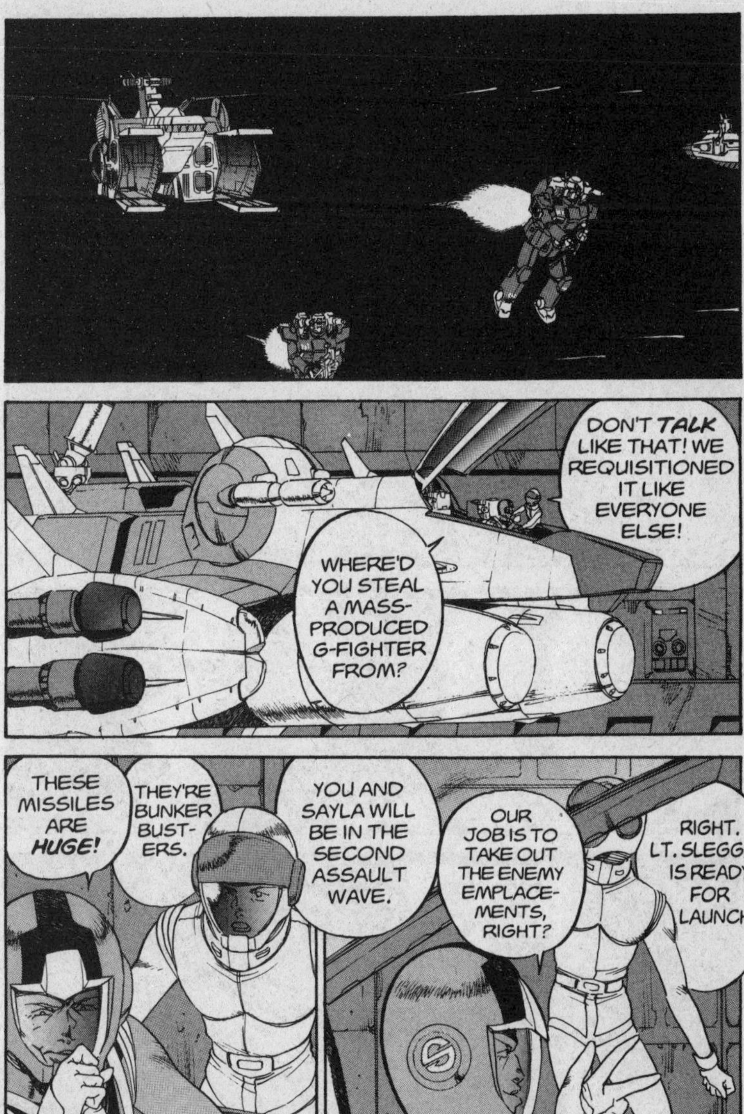
WHERE'D YOU STEAL A MASS-PRODUCED G-FIGHTER FROM?
DON'T *TALK* LIKE THAT! WE REQUISITIONED IT LIKE EVERYONE ELSE!
THESE MISSILES ARE *HUGE!*
THEY'RE BUNKER BUST-ERS.
YOU AND SAYLA WILL BE IN THE SECOND ASSAULT WAVE.
OUR JOB IS TO TAKE OUT THE ENEMY EMPLACE-MENTS, RIGHT?
RIGHT. LT. SLEGGAR IS READY FOR LAUNCH!

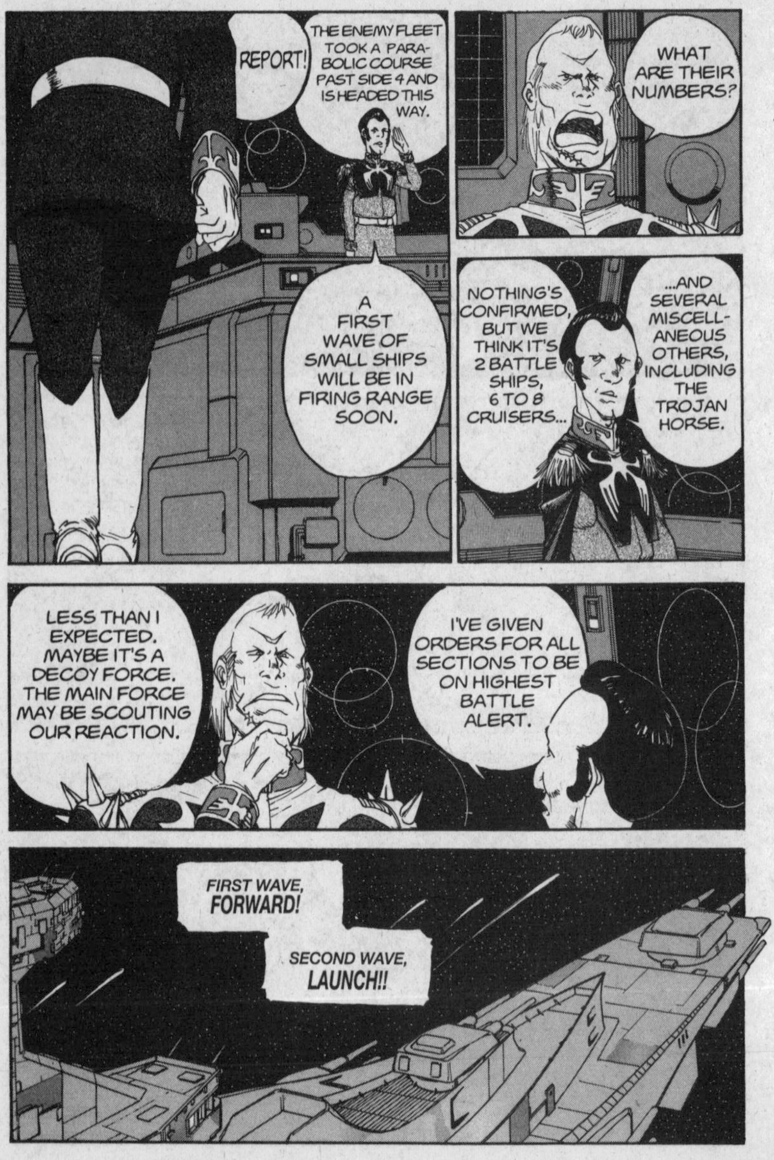
REPORT!
THE ENEMY FLEET TOOK A PARA-BOLIC COURSE PAST SIDE 4 AND IS HEADED THIS WAY.
A FIRST WAVE OF SMALL SHIPS WILL BE IN FIRING RANGE SOON.
WHAT ARE THEIR NUMBERS?
NOTHING'S CONFIRMED, BUT WE THINK IT'S 2 BATTLE SHIPS, 6 TO 8 CRUISERS...
...AND SEVERAL MISCELL-ANEOUS OTHERS, INCLUDING THE TROJAN HORSE.
LESS THAN I EXPECTED. MAYBE IT'S A DECOY FORCE. THE MAIN FORCE MAY BE SCOUTING OUR REACTION.
I'VE GIVEN ORDERS FOR ALL SECTIONS TO BE ON HIGHEST BATTLE ALERT.
FIRST WAVE, FORWARD!
SECOND WAVE, LAUNCH!!

ALL SHIPS ADVANCE TO FIRING RANGE!

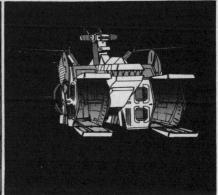

006, SAYLA, LAUNCHING!

007,
SLEGGAR,
HERE I GO.

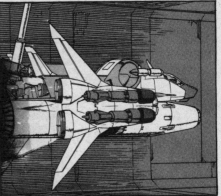

156

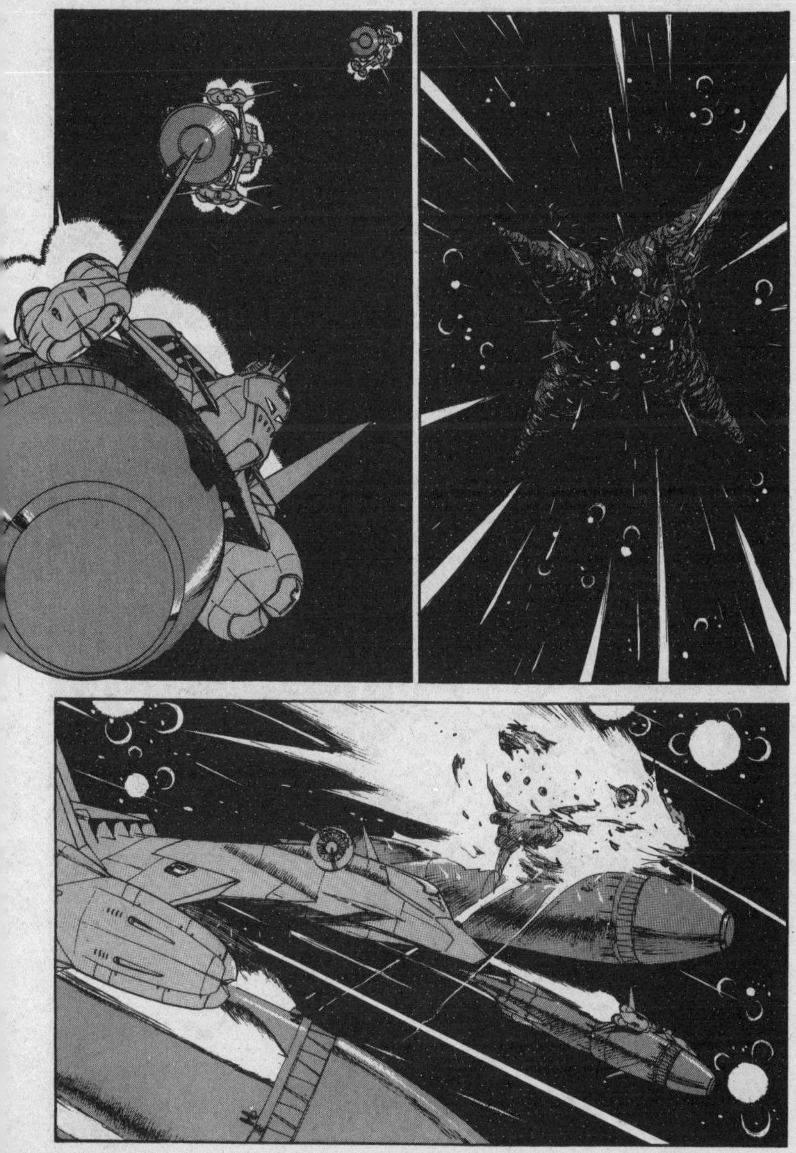

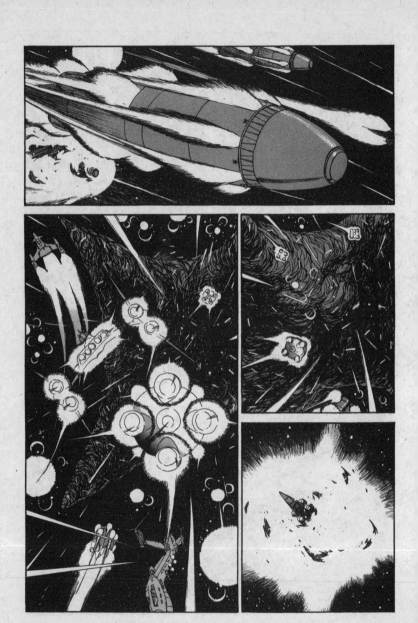

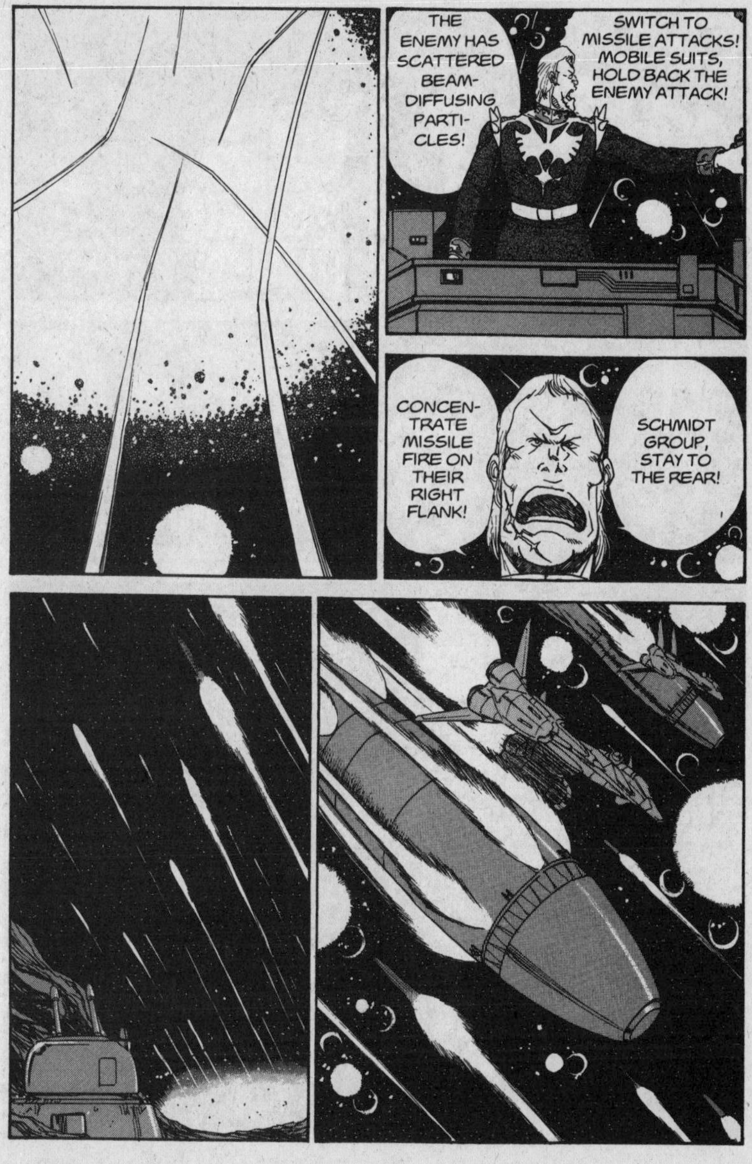
THE ENEMY HAS SCATTERED BEAM-DIFFUSING PARTI-CLES!
SWITCH TO MISSILE ATTACKS! MOBILE SUITS, HOLD BACK THE ENEMY ATTACK!
CONCEN-TRATE MISSILE FIRE ON THEIR RIGHT FLANK!
SCHMIDT GROUP, STAY TO THE REAR!

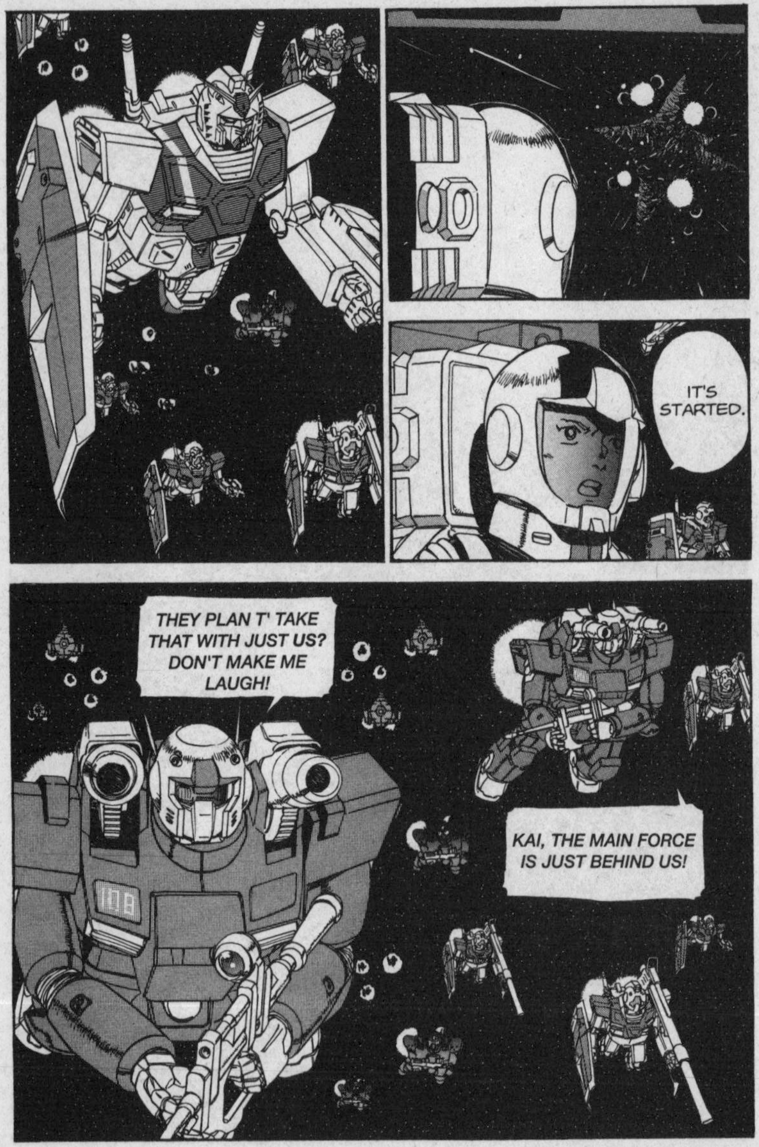
IT'S STARTED.
THEY PLAN T' TAKE THAT WITH JUST US? DON'T MAKE ME LAUGH!
KAI, THE MAIN FORCE IS JUST BEHIND US!

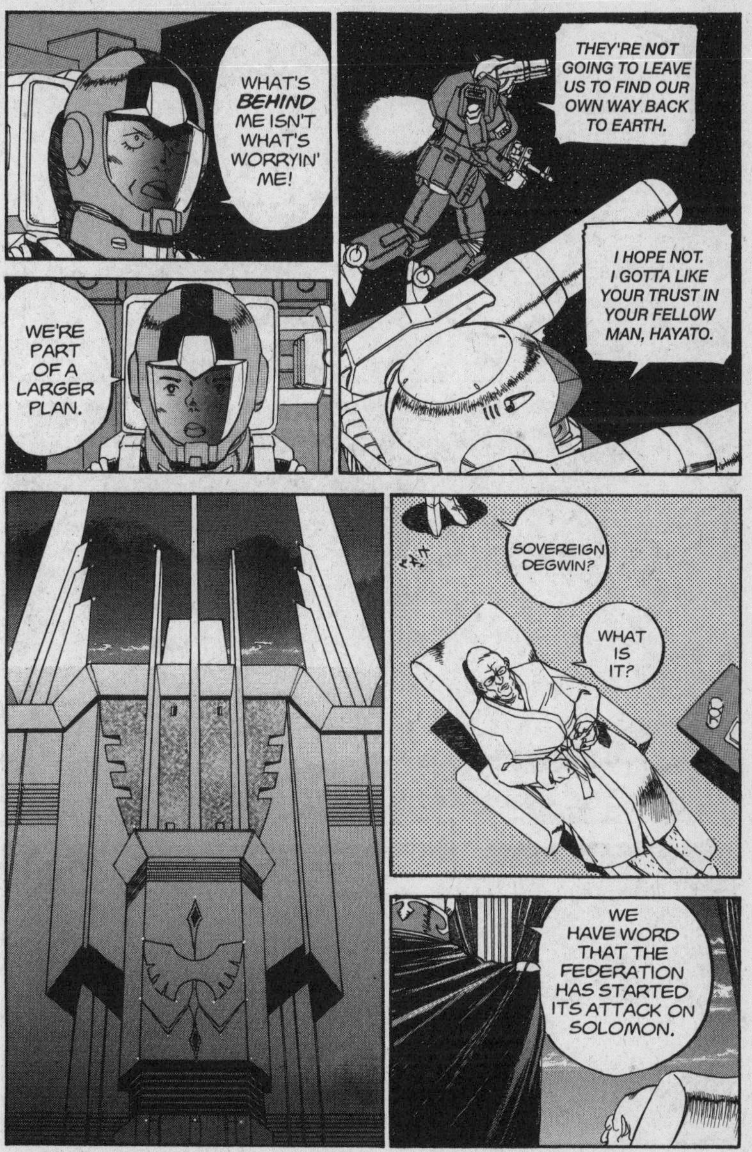
WHAT'S ***BEHIND*** ME ISN'T WHAT'S WORRYIN' ME!
WE'RE PART OF A LARGER PLAN.
THEY'RE ***NOT*** *GOING TO LEAVE US TO FIND OUR OWN WAY BACK TO EARTH.*
I HOPE NOT. I GOTTA LIKE YOUR TRUST IN YOUR FELLOW MAN, HAYATO.
SOVEREIGN DEGWIN?
WHAT IS IT?
WE HAVE WORD THAT THE FEDERATION HAS STARTED ITS ATTACK ON SOLOMON.

SO IT'S FINALLY STARTED...

THANK YOU, INSPECTOR GENERAL. HAVE THE SEALS BEEN REMOVED?

THE SEALS ARE GONE, BUT ANY GUNS FIRED IN SIDE 6 AIR-SPACE...

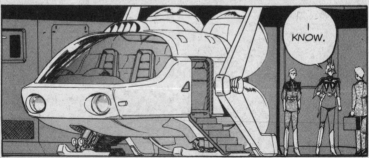

I KNOW.

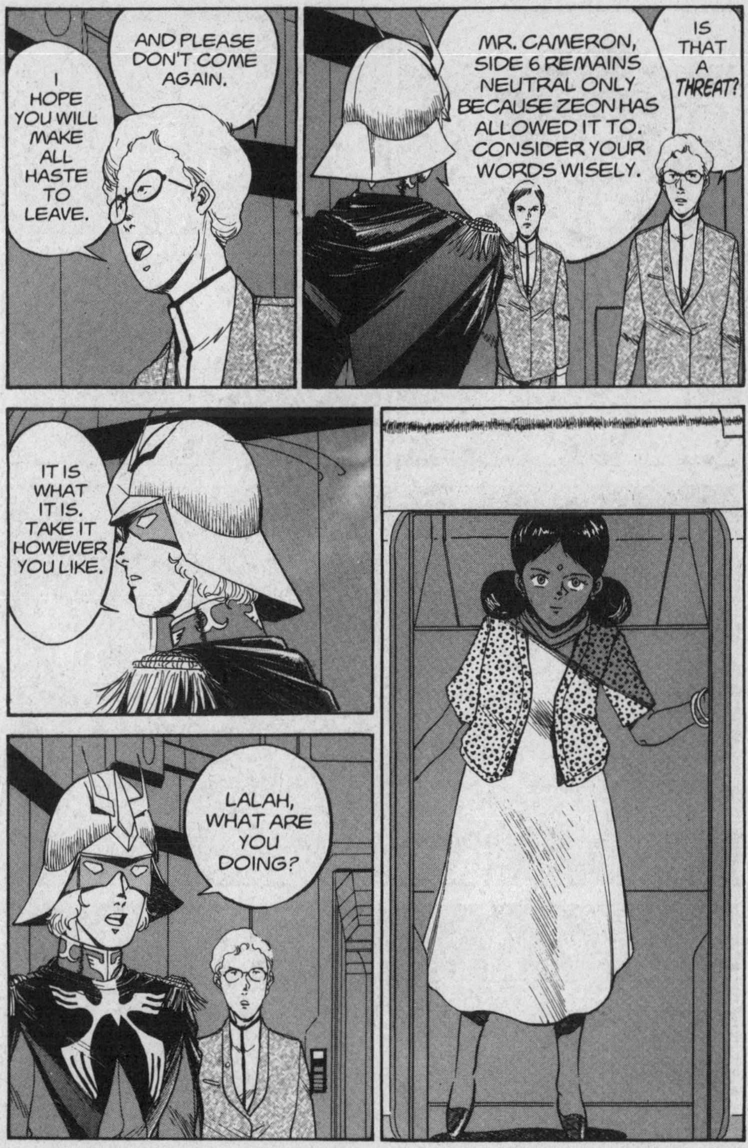
I HOPE YOU WILL MAKE ALL HASTE TO LEAVE.
AND PLEASE DON'T COME AGAIN.
MR. CAMERON, SIDE 6 REMAINS NEUTRAL ONLY BECAUSE ZEON HAS ALLOWED IT TO. CONSIDER YOUR WORDS WISELY.
IS THAT A *THREAT?*
IT IS WHAT IT IS. TAKE IT HOWEVER YOU LIKE.
LALAH, WHAT ARE YOU DOING?

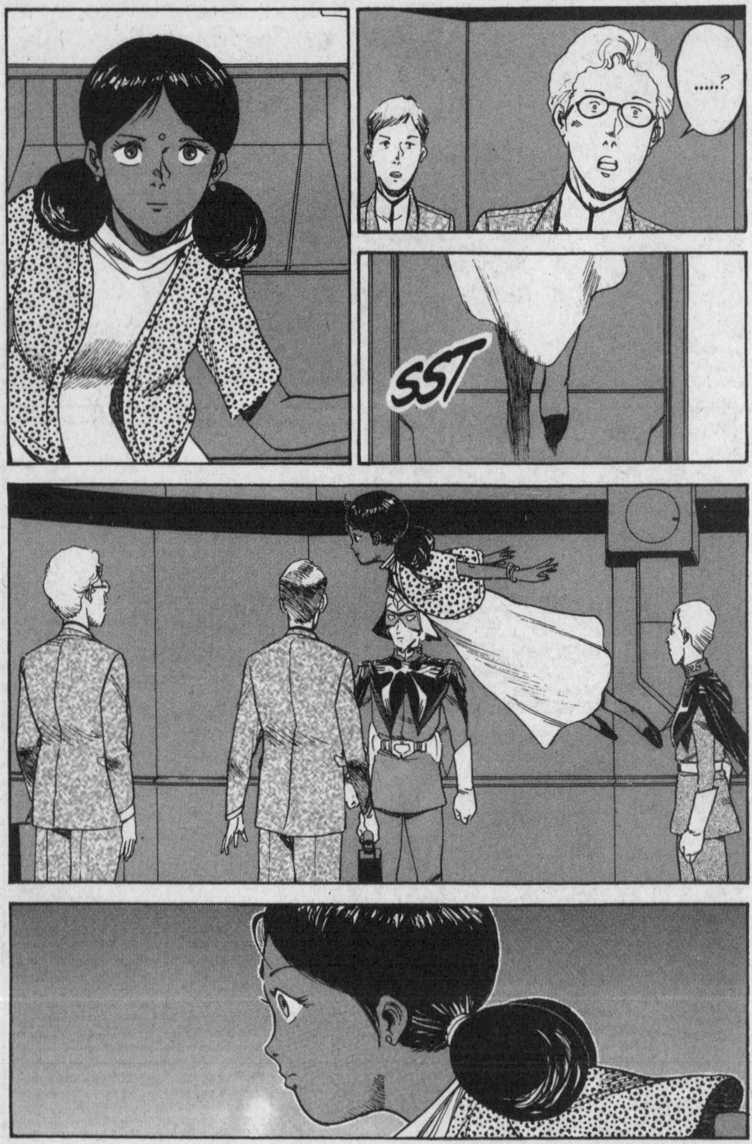
......?
SST

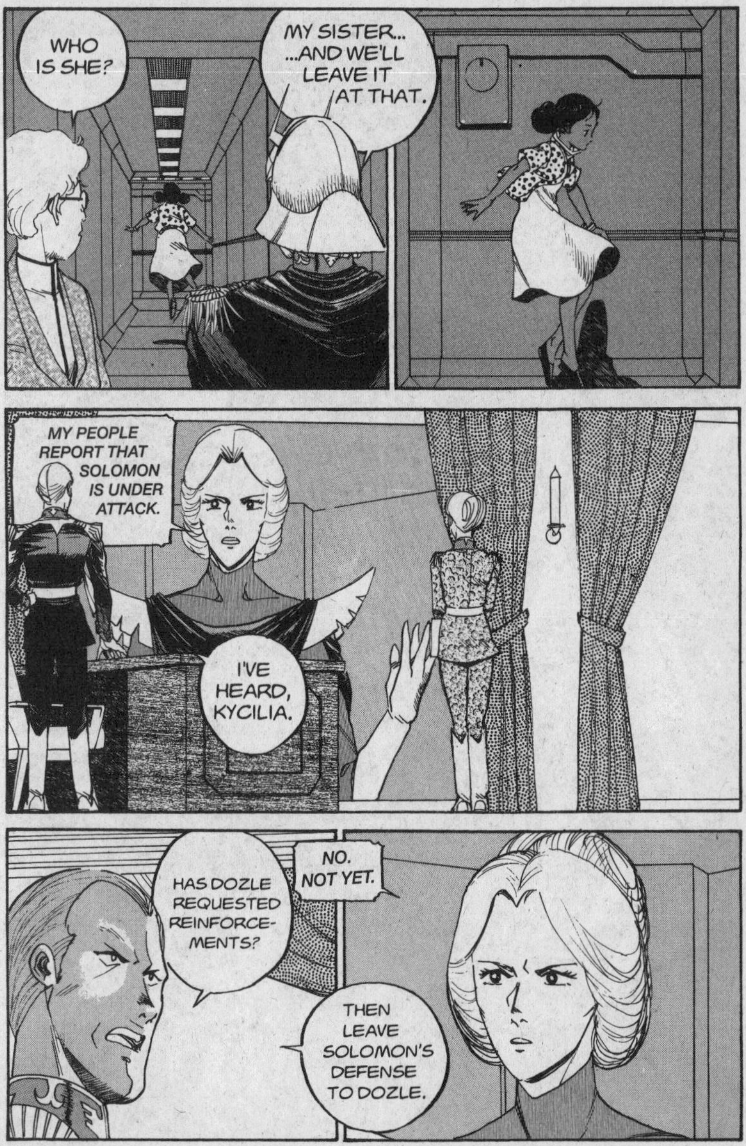
WHO IS SHE?
MY SISTER... ...AND WE'LL LEAVE IT AT THAT.
MY PEOPLE REPORT THAT SOLOMON IS UNDER ATTACK.
I'VE HEARD, KYCILIA.
HAS DOZLE REQUESTED REINFORCE-MENTS?
NO. NOT YET.
THEN LEAVE SOLOMON'S DEFENSE TO DOZLE.

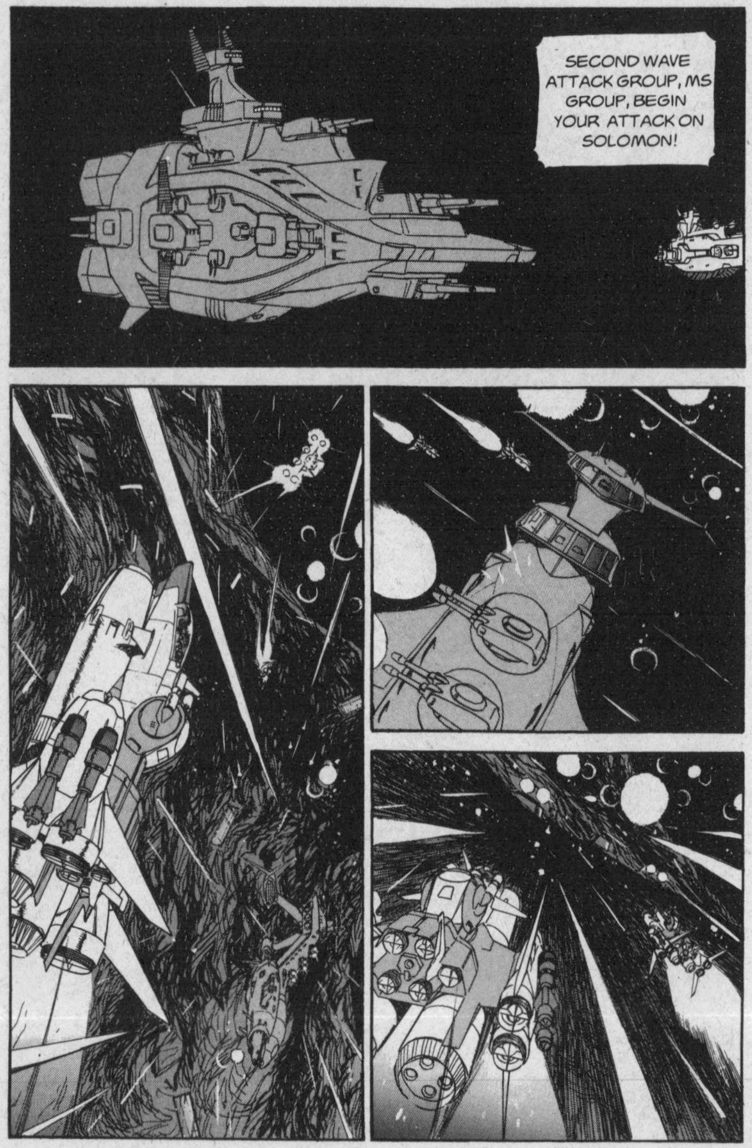
SECOND WAVE ATTACK GROUP, MS GROUP, BEGIN YOUR ATTACK ON SOLOMON!

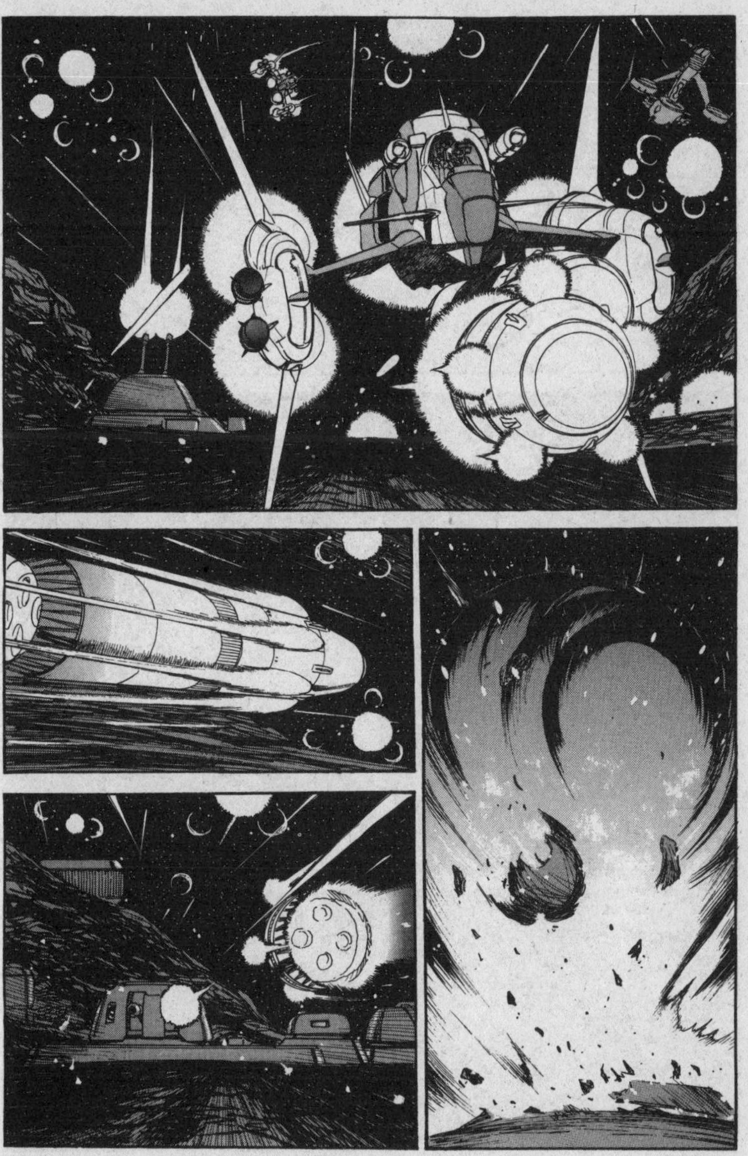

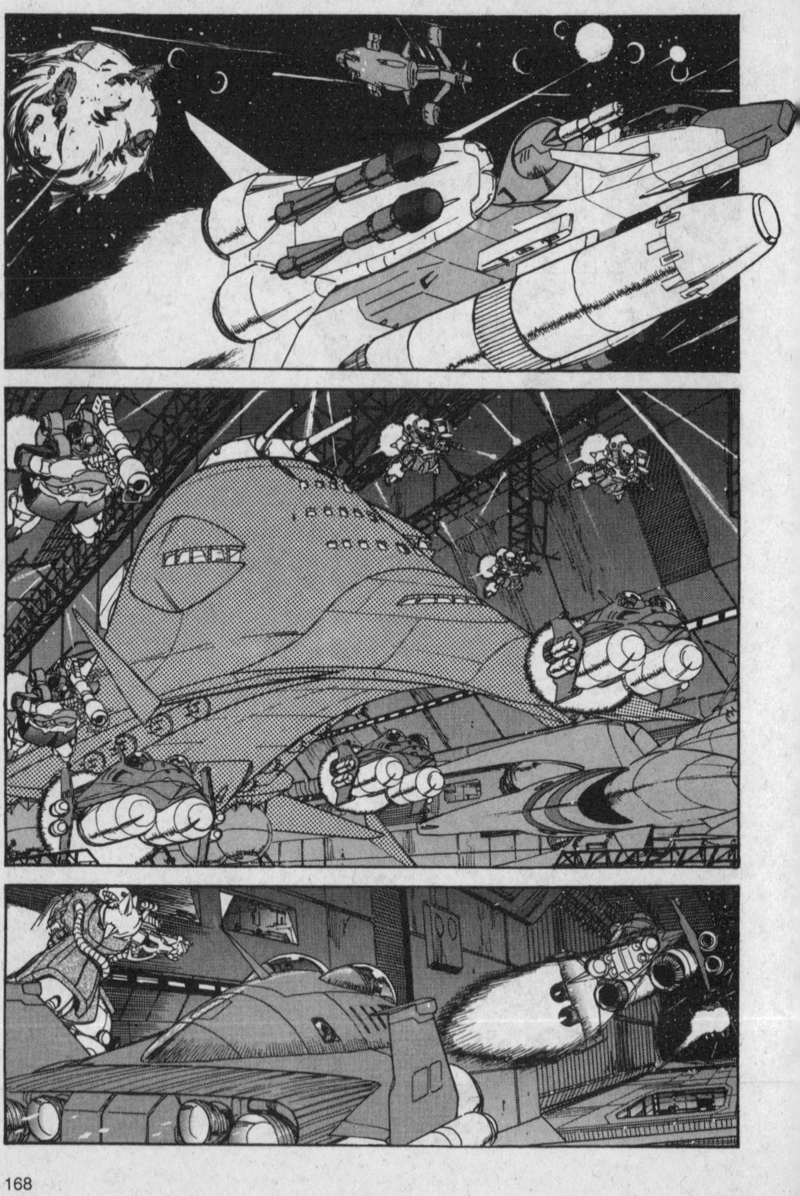

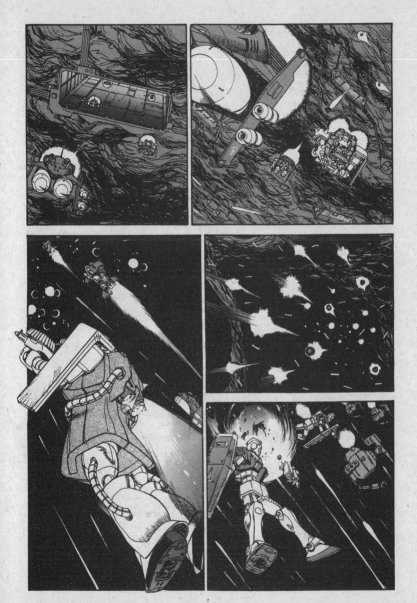

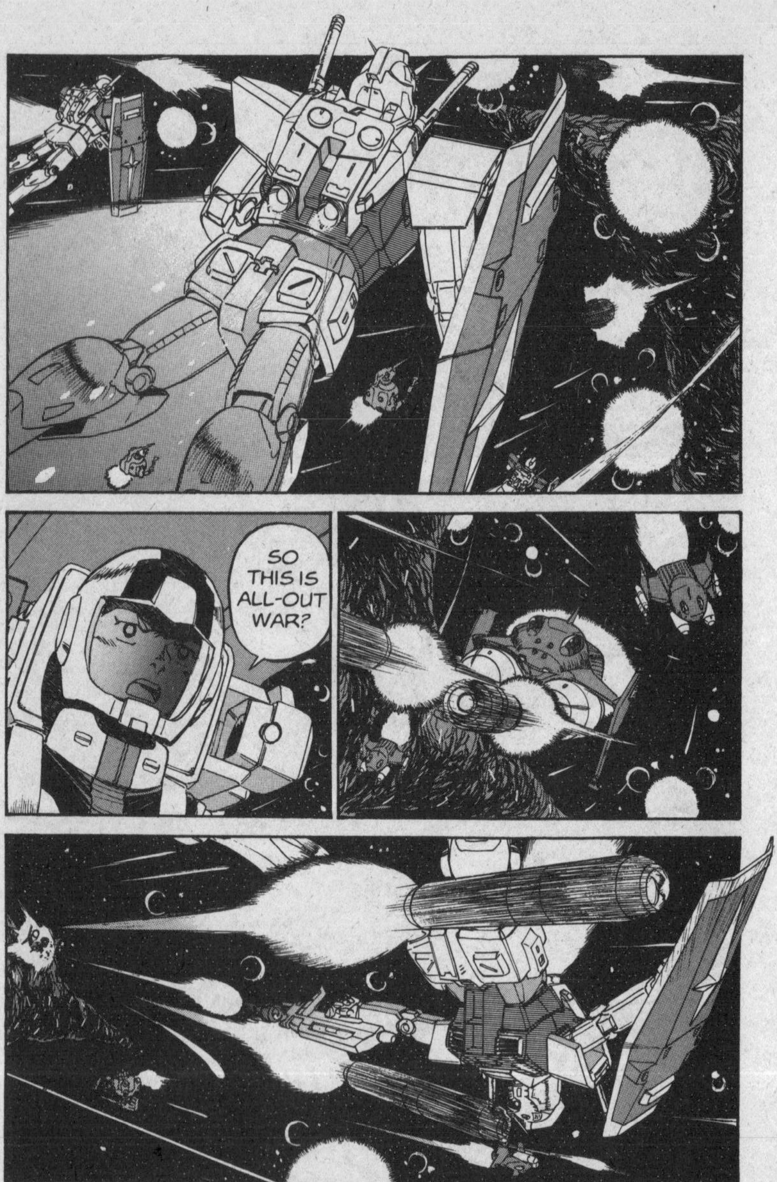
SO THIS IS ALL-OUT WAR?

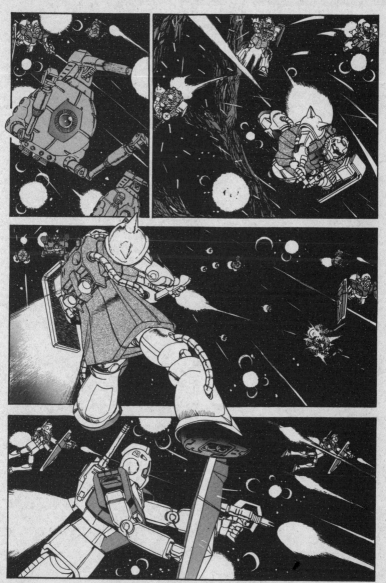

TO BE CONTINUED IN VOL. 9.

EARTH FEDERATION SPACE FORCE

Eleven months into the war, the Earth Federation has finally rebuilt its devastated space fleet. While the *White Base* served as a decoy to distract the enemy, dozens of newly-constructed warships and mobile suits launched into space from the Federation's Jaburo headquarters. Now the reborn Federation Space Force is launching an all-out offensive against the Principality of Zeon's home territory, starting with the asteroid fortress Solomon.

RB-79 Ball

Before the creation of the mobile suit, simple space pods equipped with manipulator arms were used for colony construction and maintenance. To supplement its mobile suit forces, the Federation Space Force has adapted these machines into combat-ready "mobile pods" armed with 180mm cannons. While the Ball is no match for a genuine mobile suit, its long-range armament enables it to provide fire support for the Federation's close-combat GM mobile suits.

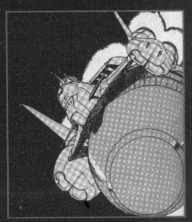

Public

In addition to mobile suits and mobile pods, the Federation Space Force is also equipped with a new line of space fighters, based - at least in their Gundam 0079 incarnations - on the G-Fighter tested by the *White Base* crew. The Public assault boat is a heavily-armored model designed to break through enemy lines and deliver its oversized missile payload. There's also a general-purpose mass-produced G-Fighter, with a tandem cockpit and attachment points for a full arsenal of heavy missiles.